MW01688571

Behind The Front Door

A Collection of Short Stories

John Powell Riley

PublishAmerica
Baltimore

First printing

The story, "The Cuppa Jo" reprinted from the August, 1998 *Naval History*, a publication of the U.S. Naval Institute.

ISBN: 1-59286-470-8
PUBLISHED BY PUBLISHAMERICA BOOK PUBLISHERS
www.publishamerica.com
Baltimore

Printed in the United States of America

DEDICATION

To the memory of my precious wife, My Little Darling, my Assia – born Anastasia Smaguine, daughter of Countess Mary von Krouse of the Russian hereditary nobility (daughter of Alexander) and Colonel Alexis Smaguin of the Don Cossacks, Goddaughter of Prince Vladimir Andronnikov (son of Michael).

She lives on in my memory.

PREFACE

I have always preferred the short story and the novella as a form of literary expression. When well crafted either can be a little gem—the essence of the writer's art. Short stories are conveniently read in one sitting or on a plane or commuter train and they can be very entertaining. One would think that this is ideal in these busy times. All too often I feel that a novel would have been better as a short story. Sometimes they seem to be short stories that have been interlarded with thousands of additional words that don't advance the plot. Because of that I am often in a hurry to finish or to throw the book aside unfinished. How often when reading novels do you find yourself flipping pages to get to the action?

Short stories have been called "an American art form." During the first half of the 20th century their popularity in America may have justified that claim, though at the same time they were also being written in Russia, France, and England. Since then, weekly magazines that once were the principal publishers of short stories have all vanished. The short story is now anything but an American art form, to our great loss, but I hope this will change in the future. The fact is, there is no market for the individual short story today. They must be sold as collections and collections are usually accumulated over a lengthy period of time. If the quality is high, they are difficult to write. Prolific writers can grind out a couple of novels a year, but good short story collections are not written that way.

The greatest writers of all time – classic writers like Leo Tolstoy, Oscar Wilde, Guy de Maupassant, Sommerset Maugham, Edgar Allen Poe, Mark Twain, Anton Chekhoff, and many others invested their talents in this superlative form of expression; the short story.

I have had the good fortune to live a full and exciting life   a Naval officer on an Admiral's staff in WW-2, a private pilot, a single handed ocean cruising yachtsman, and a career in foreign commerce. My work took me to over 70 countries in almost every part of the world. For most of my working life I lived in Paris, Madrid, Geneva, and Monte Carlo. I married the beautiful, charming, lovable daughter of a Russian Countess and a Colonel in the Don Cossacks (Anastasia "Assia" Smaguine). Characters in some of my stories provide glimpses of her unique personality.

Because of the unusual opportunities I have had, I tend to write mostly from my life, often in the first person, which is ideal for true stories. This collection is unusual in that most stories are strictly true with some names and locales changed. Knowing that it really happened as told adds, for me, something exciting, something important to a story. I am of the school that has found truth stranger than fiction. However, two stories are fictions, two others are about 50% true and one is an educated guess as to what probably happened.

I like strong surprise endings and enjoy writing about events in which *these actually occurred.* When I encounter situations like this in life I feel compelled to tell everything precisely as it happened.

Get comfortable now and read. I hope you enjoy…

John Powell Riley

CONTENTS

TUMBLEWEED

Margie looked out of the dirty, grease-stained window of Ben's Truck Stop Cafe and watched the wind-hounded tumbleweed roll past on the highway. In every direction the land was flat, dusty, and hot. The Texas Panhandle was the only world she knew. She was born a few miles down the road in a little unincorporated town through which ran U.S. 66, the main east-west highway that disappeared in two vanishing points on the horizon.

Her impression of the world beyond her dreary perspective was hazy and confused. Not even television reached this remote part of Texas at that time, and to most it is a window on the world. But Margie dreamed of what it would be like if she could travel—free as the wind. In her mind she saw places far away like Hollywood, Memphis, and even New York City.

When people stopped to eat, the magazines they sometimes left gave her tantalizing glimpses of the outside world. Without them she might have thought the whole universe was flat and strewn with tumbling tumbleweed.

Margie had almost no social life and knew only a few people. There was Ben. He was gruff. He was insensitive. He was stingy. He was also old enough to be her grandfather, and he owned the cafe. There was Sid, the only bachelor, who pumped gas at the filling station across the road. There was old Horace who delivered the RFD mail, and there were some highway patrolmen who came in for coffee and sandwiches or maybe a bowl of hot chili. Most of the others she saw were either truck drivers or people driving across the continent. Some were nice and she was sorry to see them go but, of course, they always did.

The truck drivers were generally a rough lot and Margie, whose youth and beauty were only just starting to fade, had to suffer their insulting propositions. Some though were decent men, and once a fight had broken out over how a man should talk to a lady. The nice ones were always married, and Margie was not one to fool around with married men.

Sid came in to dawdle over a cup of coffee and talk to Margie, when he wasn't pumping gas. He was a drifter. Like the tumbleweed, he never put down roots, never stayed long anywhere. He wore an old baseball cap and tattered Levis, like most people around there, and shaved every three or four days, if he felt like it. He also chewed gum constantly, a huge wad of it—his mouth opening and closing like those of the fish in Ben's tiny aquarium.

Margie had little education but she had learned to read and write, after a fashion. Sid had not progressed to that level of learning. He wasn't much, but he owned a pick-up truck and sometimes took Margie to a picture show in a little town about thirty miles down the road. There was nobody else to take her anywhere.

Behind the cafe was Ben's rattlesnake exhibition—a screened enclosure that was home to about forty rattlers of various sizes. Signs up and down the highway advertised this enticement but few people stopped to see it. Also behind the cafe were a couple of one room huts of adobe. Ben lived in one and Margie had the other. From a discarded red and white checkered tablecloth she had made curtains for the one shuttered window, and had decorated the wall with pictures cut from magazines left by customers. These she tacked to the whitewashed walls and thought they gave color and a bit of class.

In one corner was a big metal milk can, the kind that farmers used to carry milk to market—tall enough to sit on. Margie had painted it white and decorated it with a picture of a bouquet of roses she had cut from a magazine and stuck on with glue. She hid and saved her tip money in it in the forlorn hope of a better future.

Every woman has to love someone or some thing—Margie had cats. At first it was just one, but Princess had kittens and now there were four. The big yellow mother cat was everything to Margie. She talked to it, confiding her hopes and dreams, and cuddled it when she slept.

One day, cleaning up a booth, Margie found a yachting magazine someone had left. The picture of a beautiful sailboat on the cover caught her interest as nothing ever had before, and she could hardly wait for her day to end to read about boats and the far away, exciting places they go to. It would be a new picture for her wall. It was so grand, so free, with the wind in its red sails.

When at last it was closing time, Margie fetched Cruising World from a drawer under the counter and hastened to her little room. After she fed the cats, she and the four of them got into bed, and Margie at last could explore the pages that fascinated her so. There was an exciting story about a cruise along the coast of Ireland with the most breathtaking color pictures she had ever seen—all that grass of an unbelievable green, and no tumbleweed. The pictures called to her and drew her like a magnet into delightful and mystical fantasies. She went over to the milk can and recounted her savings. They came to $876.47. This was a lot of money to her. She tried to think how she could use it to live the adventurous life she longed for.

When she came to the advertising section, she saw what yachts like this sold for and her heart sank. It said to "try $80,000" for a small one she liked, or "$300,000" for a boat that looked like the one on the cover. This was more money than she could even imagine. Besides, she would not know how to handle such a boat, nor how to use the compass to get where she wanted to go—what to do at night—what to do in a storm. She hugged her big yellow cat as tears came to her eyes and blurred her vision. Finally though, in the classified section under Positions, she read this:

TWO CREWMEN WANTED 41 foot sloop Dolphin, fully found for ocean cruising, sailing to French Riviera via Azores, Gibraltar, and Balearic Islands. Departure first week in June. Owner will pay all expenses. Write Captain, Yacht Dolphin....

Margie's heart began to beat wildly with anticipation. She would mail a letter tomorrow as soon as Horace came by with his mail truck. She lay awake way into the night planning what she would say. This was her big chance. She hugged the yellow cat and talked it over with her.

At dawn the next morning, having slept on it, Margie was ready to write. Her letter went like this:

Dear Captain Riley of the Dolphin

I am 29 years old and strong and helthy. I have blew eyes and light brown hare and work as a waitress in Ben's Truck Stop Cafe. I never been on a boat an never even seen the ocean but I'm a quick lerner and you could teech me sailing real easy. I live with my fore cats. I'm tired of the same place all the time and the tumbelweeds. I'm a real good cook. Just tell me what you like to eat. I dreem to go with you to the French riviera. If you take me you won't be sory. Here is a snapshot of me taken to years ago in front of the cafe.

Yours truly,
Margie Hall

She enclosed a Polaroid snapshot taken by some customer. It showed an exceptionally pretty, smiling, young woman, rather poorly dressed, with a big yellow cat in her arms.

Now all was ready, and she waited by the side of the road until she saw Horace coming. She began waving the letter until he saw her and stopped.

If the Captain answered by return mail, she calculated she could have a reply as early as next Tuesday. When Sid came for coffee, she told him she was thinking of taking a long trip. She wouldn't say where—just, "You'd be surprised."

As Tuesday drew near, Margie could think of nothing but the letter she was expecting. Living in a dream world, she couldn't remember orders, and Ben bawled her out unmercifully in front of everyone. That night she couldn't sleep. She talked to the yellow cat in her arms until it was almost time to get up.

"Princess, just think. Maybe the captain is young and handsome and unmarried. Maybe we'll fall in love...maybe get married and sail all around the world for the rest of our lives. But don't you worry now. I'll send for you." Princess responded enigmatically with a purr, while outside the wind raced over the flat land and moaned in the crevices of her little mud shanty.

The next morning Margie kept watching for Horace with the mail. Finally she saw his truck coming down the highway, but it didn't even slow down. She ran out and watched it disappear in the distance. Swallowing hard, she told herself that the captain probably didn't answer mail the same day. If he took a day to do it, the reply would come tomorrow, but it didn't. Then she reasoned that maybe, because of a weekend, there was a delay.

Every night she read and reread Cruising World, then put it carefully away in her big milk can and talked to her yellow cat until late at night; every day she stood in front of the cafe when Horace was due to pass. Every day he did pass, but without stopping. He just waved his hand and kept on going.

Margie began to understand there might never be an answer. She didn't know if she could face that. The last day of June she was still standing forlornly by the road, her yellow cat in her arms, and Horace again sped on with a wave of the hand. Margie ran to her little room and threw herself on the bed, struggling to hold back the tears. Princess regarded her with dismayed incomprehension. Soon, Ben's angry shouts roused her and she dragged herself back to work.

She saw Sid amble across the road, stopping twice on the way to let tumbleweed roll past in heavy gusts of wind and dust that made him stagger. He hadn't shaved for days and came in, jaws working hard, as usual. He wasn't looking his best, whatever that might be. After glancing around for Margie, he took his usual place at the counter. She brought his coffee automatically, struggling to bear up under a heartache tearing her apart.

Sid shoved his grease-stained baseball cap to the back of his head, and after shifting his wad of gum from one side to the other with his tongue, he said: "Baby, this is your lucky day. You and me's goin to the movies tonight over in Adrian.

Seeing Sid was a crushing blow. Clear to Margie in an instant was her bleak destiny, her profoundly lonely lot in life, in every dreary, dismal detail. Margie couldn't hold the tears back any longer. She ran to the booth in the corner, covered her face with her hands and put her head on the table. Her sobs came from the very depths of her miserable soul.

Sid turned to Ben, astonished. "Whud I say, huh? Whud I say?"

"Damned if I know," replied Ben. "Hell, ya never kin figger a woman an they ain't no use a-tryin."

"What's 'a matter with ya Margie? Jeez I thought ya'd want 'a see the pitcher—it's called, *Red Sails in the Sunset.*"

THEODORE AND ARLENE

When I lived on my boat in Monte Carlo, I was often awakened by the roaring of lions in Prince Rainier's zoo, which overlooked Fontvielle harbor. On those occasions, I sometimes lay in my bunk speculating on the motivations of beasts making such terrifying noises. The lion, I decided, trying to think like one, was attempting as best he could to assert what he considered to be his natural authority. He was just trying to hold onto a little of his male pride by pretending. Actually the poor old guy had big problems. There he was, so magnificent—created by nature to be the king of beasts, but condemned to spend his life in jail, caged up with a mate he didn't choose. As for the alpha female, she obviously didn't understand him, didn't see him as just a big pussy cat. She fiercely protested the arrogance of his majesty and seemed to consider him as the quintessential male chauvinist while he appeared convinced she was a feminist, with sharp claws.

My thoughts would eventually return to the human race in search of specific analogies. I didn't have to look far. Arlene and Theodore invariably came to mind. They gave me a feeling of oneness with the creatures of the universe. We are not all that different.

Theodore and Arlene lived in New York City and owned a small but luxurious apartment in La Napoul, in the French Riviera. It was what the French would call a bijou—a gem. In it they spent about one month of each year. He was a prominent surgeon, about to retire, and she had at one time been a partner in a law firm. Now she only threatened lawsuits—a new one each week.

Every few years, Arlene flew to a clinic for a face lift by one of the world's greatest plastic surgeons. She confided this to me after a few drinks. I must say the effect was miraculous. With her exceptionally fine, silky, blond hair, flawless, creamy complexion, and her perpetual youthfulness, she looked more like her husband's daughter than his wife. She was decidedly attractive.

The years had not been as kind to Theodore. The strain of piling up a huge fortune, despite ever mounting bills for malpractice insurance, had prematurely aged him, and a few strange foibles had taken root in his personality. For instance, he had acquired a definite preference for fish rather than meat. Carving and serving meat at the dinner table was something he tried to avoid because it reminded him too much of what he did all day. He told me he once dramatized his point of view by donning latex gloves, a mask, and the green attire he wore in surgery, to carve a roast. Arlene was not amused however and made it clear she liked red meat—as rare and bloody as she could get it, so that's what they usually had.

Both had what psychologists call "type A personalities." They had lots of adrenaline—both were aggressive, competitive, and constantly keyed up.

The one thing they each enjoyed was putting on smart dinner parties, and I was usually invited. Everything would always be beautifully prepared and presented and the guests were often interesting. Even more so were the host and hostess if one is fascinated by the oddities of the human species.

The last time I attended one of their parties, I arrived early. They always asked me to come in time for cocktails. Other guests, being European, were invited only for dinner as was the custom in France.

When I announced my arrival by a knock, Theodore opened the door with a flourish and greeted me with a gracious smile. Arlene stood behind him. She was something to behold, all dressed up in a flowing white gown like a princess. Her favorite Frank Sinatra tape was playing softly in the background, which added warmth and sentiment to the ambiance. Theodore, who could not carry a tune and disliked music, suffered through this uncomplainingly but with, I think, a conscious effort which showed sometimes in his eyes.

"Well. Good evening, John," he said, "Come in, come in. It's real good to see you again. How about a Scotch on the rocks?"

Arlene's lips became straight and compressed as if she were getting ready to blow a trumpet. "Theodore, what's the matter with you?" she shrieked. Can't you ever do anything right? Don't you know John always drinks bourbon, not Scotch? If you can't remember these things, why don't you write them down?" This was said in the harshest possible tone of voice as if admonishing a willful and rather stupid child.

"Either will be just fine," I said, hastening to move out of the line of fire.

Theodore was ready with a lightening riposte. His face turned the color of a boiled lobster and he roared back, "All right for Christ's sake. You don't have to yell at me like a fishwife. I'll bet you don't even know what kind of wine John prefers." Score: Arlene one, Theodore one. The party was off to its usual start and both were now set to parry and thrust in verbal combat, and to draw blood.

One of the high points of the evening came later, after the other guests had arrived and we were seated around the table. It ended a period of time when Arlene had tried to control and censor everything Theodore said and did, using subtle signals—as in dressage—that is to say by owl eyed disapproving glances, by sighs, by an occasional raised eyebrow, or by a kick in the shins under the table. None of this had worked very well for the alpha female and I judged by her expression that her temper had risen ominously. I think we all sensed it except Theodore, or so it seemed.

They had been snapping and snarling at one another all evening and there had been several minor shouting matches but now the time had come for the decisive battle, the main act of the drama, the denouement. Something had pushed Arlene beyond the critical point and she suddenly cast subtleties aside and with catlike speed went for the jugular vein.

"We are total opposites," she announced. "We really get on each other's nerves. Theodore and I just can't get along. I don't know why I ever married him. I don't know how we have put up with each other for thirty years." She explained this as if we might never have guessed it.

Shocked by Arlene's bold hostility, we all looked in breathless suspense at Theodore. How would he react? He had just finished sharpening his big carving knife and I suspected Arlene's outburst had been a show of bravado on her part. It was as if she wanted to prove she wasn't afraid of her husband, by taunting him while he held the razor sharp weapon in his hand and looked as if he wanted to kill her. Arlene was like the matador who risks death to show contempt by turning his back on the bull before killing it—or being killed by it—defying the beast as it stands, still powerful, but with drooping head and hatred in its blood-shot eyes.

Theodore, clear minded and sober, had anticipated her battle plan with the brilliance of Wellington at Waterloo and he was ready to spring the trap. A good tactician always has a contingency plan ready. "Thirty years, 349 days, twelve hours, and thirty-five minutes," he thundered triumphantly in slowly spoken but emphatic words, exaggerating the precision of his diction to achieve maximum dramatic effect. He shook with rage, and flourished the carving knife threateningly in Arlene's direction. His eyes bugged out and the whites showed full circle. Arlene did not waiver. She had guts. Magnificent thespians, both of them. They sat staring at one another, their unblinking eyes locked in contact, each determined to not be the first to look away. I let my fork fall to the marble floor to end the contest.

But Theodore was out to win now and in a surprise attack he shot back the ultimate insult, "Yes, almost thirty-one years but it seems more like a hundred and thirty-one." Score another point for Theodore.

"I don't care what you say. My Snubbins loves me." Snubbins was a 14 pound 18 year old yellow tomcat. Big, round, piteous tears trickled down Arlene's cheeks taking with them some mascara to paint two black stripes like the markings on the face of a cheetah. Into those tears she doubtless poured a lifetime of who knows what frustration and broken dreams. My heart went out to her.

Theodore had sensed victory until this moment, but he now looked confused. Though he had the advantage of near sobriety, he didn't seem to know what to do with it. The history of man's relationship with woman was repeating itself. Tears. Woman's secret weapon. Woman's strategy of last resort. Woman's final argument. Woman's symbolic last word.

This presaged the end of a typical evening though the main course had yet to be served. Arlene got up uncertainly from the table and staggered to a chair, then made it from chair to floor lamp. Finally reaching the sofa on the terrace, she flopped down and passed out. Cocktails and then wine had been too much for her. The thought crossed my mind that Theodore might have given her a Micky Finn—easy enough for a doctor to do, but I feel sure he didn't.

He was now a subdued man. The Frank Sinatra tape came to an end. Silence replaced dinner music and there was something sad about that silence.

Theodore started to carve the roast, then thought better of it and carried it back to the kitchen for dissection. It may have occurred to him his reputation as a surgeon would be in jeopardy if he botched the job in front of his guests. A surgeon may not like to have his dexterity, or lack of it, put on display and subjected to critical judgment—the dinner guests watching like interns in a teaching hospital. Besides there was the possibility of unpleasant connotations that might diminish appetites.

When they could, the others thanked the doctor for "a very pleasant evening," made a futile bow in the direction of their unreactive hostess, and departed. After they had gone, I also left. It was how every party ended.

Leaving the building, I glanced up at their second floor terrace just in time to see Theodore tucking a quilt around Arlene so she wouldn't catch cold. He wore an expression of deep concern, and of something else too. Could it have been lingering affection – or even love?

Lions in the zoo and some couples are indeed very strange beasts but I don't think their snarls are always as menacing as they sound.

THE BEAUTIFUL PEOPLE

"Hello. Is this Mr. John Riley?" The man on the phone spoke perfect English with only a slight French accent.

"Yes it is."

"My name is Maurice Rousseau," said the caller. "I own companies with offices and manufacturing facilities in Stockholm and Antwerp. I understand that your firm makes a wide range of radio communication equipment. Maybe we can do some business, but that is not why I am calling now." He hesitated a moment. "You are an American are you not?"

"Yes, I am."

"Mr. Riley, as you don't know me this is going to seem a very strange request, but I would be extremely pleased if you would come for dinner at my home Sunday night, if you are free. It is terribly important—there will be an American couple there—friends. I can't even begin to tell you how much it means to us for you to come. I promise you a very good dinner. Please say you will be there. My home is not far from your Monte Carlo apartment. I live in the mountains above Beaulieu."

Monsieur Rousseau had thoroughly aroused my curiosity at that point and as I had nothing important planned for Sunday night I accepted his invitation with thanks.

"My place is a bit hard to find and not simple to enter. To make it easier for you let's meet at the Hotel La Reserve in Beaulieu at seven sharp. Say by the concierge. Please don't be late—we are having soufflé and it must be served right out of the oven as you know. You can follow my car up to the villa."

Sunday at seven I stood near the concierge's counter in La Reserve, one of the most fashionable and expensive hotels on the Riviera—still wondering what it was all about. My thoughts were interrupted when I heard a man greet the concierge amiably.

"Bonsoir André. Ca va?"

He then turned to me with a pleasant smile and said, "Good evening. You must be Mr. Riley. Allow me to present myself, I'm Maurice Rousseau."

We shook hands. I had met my host at last. Monsieur Rousseau was probably about 35, well over six feet, and tastefully dressed in tan sports coat and slacks. He had an athletic build, a deep suntan, and was clean shaven. His poise was that of a man well-born, and he made an excellent first impression. We chatted a moment before getting into our cars. Rousseau said he was an international dealer in arms, and his wife, Astrid, was from Sweden. The guest of honor, he said, was a close friend from America—in the electronics business. Clearly he was anxious for this to be a memorable evening and I assumed that the American was probably important to him in business. I still didn't know why I had been invited. There was some mystery here, and I couldn't imagine what it could be. He was evidently not yet ready to explain.

"Oh say, we'd better get started. I think I told you, Astrid is making her soufflé tonight and if it falls because we are late, I'm in real trouble." He made a wry smile and began walking to the door, feeling in his coat pocket for his car keys.

I followed his red Alfa Romeo sports car, which he drove top down despite the slight chill in the fall air, and we headed up a road that looped back and forth several times as it ascended the steep mountain where the Alps come right down to the Mediterranean sea.

As I drove, I tried to make some sense of what I knew so far. He was an international arms dealer. I didn't like that. Strange, he didn't look like a man who made his fortune selling rifles, machine guns, mines, mortars and grenades in third world countries, no questions asked. No wonder he didn't tell me his business when we spoke on the phone. Increasing curiosity prevented my turning back.

Just before we reached the moyenne corniche, the middle one of three highways that follow the coast, Rousseau turned sharply left into his private drive and waited for the radio controlled gate to swing open. I could see nothing of his villa yet because of a high brick wall surrounding the property. We then continued on a gravel road that wound first past a large swimming pool and bath house on the left, then swept on up the mountain side to a parking area.

The villa was magnificent—spacious and rambling. It had an imposing entrance with porte cochere; huge windows faced southeast toward the sea 3000 feet below. When I got out of my car, I paused to appreciate a panorama that looked like the background scene for a motion picture. The atmosphere was clear, and the brilliant sparkling stars came right down to the sea horizon. In the dim light I saw a large oval shaped plot of lawn with floral border between the villa and the pool, but the rest of the landscape was wild—covered mostly by low native shrubs and cactus gardens.

Rousseau led the way through a foyer and then left into a large tastefully furnished room where we took seats by a fire that was crackling on a huge raised stone hearth. A faint trace of wood smoke pleasantly scented the air and whetted my appetite. The room was both spacious and cozy, combining rustic and Scandinavian modern decor. Numerous bouquets of cut flowers added warm color accents, making the ambience as charming as a picture on the cover of a home magazine.

"Well, the others are not here yet John, what can I fix you to drink? I'm going to have a dry Martini."

"That will be fine," I said, a bit surprised. Usually the French strongly disapprove of cocktails before dinner, thinking strong alcohol before dinner will diminish their ability to appreciate the food and wine.

"Do you spend much of your time here, Maurice?" What I really wanted to say was, "Why did you invite me here? What's on your mind?" I thought if I got him talking he would eventually get to the point. "You mentioned having offices in Stockholm and Antwerp."

"Yes, but I run everything from here. In fact my main office is in the bath house we just passed driving up to the villa. I spend my days by the pool. Business is just making phone calls and dictating letters to my secretary and I can do that better by the pool—me in my swimming trunks, she in her bikini. We work a while and then dive into the pool and swim a few lengths. I think work should be fun, don't you?" It was a rhetorical question, and not needing my reply nor waiting for one, he continued. "However in Stockholm I have a toy factory and the Antwerp plant manufactures only weapons. I go to each of those cities once a month."

I wondered if he had swimming pools for offices in those cities too. It must be nice, I thought, conducting business in such a casual way—living the life of a Sybarite full time and accumulating great wealth without seeming to half try. But I also wondered if he slept the untroubled sleep of a man with a clear conscience.

An attractive young woman built like a high fashion model approached and we rose to greet her.

"John, I'd like to present my secretary, Sabine."

"Enchanté," I said, and it crossed my mind that Sabine in a bikini would be rather distracting. She not only had all the measurements of a mannequin, she dressed like one—a tanned, wind-blown brunette type with an engaging smile and direct gaze. If his wife was not jealous she had to be strikingly attractive herself. Sabine declined a cocktail—said she just wanted to say hello, but was helping prepare the dinner and had to get right back to the kitchen.

When Sabine left, his wife came to meet me. Like so many Swedish women, she was stunningly beautiful, and her musically accented English had great charm. Astrid was tall, straight, blond, blue eyed, and decidedly alluring. It worried her that the soufflé would be ready in five minutes and would be ruined if it could not be served right out of the oven.

Fortunately, just at that moment the guest of honor, Bob Merrit, arrived with his charming young wife. Bob was about Rousseau's age and had conspicuously red hair. He came in grinning, but one foot was bandaged and he was using a crutch.

"How was the skiing today?" I asked.

"I zigged when I should have zagged," he said, laughing, but didn't offer any other explanation.

Bob's wife, attractive and petite—I have forgotten her name—was somewhat younger than he. She was running a comb through her long blond hair when she came in and I assumed they, like Rousseau, had driven with the top down. I noticed she stayed close to her husband and was unusually attentive. Like newlyweds, though they were not, they held hands much of the time, occasionally gazing silently at one another, speaking only with their eyes.

Bob said he was from Rhode Island and planned to open a marine electronics company in Monaco. I wondered what that had to do with Rousseau's line of work. Was there a connection there? Or did our host think I might be able help Bob in some way? Well, I was sure I would find out before long.

"Everyone to the dining room right away please. Time, tide, ships, and soufflés wait for no man—and no woman either. Maurice, open the champagne." It was Astrid's voice from the kitchen, where she had rushed to inspect the soufflé. I liked Astrid. You can never define charm, but she had it—and she was a gourmet cook too.

It was a gathering of outstandingly attractive people. They were what journalists would call "the beautiful people." They had youth, money, education, background, and it seemed, not a care in the world. Fortune had smiled on them all. Perhaps I was a little envious, and I remember wondering how well their lives of privilege had prepared them for the heartbreaking misfortunes that befall the less fortunate people of the world. Put to the test, would they be found wanting?

The food, the champagne, the elegant atmosphere of candle light, the sparkling crystal, the polished silver, the witty and scintillating conversation, the carefree laughter—it all combined to make an unforgettable evening. Bob held us all enthralled by his amusing stories—his wife by his side, looking adoringly at him and laughing appreciatively at his wit and humor. I think they were holding hands under the table.

"Listen," she said, when we started to talk about sailing, "Bob here is really a sailor. He is the best I have ever seen. They just don't come any better." She looked around the table as if warning us not to challenge her statement. I thought that sounded a bit extreme, but it was good to see a wife so devoted to her husband.

Later Astrid brought in a baked Alaska and Rousseau served a chilled dessert wine with it—after that an espresso. We remained at the table for a while talking and sipping cognac.

The evening was still young when Bob and his wife got up, saying how much they had enjoyed the evening; but he felt a bit tired and wanted to turn in early. "And besides little Annie, our three year old, won't go to sleep until I come home and tell her a story." I also prepared to leave.

"Don't go yet, John." Rousseau whispered to me. "Stay and have another cognac. I have something to tell you."

When the Merrits had gone, I waited, eager to hear at last what was on Rousseau's mind, but if he had exploded one of his grenades behind my back, he could not have shocked me more.

"Bob just had his last dinner party. Astrid and I wanted so much for him to enjoy it. He will never go out to dinner again. He will be dead in three days."

I was stunned—absolutely astounded and saddened, both for Bob and for his adoring wife. Rousseau then went on to tell the rest, his eyes occasionally glistened and his voice shook with emotion.

"Bob is the only son of an immensely rich father—a domineering New England industrialist. He and his father have never gotten along. When Bob became ill, doctors diagnosed leukemia and advised immediate chemotherapy. His father took charge and arranged for the best care that money could buy at the Mayo clinic, but Bob and his wife didn't believe in doctors and he refused treatment. He said he would go instead to Monaco, open a marine electronics store, and put his trust in prayer. His father couldn't change Bob's decision, despite the fact that medical science had recently advanced to the point where they could sometimes cure this terrible disease—but only when treatment was started without delay."

I sensed that this was not the whole story and still didn't know why I had been invited. When it became clear that Rousseau would not say more, I thanked my host and hostess for an enjoyable evening and left.

Driving home, I thought about Rousseau's approach to life. I couldn't help liking him, though his way of making a living shocked me. I had seen the depth of his human feeling, his kindness, and his compassion. I wondered at the contrast between his two businesses. He made toys that brought pleasure to little children but sold weapons that caused untold suffering and death. Did the toy business give him a better self image or was it a hedge to improve his chances in the hereafter? Whatever the answer, there was a decent streak in him, along with the sinister. We humans are complex, often enigmatic, creatures, I thought.

Exactly three nights later Rousseau phoned again. His voice was heavy with emotion. "Bob just died."

I sat in stunned silence for a moment. I couldn't believe it. A feeling of profound sadness swept over me. Finally I asked something that had been troubling me since that night, "How did you know Bob had only three more days to live?"

After some hesitation he said, "I've known him since we were college room mates in the States. He was my best friend. We had no secrets from one another. Bob was in constant pain, suffering terribly." Rousseau stopped.

I waited, saying nothing as I began to sense the incredible truth.

"He took an overdose of sleeping tablets. I can tell you now that when we all had dinner together, only you were unaware of what he was going to do.

Have you wondered why it was so important for you to be with us that night? We needed someone who didn't know—someone to help us keep up pretenses."

THE CENTERFOLD GIRL

I never was sure which intelligence agency Pat worked for. He would only speak of those he had been with in the past—the FBI where he started his career and then some special branch of US Army Intelligence. I suppose he had to have been with OSS, the forerunner of CIA, when I met him. I was in the Paris office of my company then and he was going with my English secretary, Victoria.

There was an aura of mystery about Pat which I think he cultivated. He never gave away any trade secrets but liked to impress me with grim reminders that he was involved in deadly serious intrigues and already had more bullet holes in him than he cared to think about. If he was somewhat melodramatic, I made allowances for it. He was the real thing—big, powerful, tough, and professional. Even his father had been a sheriff, shot dead in the line of duty.

When he married Victoria, I went to London to attend the reception. Two of Pat's friends were with him—one a tall, brooding, silent man of about thirty, who in many ways resembled Sean Connery. I noticed he spoke to almost no one but sat off to one side sipping a sherry in solitude. A month later Pat told me this friend had just been killed behind the Iron Curtain—in Hungary or Czechoslovakia—I wasn't sure which. The other friend was a black man whose name was Ben, if my memory is correct. Pat and Ben worked as a two man team and it was clear that they regarded one another as if they were brothers.

Preparations for this kind of life were extremely rigorous according to Pat. I remember, for example, being impressed at the emphasis on memory training. Pat had to notice, and remember almost everything. He would be shown a table with thirty or more objects on it for a few seconds, and then told to list everything he had seen. As a result of this training he seemed phenomenally alert at all times. He said that during every moment of his waking life he looked for opportunities to practice and enhance this ability, knowing it might someday save his life.

I remember having lunch with Pat once in a little Japanese restaurant in Paris. We gave our orders and the waitress left the table.

"Could you describe the waitress' ears?" he asked.

"Hell no." His question astounded me.

"You should notice these things. Ears are as distinctive as fingerprints and more useful for identification because they're usually easier to observe. No two people have ears that look the same."

Pat leaned toward me and spoke in a low conspiratorial tone. "Notice this girl's ear lobes especially. They are most unusual. She could have extensive plastic surgery and completely change her face as well as her hair color and its style, but even fifty years from now I could still recognize her."

Was he only practicing what he had been taught, or was the waitress a foreign operative? It occurred to me there might be some sinister reason we were in that particular restaurant. When the girl came back I looked so intently at her ears I believe I scared her.

Pat was always enveloped in an aura of intrigue. I think that's one reason I enjoyed his company. When I was with him I felt I was somehow participating in a real life drama, and anything could happen at any moment.

One day my fiancée and I went to Pat and Victoria's modest little apartment for a dinner of poulet roti, pomme frit, and the season's nouveau Beaujolais. The tantalizing aroma of delicious food made me ravenous, but just as we were sitting down to eat, the phone rang.

"It's for you," Victoria said. Her voice was cold and resentment showed unmistakably in her expression. She shoved the phone brusquely at her husband.

He mumbled, "Pat here...yep...right...OK, ten minutes." His face betrayed nothing as he left us and went into the bedroom.

Victoria said this happened routinely. She grumbled that the dinner party was ruined. Pat would leave, she said, and not tell her where he was going nor how long he would be gone. She said she knew better than to ask. Sometimes he would be gone for a few hours and at other times for weeks. Once it had been for well over a month, without any word from him. It wasn't his fault really. He had to follow orders exactly. His survival and Ben's depended on it. He was government property. His life was not his own.

About ten minutes later Pat returned dressed as a filthy stumble bum. He gave Victoria, now a frigid marble statue, a quick peck on the cheek.

"Sorry," he said and was gone.

"When he dresses like that he doesn't come back for weeks." The bitterness in Victoria's voice made me wonder how long the marriage would last.

He may never come back, I thought.

A month later the Herald Tribune carried a story on its front page concerning a major coup won by the NATO allies in the back alleys and underground dens of Algiers' Casbah. Two American agents, one white and one black were responsible for the victory. It was the largest roundup of the free world's enemies in years. Victoria, momentarily proud, told me the men were Pat and Ben. Pat had no comment.

Soon after, I married and went with my wife to live in Madrid. Although we tried to keep in touch with Pat and Victoria, we lost contact because of their, and our, frequent moves.

Years later when I was in Rochester, New York, something reminded me of Pat and it occurred to me this was where he grew up. I reached for the phone book and sure enough his mother was listed. From her I learned Pat was still alive and well and living in Boston. I couldn't wait to ring him up.

In an enthusiastic rush of words he said, "Damn. It sure is good to hear from you John. How the hell are you any way? How about coming over for dinner? I guarantee you the biggest and best lobster you ever ate." We set a date and Pat met me at the airport. He looked about the same, butch haircut and all, except now he was ebullient and happy. I had never seen him like that before.

Driving to his apartment, he brought me up to date. He and Victoria had long ago divorced. This didn't surprise me. He had recently remarried. Again I was not surprised. Pat added, "It was the move to a small town in Maine that was more than Victoria could take."

My imagination filled in the details. She had been raised in London's elegant Mayfair district and in Paris. Having to languish out in the middle of nowhere on Pat's meager pay, while wondering when or if he would come home was not her idea of living.

He told me he took early retirement a few years later and said, not without a touch of pride, "I had four knife scars and 7 bullet holes in me." The expression on his face challenged me to top that. I smiled. The same old Pat…but I didn't doubt what he said was true.

He said he was in great demand because of his background. A head hunter found him a job as Vice President, In Charge of Security, with a major corporation. They owned several hundred discount stores scattered across the nation and their losses due to shop lifters and dishonest employees amounted to millions of dollars a year, according to Pat. They could afford to pay plenty for his expertise—a salary many times what he made before. At last he was affluent and able to enjoy a normal life.

When we arrived at his apartment I met Pat's young auburn haired wife. She was startlingly attractive in every way. Sharon, half Pat's age, had a perfect figure, a complexion as smooth and unflawed as a ripe peach, and eyes of deep-sea blue. She was charming, vivacious, and had the knack of surrounding herself with beauty. It showed in the furnishing and decoration of their apartment. A fire crackled on the brick hearth and I looked around admiringly at the teak, the black leather, the bright hued pillows, and ceramic color accents. Their home was the epitome of quiet elegance, thanks to Sharon's taste and Pat's newfound prosperity. The atmosphere was that of a happy household, the American dream come true, and I was glad Pat had finally found contentment and security, which he so deserved.

During the delicious lobster dinner I looked at Sharon and asked, "How did you two happen to meet?" It probably sounded like polite conversation, but I was curious to know because of the difference in their ages.

"Oh, we met in the Boston Playboy Club. I was a bunny there—you know serving drinks and that sort of thing."

"Really? I've never been in one of their clubs but I have a friend who thinks it's a good place to spend an evening…soft music, excellent food, honest drinks, and very pretty girls."

"Do I look familiar to you?" she asked. In retrospect I realize Pat knew what was coming and it seemed to amuse him.

I was baffled by the question. "No, I'm sorry. Should you?" I dipped a big chunk of lobster in a bowl of hot butter.

"I guess you don't read—I say read for want of a better word—*Playboy* magazine. I was the centerfold girl in last year's March issue."

The lobster on its way to my mouth stopped in mid air until hot butter ran down my sleeve. I thought at first she was joking but both she and Pat assured me it was true. I thought it out of character for Pat to approve of this, but his expression suggested he was more proud than embarrassed—or at least was trying to convince himself that was the case.

"If you think I'm kidding, check it out," she said.

"I'll take your word for it."

"Shall I tell what happened last week?" Sharon asked Pat. He grinned and nodded.

"OK. Last week Fred dropped in. Fred is one of Pat's plain clothes security men. The three of us talked, played music tapes for a while, relaxed and drank beer. Finally I said I was going to bed and I left them."

I wondered what was coming. I gathered it was going to be an amusing story.

She continued, "There I was getting undressed when I turned and saw a man watching me through the window." Sharon laughed and could hardly go on. Pat also joined in, but his smile now looked crooked and unnatural. I wondered if he was trying to conceal his embarrassment, as people sometimes do. "I ran as fast as I could, forgetting to put on my robe—imagine—and told Pat and Fred what had happened. I was so scared I couldn't even remember what the guy looked like."

Pat spoke up. "Fred and I ran for the door. At the same time I told Sharon to dial 911. Report. Say two men are in pursuit and describe us. Off we went like bats out of hell. I told Fred to go out the back. Said I'd take the front. We would both circle the building counter-clockwise."

Sharon resumed the telling. "OK, I dialed 911 and did like Pat told me. Then nothing happened for a long time. Eleven thirty became 1 a.m. Still no word. I figured Pat and Fred were out there going up one street and down another trying to find someone suspicious."

Pat interrupted. "John, you are not going to believe this. Here I am with Fred and we are out there beating the bushes when up comes a police patrol car and out hop two cops with drawn revolvers. One guy says to the other 'that's them all right—the guy wearin jeans with an orange windbreaker and the guy wearin a yellow and black horizontally striped T shirt and black corduroy pants.' My God, what dumb bastards. I told 'em who I was and they didn't believe me. I didn't have any identification on me and neither did Fred, so they took us down to the police station, booked us as peeping Toms, and locked us up. I said I wanted to phone my wife and they said 'never mind we'll do it.'" While he was telling me this I noticed Pat's face had turned the same color as the lobsters. He still wore the smile of mortification. Pat probably could visualize headlines in the morning paper, EX-OSS HERO A

PEEPING TOM. "Sharon, you tell the rest."

Sharon was laughing so hard now she couldn't go on for a moment. Tears were streaming down her cheeks but finally, with an effort of will, she continued, "Well I finally got a call from the police sometime after 2 a.m. and they said, 'We've got 'em ma'am. They're dressed just like you told us.' I said, 'My God, maybe you have made a mistake. I'll come right over and see who you've got.'"

Sharon had my full attention now.

"This is almost unbelievable. I got dressed and got in my car to go to the police station. When I started it, the engine sounded OK but after I went about two miles it conked out and wouldn't restart. Out of gas. At that time of the morning there was not a house in sight with a light on. After a lot of bell ringing and pounding on doors, I finally found one person who would answer, but he wouldn't let me in to use the phone—just promised to call a cab. I won't go into any more details but poor Pat and Fred spent most of the night locked up in jail. The police had misunderstood everything I said when I called 911." It was clear Sharon thought nothing could have been funnier.

I sensed instantly this whole thing had to have been a cruel prank. There were too many improbabilities. Although I could neither recall all the things on the table that night nor describe Sharon's ears as Pat no doubt could, of one thing I was sure—this was a mean hoax—which was more than he knew.

I returned to Rochester on the late night flight and didn't hear from Pat again until months later. When I did, I found him changed—no longer the cheerful, happy man he had been.

I learned that the police had been suspicious. All calls to 911 are recorded on tape and a detective played back Sharon's voice as she reported the two peeping Toms, one dressed like Fred and the other like Pat. A check of her credit card records showed she had filled her car with gas the day before all this happened and could not have run out of fuel as she pretended. Finally Sharon confessed, angrily accusing them of not being able to take a joke. She was arrested for falsely reporting a crime, a serious offense; taken to jail, booked, fingerprinted, and locked up. Pat bailed her out, paid her legal expenses and finally the steep fine, but said he could never feel the same toward her again after the way she humiliated him.

I never could understand how Pat, with all his professional training, failed, in this instance, to see what should have been obvious to anyone. Probably he didn't want to see. Perhaps his love for Sharon blinded him, as love is known to do.

I guess he knew what I was thinking. At least I got this impression when he added sadly, “One thing they forgot to warn me about…logic sort of flies out the window when emotion comes barging in the door.”

ABRACADABRA

It was Hank's first trip to the Orient, a part of the world that had fascinated him since he was a child; and as he boarded his flight the words of his boss were still ringing in his ears, "Get Sakamoto to sign this agreement and I'll promote you to Vice President."

After takeoff, a tiny JAL stewardess, in a lavender kimono and white obi of spectacular splendor, brought him a "happy coat" to wear during the flight—or did she call it "a hapi coat"—he wasn't sure. It was black, white, and red; and made in traditional Japanese style. The stewardesses fascinated him. They reminded him of little oriental dolls.

Hank opened his briefcase and took out the proposal he had to present, intending to look at it one more time. But as he sipped a bourbon on the rocks and munched roasted peanuts, his mind went back to the events of two days earlier when he and Harrison had sat facing one another, a coffee table between them, in the CEO's opulent office.

Harrison, the CEO, an abrupt and often ruthless man, had sent for him, and he waited to hear what the boss had on his mind. One never knew what to expect from the man. He was a tall rangy individual with a fringe of red hair around his bald head, and a fiery temper. Deep voiced and barrel chested, he had the abrupt manner of one who always had his way—one who gave orders and did not tolerate any argument. On this occasion it suited Harrison to greet Hank in a friendly enough way, however. He told him to sit down, and had his secretary bring some coffee.

"Hank, I've been in a board meeting all afternoon, discussing distribution problems in Japan. We damned well better get a new color-film processing plant there or we'll lose the market completely, but we can't get Sakamoto to approve the funding for it."

"I know. I'm aware of the problem." It seemed to Hank an appropriate response and it was.

"Oh you are, are you?" The CEO's irritation showed in his tone of voice. His face began to flush—an early warning of trouble. "Do you know how much our gross revenue is down in Japan, during the second quarter?" He had this way of firing questions at people in an intimidating manner making them understand they were being tested and their whole future depended on the answer.

"Yes, 18.7 percent," said Hank. "During this period, the Japanese economy grew at an annualized rate of just under eight percent." Hank was not reading from notes; he had done his homework. "We are fast losing that market because our competitors can rapidly process color film, including both theirs and ours, and we can't even process our own without unacceptable delays and quality problems. I'd also like to say that we need more than a new color processing plant there, in my opinion."

Interest replaced irascibility in a sudden mood swing. "What do you mean?" asked the CEO, surprised by Hank's reply.

"Since we are starting to diversify into many film and optically related fields, it's vital that our Japanese dealer invest heavily in building and staffing a new training division. That's every bit as important as the new processing plant. Both are essential. As an inducement to get on with an overall plan, we could offer to train his instructors without charge, with the proviso that he doesn't delay his decision beyond some date that we should spell out clearly."

If Harrison agreed with Hank, he gave no indication of it; to do so was not his style. Hank had just identified a need that nobody else on his staff had mentioned—it was one of those things that was immediately obvious, when you thought about it, but clearly nobody else had done so.

Hank had joined the company at a low level only seven years before and now he was already a department head in one of America's largest corporations, reporting directly to the CEO. He had scored almost unbelievably high on the IQ test administered to new white collar employees, and that probably had something to do with his rapid rise, but just now it was Hank's remarkable ability to handle people that interested Harrison. This first came to the CEO's attention when, by sheer force of his personality, tact, and charm, Hank averted a strike. Labor relations had been relatively cordial since then.

"The reason I wanted to see you," the CEO continued, "is that I am sending you to Tokyo to see if you can persuade old Sakamoto to build the new facilities. Bill wanted to go but I turned him down—told him I need my Executive Vice President here, not on the other side of the world. Whether he likes it or not, I think you are the man for this assignment. Hope I'm right. I want you to leave Friday. Any personal reason you can't?"

Hank glanced momentarily at his pocket agenda. "I can change some meetings and postpone a trip to D.C. Friday's fine with me."

"Good." The CEO paused long enough to drink some coffee, while he considered his next remark. "Sakamoto's a complete enigma to all of us—like an old Samurai, powerful man but short, stone faced you know, speaks only Japanese—you have to communicate through his interpreter whose English is just so-so. Did you meet him on either of his visits here?"

"Yes. I sure did," Hank said this with a wry smile

Harrison mimicked the stiff countenance of the Japanese, "Never laughs, never even smiles...."

"That's true but, maybe his sense of humor is just different from ours. Perhaps we don't laugh or even smile at the same things."

"Maybe so but damn it, Hank, he never even changes his *expression.* You never know what the old bastard is thinking. Both Bill and I tried to reason with him when he was here, but we got nowhere." Harrison's face was beginning to flush with anger as he recalled his last meeting with the old Japanese.

"You may not even be able see him," he continued. "It wouldn't surprise me at all. He's so rich and so powerful that, in his own country, he's almost completely inaccessible—even to visitors from overseas. Make no mistake about it, this is a tough assignment, but we can't give up. We have to keep trying."

"Well I think he'll at least *see* me," said Hank. "During his last visit, he and his entourage came to dinner at my home and I cooked for them in the Japanese style. I am a chef by hobby and my specialty is oriental cooking. Sakamoto seemed surprised—ate everything and accepted more. You're right though, he's a cold, hard character. I can't say that I succeeded in warming him up. I didn't. I learned a few things that don't work with him—that's all."

"I must say, your interests are a bit off-beat. I keep hearing new ones. I'm told you started your career on the stage. Is that right?"

"Yes, in a manner of speaking. Hank smiled as he recalled a flood of pleasant memories. "I was very young, seventeen or eighteen, when I started.

Times were hard then and I had no money for college…couldn't get a job, so that's what I did for five years. It paid well and was fun."

Harrison looked appraisingly at Hank. Anyone could see that he was still slim and well proportioned; had dark, wavy hair; and had a well modulated voice with a ring of authority, which had a mesmerizing effect on people. His gray eyes were his strongest feature. They gave him an almost hypnotic presence that people noticed and could not forget—not even Harrison.

"Well I must say you have done pretty well Hank, considering your unorthodox path to success." Harrison leaned forward as if to dramatize his next words. "You *could* do even better. You know my policy; I believe in incentive. I have an agreement here." He held up a thick brown envelope. "If you can get Sakamoto to sign this, I'll promote you to Vice President and, of course, increase your stock options, salary, bonus, and other benefits accordingly. But if you come back empty handed—well there's no pay-off for good tries no matter how clever they are. Any questions?"

Hank shook his head negatively and held out his hand to receive the document. The CEO tossed it to him and stood up, indicating that the meeting was over.

His last words would have been, "Good luck. You'll need it," but as Hank reached the door a sudden thought prompted Harrison to say, "Wait a minute. Better give me back that envelope. I just thought of something I want to add. I'll have this sent down to you first thing in the morning."

Harrison called in his secretary as soon as Hank had left and dictated something concerning a new training division to support planned diversification—adroitly rephrasing Hank's idea to make it his own. Having done this, he promptly forgot where the idea came from—something he had learned to do early in his business career.

"Fasten your seat belts prease. Air ahead is bumpy." The announcement brought Hank back to here and now. He was in a section where the seats faced one another, an unusual arrangement featured by some airlines at that time. Opposite was Jimmy, a little boy of eight, and his mother. The stewardess had given the little fellow some plastic JAL Pilot's wings to pin on his coat and as small boys often do, he dropped them on the floor. In an instant Hank picked them up, but instead of returning them, he grinned and passed them quickly back and forth between his hands for a moment. He then held up two clenched fists and said, "The hand is quicker than the eye. Guess which fist it's in."

Little Jimmy returned Hank's grin. "The right one."

"Good guess, but you are wrong." He opened his right hand, palm up. No wings.

"I meant *my* right—that would be *your* left," he said, surprising Hank with his quick wittedness.

Hank laughed. "Smart boy! But you are still wrong." He then opened his left hand palm up. Again no wings. "But I think they are in your coat." He reached over and, to the little fellow's astonishment, plucked the wings out of a pocket.

"How'd you do that? How'd you do that?" little Jimmy shouted excitedly.

Hank showed him. It was simple in principle but required a dexterity that had come only after years of practice and a five year career as a vaudeville magician-hypnotist.

After a delicious dinner and some hot saki he put down his chop sticks and dozed off, watching Jimmy's futile attempts to duplicate the trick. Unlike many people, he had no trouble sleeping during long flights; and rarely suffered from jet lag.

Hank was awakened later as the plane was on its final approach for a landing at Tokyo's Narita International Airport. His charming little stewardess was making a last announcement.

"Prease put your seats in the uplight position for the randing. Thank you for frying Japanese Air Rines.... Put your laincoats on. The wezzer on the glound is crowdy and lainy." Hank smiled at the stewardess' difficulties with the L's and R's of the English language.

A limo-bus brought him to the Imperial Hotel at what would have been his normal bedtime if he had not reset his watch, but he wasn't sleepy. His mind was racing, trying to deal with a flood of exotic impressions of sight and sound, so he decided to explore the city on foot. He could sleep later.

The concierge gave him a street map, after carefully marking the location of the hotel.

"Are there any parts of town that I should avoid? ... places where it would be unsafe to walk alone late at night." Hank asked.

"Don't understand," was the reply. "What do you mean *unsafe?*"

"Street crime...I'm talking about street crime."

"No. No stleet clime."

"What do you *mean* no street crime? Tokyo has a population of almost nine million. How can you *not* have any street crime?"

"We make law against it—it is forbidden." The concierge sucked air in through his teeth and looked up at Hank through large, thick, horn rimmed glasses. Hank had no more questions, but he knew then that he had a lot to learn. *When we first contact intelligent creatures from outer space I know now just how it is going to feel, he* thought. Hank had a passion to know and understand the Japanese people and their culture.

He walked the streets of the Ginza district observing—gathering first impressions. The picturesque atmosphere excited him. He had an impression of bright lights and also of places that were dark and mysterious—of vivid color, of smoke-borne, tantalizing cooking aromas; of thousands of banners marked with immense artistic pictographs of the Japanese language, of tinkling bells, and of wind chimes.

He heard quaint, weird sounding music made with bronze bells, six stringed zithers, and bamboo flutes. Sometimes he could also identify wooden gongs, cymbals, plucked stringed instruments, and pieces of wood struck together. Just moments later and a few steps farther on, he heard familiar western music. The ancient traditional culture made an unblendable mix with the new.

Most people wore occidental clothing, but he saw a few women magnificently and expensively dressed in kimonos, so carefully made up and coifed that they looked like oriental paintings. They were often escorted by Japanese men in elegantly tailored tuxedos.

Well behaved young people were everywhere, wearing casual western clothes, like teenagers the world over, except that they were immaculate. Men were usually diminutive by western standards but from time to time Hank saw one who was well over six feet tall. At four in the morning he returned to the hotel exhausted, but exhilarated.

Sunday morning Hank's phone rang. Sleepily he picked it up and heard:

"Good morning Hank. I have good news." It was the voice of Robert Hiroshi Nakagawa, a man in his early thirties, who worked for Sakamoto. "You have an appointment with Sakamoto Monday morning at eight. You're lucky. In Japan everyone hears 'Sakamoto' all the time but only rarely does anyone see him face to face. Just tell the taxi driver to take you to the Sakamoto building. His office is in the penthouse."

"Good. Thanks for calling me. Where are you now?"

"In the lobby of your hotel."

"Great. Come on up and have breakfast with me."

Hiroshi was a Nisei American, born and raised in San Francisco. He had a degree in Chemical Engineering from Stanford and an M.B.A. from Harvard. Closely related to Sakamoto on his mother's side of the family, he had spent many summers in Japan, staying with the old man. Hank was glad Hiroshi was there to help him understand, at least a little, the Japanese culture—to instruct him in some of the more important aspects of etiquette, such as how and when to bow—things like that.

It worried Hank that he still had no strategy for accomplishing his mission. Robert, or "Hiroshi" as he was called when in Japan, confirmed what Hank had already been told, that Sakamoto was one of the richest and most powerful men in the country. He was Chairman of the Board and held the controlling interest of a giant holding company that owned a major shipyard, several industrial chemical factories, a pharmaceutical company, two electronics firms whose products were household names familiar to every American; and a trading company which held the franchises or licenses of almost every leading technical firm in the motion picture business—its products included everything of film or optical nature used by the motion picture industry.

Hank ordered breakfasts to be served in the room and they sat by a large window from which they could see the tall Sakamoto building which stood as a monument to the man whose name it bore.

"Hiroshi, can you give me *any* advice? The presentation I am going to make tomorrow is extremely important to the company and to me personally. What, I wonder, is the key to success? I feel that it's important for me to know everything you can tell me about Sakamoto. What are his interests aside from business? What is he really like? What makes him tick, as we say?"

Nakagawa, elbows on the table, rested his chin on his hands and sat with eyes closed for a while. "That's a good question, Hank. You can call me Bob, by the way. Only the Japanese call me by my middle name. I don't know what to tell you. As you know, I've lived with him off and on when growing up but I really can't say I know him at all. He is rather formidable. Nobody ever knows what he is thinking—not even Japanese people."

Bob was deep in thought. Hank remained silent and waited. He sensed there was more to come.

"I guess all I can advise is that you come to the point quickly. Say what you have to say to make clear what you are proposing, cover everything but don't repeat yourself. He is a very busy man and gets angry with people who waste even a minute of his time. Watch his hands and if he gets nervous fingers—drums on the table or something like that—it means he is impatient and getting angry. Get on with it fast or you are finished."

None of this helped Hank. These were generalities that every experienced negotiator understood anyway. Well, in any case, he reflected, he liked challenges and that's what he had now.

Hank had a strong conviction that if a deal made sense to him and he believed it was in the best interest of both parties, he could *always* find a way to sell it, if he could just think of the angle—the all important key to the sale. He had never failed before to find it, but there was a first time for everything. Never before had he negotiated a contract with Sakamoto or anyone even remotely like him.

Hank tried his best to find a strategy that he would instinctively recognize as the *key,* but it eluded him. Nobody, it seemed, knew what made Sakamoto tick. Under the circumstances he had no choice but to play it by ear. It was utterly contrary to his every instinct to do that, but he had no choice.

The next day Hank arrived at the Sakamoto building a half hour early, to be sure that traffic delays didn't make him late. He walked up and down the street until ten minutes before the appointed time and then went in. A receptionist took him in the private elevator, to Sakamoto's large and sumptuous penthouse office. The room was furnished mostly in Western style and the old man was seated near a large picture window where he could look out over a panorama of the Ginza district where Hank had been the night before.

Sakamoto got up, looked impassively at Hank and bowed from the waist. Hank bowed from the waist. It pulled his muscles as painfully as it would have if he had to bend over and put his hands flat on the floor without bending his knees. Only one other person was present, a very pretty, beautifully dressed young Japanese woman—the interpreter. When the bowing was over, tea was brought in and poured. Sakamoto was following the mandates of Japanese tradition but Hank noticed that before the usual polite talk, required by Japanese etiquette, was finished and the tea drunk, Sakamoto was already starting to get "nervous fingers."

Hank took that as his cue and began his presentation immediately, but Sakamoto stopped him and led him into an adjoining room in which there was a long table and many men.

After introductions and seemingly endless polite but formal bowing, Hank was seated on one side of the table—Sakamoto and his board of directors sat on the other. Off to the left at the end of the table was the interpreter. Hank got right down to business. He told Sakamoto to interrupt him immediately at any point if he had any question or comment, then began by pointing out the steady decline in the company's Japanese market, and competition's up-trending profits. He assessed the cause, urged the construction of the new color processing plant and the new facility for training and service, gave a concise description of the agreement he had brought with him, and expressed the hope that Sakamoto would accept and sign it. He had talked just under 25 minutes when he finished.

The thick, stubby fingers had ceased their drumming on the table, but during his presentation and after it, Hank saw not the slightest clue as to what effect, if any, his presentation was having on Sakamoto. The old man sat as impassive as a Buddha sculpted in granite, his eyes closed, or perhaps they were mere slits that seemed closed. Hank looked at the others hoping for some reaction but saw a sea of faces as much alike one another and as enigmatic as the statues on Easter Island.

The only response was silence. After a moment Hank, in his anguish, feared that Sakamoto had gone to sleep. He could not have been more wrong. Sakamoto suddenly stood up—so did Hank, by reflex—and turning to the interpreter uttered a series of abrupt commands in a raucous, acerbic tone of voice, with a whip lash delivery like a medieval Samurai that Hank had once seen portrayed on television.

The interpreter said, "Mr. Sakamoto says he must go to Osaka tomorrow morning on urgent business. However, he invites you to join him for dinner tonight. He will send a car for you at eight p.m."

Sakamoto bowed. Hank bowed. The interpreter bowed, the directors bowed. Hank bowed a few more times and left. His back hurt and he had a headache.

On his return to the hotel, Bob was waiting for him. Seeing the expression on Hank's face, Bob couldn't help laughing. He said, "Well, now West meets East."

Hank managed a grim smile and said, "Thanks for being here, Bob. Come on, let's go to the bar and have a drink. I need one." Fortunately the bar was only a few steps away.

"Two vodka Martinis," said Hank. "And what will you have, Bob?"

"Nothing thanks. I don't usually drink at this time of the day."

"Neither do I, but today I'm making an exception."

"The old man is really something, isn't he?" Bob said that with sympathy, but he was still smiling. "Want to tell me about it?"

Hank described the meeting. "Does it look encouraging that he has asked me to dinner? Does he just want to think it all over and then negotiate details at dinner?"

"No Hank. In Japan it is very bad form to discuss business at dinner. I hate to say it but you have struck out like everyone in your company has done before you. I'm afraid you were licked from the start."

"Well then why does he invite me to dinner? Isn't that some sign of interest?"

"Not at all. It's required by custom. He'll undoubtedly take you to his favorite geisha house. It's a good excuse for going himself—one thing he enjoys. He told you he will go to Osaka tomorrow morning. Maybe he will and maybe he won't. You must interpret that as 'There will be no further meetings. I don't want to discuss this subject again.' No, you have lost, and I hate to be the one to tell you."

Hank was silent for a while thinking. *The show's not over yet. There's still one more act.* He said, "Well now I have learned two things about Sakamoto since I saw you last. He has little respect for women. I noticed his unchivalrous behavior toward the pretty little interpreter today—his harsh way of speaking to her—and I could see that she was actually afraid of him. Now you tell me he likes to go to geisha houses. Hmmm." At last, some pieces of the Sakamoto jig saw puzzle.

"Bob, correct me if you think I am wrong, but Sakamoto impresses me as a man who dislikes women. He isn't polite to them. He never married. He may like to flirt with the geishas but I'll bet they are only sex objects to him. My guess is that he doesn't really like them."

"I think you may be right there, now that you mention it."

"Now, *if I am* right, the kind of humor he thinks the funniest, is that which is at the expense of a woman or of women generally. Have you ever seen him laugh? If so, what was he laughing at?"

"Let me think a moment." Bob leaned back and looked up at the ceiling as he searched his memory. "Yes, by golly, you are *exactly* right. I was with him one night when a geisha was dancing. She had drunk a little too much saki, slipped and almost fell. That is the only time I ever saw him laugh."

Promptly at eight o'clock that night a limousine called for Hank and took him to a geisha house. There he found Sakamoto waiting, with four men of his staff. After much bowing, each man took off his shoes, went into a large tastefully decorated room, and sat cross-legged on mats around a low table. Sitting that way was torture for Hank's already aching back and knees. Six geisha's, their faces painted white and looking like porcelain, entered wearing the most beautiful kimonos and obis Hank had ever seen. Bob had told him that these kimonos cost thousands of dollars each.

Things started off sedately with a tea ceremony to which Japanese attach great importance. Later, they served various delicacies and hot saki, all of which Hank found delicious. The geishas were all vivacious and animated, each trained to sing, dance, and play various instruments, which they proceeded to do. As the Japanese men consumed more and more saki, the songs and conversation might have become somewhat ribald at times. Hank couldn't understand a word spoken but he sensed this by the way the men snickered and looked at one another like naughty school boys.

He decided that now the right psychological moment had come. Hank, the epitome of insouciance, and forsaking all caution, withdrew two large red silk handkerchiefs from his pocket and proceeded to whirl them around above his head to get attention. Soon there was silence as interest focused on him. He then tied the corners of the two handkerchiefs together and pulled the knot tight. Next he held them up for all to see, and demonstrated that they could not be pulled apart. This was to prove that the knot was real before he handed them to Sakamoto for inspection.

When they were returned to him, Hank proceeded to gingerly poke first the knot, then the rest of the silk handkerchiefs down the décolleté of Sakamoto's favorite geisha who sat between them. The men watched in silent fascination, their faces, as usual, betraying nothing—a few of the geishas tittered nervously. Finally nothing of the handkerchiefs remained visible except two corners protruding from the top folds of the geisha's kimono.

Now all was in readiness. Hank hoped for the best, and took a deep breath—he realized he had not been breathing for some time. He grasped one of the red handkerchief corners and, with the aid of someone acting as interpreter, conveyed to Sakamoto that he was to take hold of the other corner and at the third magic word they both were to yank the handkerchiefs out. Sakamoto nodded gravely. At least Hank had his attention.

Hank emphasized the count with dramatic gestures. "ONE... TWO... ABRACADABRA!" Both Hank and Sakamoto yanked hard and out came the two big red silk handkerchiefs with a brassiere tied between them. The victim instinctively clasped her hands to her breasts, a look of astonishment on her porcelain face. There was an audible gasp from all of the other ladies from that "world of flowers and willows."

For an agonizing moment there was no other reaction from anyone. All, including Hank, looked intently at Sakamoto. *His* face registered what one might describe as almost round eyed amazement. Then the old Japanese began to shake convulsively and this uncharacteristic reaction developed further into a roaring, almost hysterical laughter. Obviously relieved, the others all joined in.

Sakamoto rocked from side to side and back and forth. Tears streamed down his cheeks. Finally he went right over backward and rolled on the mats that covered the floor, convulsed with laughter, still holding the red handkerchiefs with the brassiere tied between them.

When he could, Sakamoto got to his feet, and tried to regain some measure of his usual composure but he seemed to be having great difficulty suppressing a smile. He took Hank by the arm and led him off to a private room nearby, where he said in perfect English, "Mr. Shipman, I want you to meet me at my office at nine o'clock tomorrow morning. I will give you the contract you want—signed."

When Hank got back to his hotel that evening he sent a telex to Harrison, the CEO of his company. This was the short but exuberant text:

"I found out what makes Sakamoto tick, signed H. Shipman, *Vice President.*"

SEPTEMBER, REMEMBER

One of the Anderson's few friends summed it up with malice, but rather well.

"Fred's passion is rare books, but he can't discuss them with Doris. She, just as passionately, enjoys soap operas, chocolate bonbons, and her little terrier, Yappie—all of which turn him off. The Andersons were never a well matched couple in the first place you know, but now they've drifted as far apart as the earth's poles, and the atmosphere of their home has become just as cold."

Through the years, Fred had collected many rare editions. Most of them had increased in value and he looked forward to becoming a rare book dealer when he retired. On Saturdays, he usually made the rounds of Boston's used book shops, always alert to discover valuable first editions that had somehow been overlooked by the proprietors. The inevitable finally happened. He met an attractive woman who owned one of these shops.

Michelle, about ten years younger then Fred, was a woman of striking appearance and vivacious charm. She had come from Paris when her husband died to live with her father who ran the Boston office of a French shipping company. Fred liked her cute retroussé nose. It suggested, not without reason, an impish light heartedness. She had that chic for which many French women, particularly those of the upper class, are famous; her wardrobe and accessories came from Paris' famed rue Faubourg St. Honoré. Her eye-catching measurements were those of a mannequin, a high fashion model, which she had been until recently. She had lively brown eyes, high cheek bones, and mobile features that showed spirit, animation, and aristocratic distinction all at the same time. He was instantly captivated.

"Michelle," he said one day, "I think you have a first edition of Boswell's *Life of Johnson*. I hope it won't cost me an arm and a leg."

"Mais non Fred, not any longair." Her face registered deep regret. With arms extended sideways, the palms of her hands up, she shrugged her shoulders in a Gallic gesture of despair. "Eet 'as been sold, but I 'ave seen anuzzair Boswell een a small shop somewhere out of zee town. Let me theenk now…was eet een Brockton?…Or Sharon?…or Holbrook?" (She pronounced it 'Olbrook). "But we close zee shop now. I theenk about eet. Next time you come, maybe I remembair."

"Look, I have an idea. Why don't you close shop? Then we can go somewhere for coffee? Maybe zen you weel remembair." Fred said this, mimicking her accent, and gave her his most charming smile. "It's important to me. I'd like to buy it, wherever it is, before someone else does." He looked imploringly at her. She must have liked his graying temples and the way he smiled. Perhaps she thought how distingué he looked.

During coffee he told her of his passion for collecting and reading short stories as well as biographies. He described enthusiastically his first editions of O. Henry, H.H. Munro, Maugham, Chekhov, Guy de Maupassant, and P. G. Wodehouse. He again brought up the Boswell book and asked her to try hard to remember where she had seen the original edition. First editions of Boswell were, he said, climbing steadily in value, like a good sound stock, and he wanted any he could get at a reasonable price. Incunabula, books printed before the year 1500, as well as very old holographic manuscripts were, he thought, the best investments, but he didn't have enough capital to afford them. When it was time to part, Michelle still could not remember precisely where she had seen the book he wanted, but offered to ride with him the next day, which was a Saturday, to help him search for the volume. That is how it all started.

Whether they found it or not was soon of secondary importance. What counted most was being together, engrossed in activities fascinating to both. Soon Fred became obsessed with Michelle's beauty and exotic charm. He decided he could not live without her. For the first time in his life, he might be in love—at least it must be what they call love. No woman ever interested nor attracted him both physically and intellectually as she did. At first Michelle had trouble with his being married, but her interest soon deepened into fervent passion. Their relationship got beyond her control before she realized what was happening. Often during the day she made a short quick phone call.

"Fred Darling, I just called to geev you zee beeg keess," she would say, and then hang up. Soon he was getting several "beeg keesses" every day. He liked her way of letting him know she was thinking of him.

Fred wanted to be rid of Doris and the sooner the better. He came home one night and walked decisively into the house. If Yappie, her little white terrier, had greeted him, Fred would have given him a vicious kick.

"Doris sit down," he said as soon as he saw her. "We need to have a serious talk." His wife did as he told her, an expression of deep concern on her face. "Our marriage has become a farce—you can surely see that. We have nothing in common. We can't talk. We don't like the same things. We have no social life. I can't imagine why we ever married. I don't love you, and you don't love me. I can't take it anymore. I want a divorce. I want to remake my life." He had said what had been on his mind for a long time, and now he felt better, as if he had taken the first step on a new road to happiness.

Doris was stunned. Fred's words knocked the breath out of her. She sat for a while unable to say anything. Shock, profound sadness, and humiliation showed in her eyes and on her usually impassive face. Her lower lip quivered uncontrollably and tears coursed down her cheeks. At last, when she could, she said, "Oh Fred, do you have any idea how this hurts me?"

He had expected anger and would have preferred it.

She continued. "How can you imagine I don't love you?" Her voice shook with deeply felt emotion. "I haven't said it in so many words, but I didn't know I had to. I thought you understood. You are all I have in this world."

Fred felt no compassion. Desperation, yes. Compassion, no—none at all.

"Doris, I love someone else and she loves me. We're going to be married. It's that simple."

"You must not break up our home. I won't let you. It's just one of those mid-life crises some men go through. You will get over it. I will not agree to a divorce. You have spent nearly all of my money. I'm not criticizing you, but what will become of me if you leave me? How will I live? And besides, what you ask is impossible. You know as well as I do, divorce is not permitted by our church. What can you be thinking?" Yappie cocked his head to one side and with his paw let her know he was there.

What she said about money was true. She had been a wealthy woman when they married, but now Fred had spent nearly all her money on his book collection. Remarriage was for her an unlikely option. She was 15 years older then he, grossly overweight, plain, and wore her white hair in a bun.

Fred left the house and drove off in his car—desperate and furious. He was forty, slender, muscular, and athletic...a rising middle management executive in a publishing firm. Most women would say he was good-looking. He had married Doris because she had money, she was a good housekeeper and an excellent cook, and she was like his mother on whom he had been overly dependent, but none of that mattered to him now. He wanted a wife, not a mother.

As for the church, if he had to commit apostasy, so be it. His attitude toward religion, in any case, was more profane then genuine, more proforma then heartfelt. He wanted Michelle and would stop at nothing to get her. His cold indifference to Doris turned to blind loathing. He began to sweat and tremble in a paroxysm of violent hatred so intense it might be considered madness. She was standing between him and everything he wanted. Fred saw only one solution to his problems. He had to kill her. The thought brought with it the pleasure of anticipation. From then on, he could think of nothing else.

Months before, each had taken out a $1,000,000 insurance policy on the life of the other. He was glad now he had insisted on it. She had no way of knowing he let the policy on his own life lapse shortly afterward. Now, having decided to murder Doris, he would not shrink from insurance fraud, but his planning had to be meticulous in order not to attract suspicion. Soon he would be able to afford an elegant home, more rare books, and he could marry Michelle.

Fred studied the insurance policy carefully, paying special attention to the accidental death stipulation. It read: "If death is accidental, double indemnity will be paid to the beneficiary." $2,000,000! He convinced himself that all well planned murders look like accidents.

It occurred to him that a large policy on Doris and none on himself would look suspicious. He also knew he had to tell Michelle that he and Doris were planning a divorce, or he might lose her.

On the way to the office the next morning, Fred paid the lapsed premiums to reinstate the policy, with Doris the beneficiary. When he thought about the risk he was about to take, he felt no fear, but instead a strange euphoria and a compulsion to get on with it. Up to a certain point danger exhilarated him, as it does an acrobat who performs on the high wire without a safety net. He realized, however, he must prevent Doris telling anyone that he had asked for a divorce. That might raise suspicions. There were a lot of things to consider. He had to be extremely careful.

Fred made an excuse to leave the office in mid-morning and returned home, stopping along the way to buy a gift for Doris. He was the epitome of dejection when he came in.

"Doris I didn't sleep all night."

"Neither did I."

"At the office I couldn't get my mind on business. I had to come home and put things right between us. I wonder if you can ever find it in your heart to forgive me. I don't know what came over me last night. I didn't mean a word I said, and there isn't another woman. I just said that. I don't know why."

"Oh Fred, I wanted to believe you didn't mean it. I'm so relieved."

"Maybe it's because of the strain I've been under lately." He closed his eyes and rubbed his temples with the fingers of both hands to dramatize the point he was making. "I desperately need a rest and a change of scene. What would you say to a trip together somewhere? I still have some vacation coming…time for one last cruise before I lay the boat up for winter. Let's sail up to Gloucester for a few days. Just the two of us and little Yappie."

"Well, as you know, I'm not much of a sailor, but it would be good for us to have a change of scene, and I know how much you enjoy sailing Leprechaun."

"Good then, I'll call the office, and we can start tomorrow morning."

The next day Doris was up early packing a box of everything needed to make Fred's favorite dishes. She had worked late the night before, planning what they would have for each meal during the four days aboard Leprechaun. She packed a bottle of champagne and checked it off on her stores list under "Sunday night special anniversary dinner." Doris hummed as she worked. Fred's mood was also bright and cheerful; he had not been like that for so long.

When they reached the harbor, Fred checked the latest weather forecast. There was a small craft warning, but he decided to ignore it. He topped off the water and fuel tanks, took off the sail covers, and stowed them. Too crafty to put on the wrong act at a time like this, he shouted high spirited greetings to all he saw. When Doris finished walking Yappie, who would have to hold his water now for longer then usual, they shoved off.

Leprechaun proceeded under diesel power until she was clear of harbor traffic; then Fred cut the engine and set the sails. The contrast was dramatic;

in an instant all was quiet and the boat stopped rolling as the sails filled and she heeled gently. Fred lit the diesel-burning heater to make the main cabin warm and cozy. When the last of the channel buoys was abeam, he carefully noted the departure in the log. He passed Deer Island and Fred changed course, not for Gloucester, but instead for a point several miles off Marblehead.

Yappie, a poor sailor, crawled into the forepeak and went to sleep.

"When will we get there Fred? I'm a bit concerned about poor little Yappie."

"Depends on the wind. Not until late tonight in any case."

Doris yawned. "Being on the sea makes me sleepy. I think I'll take a nap. Call me when it's time to fix dinner. It won't be a hot one. We're just having cold cuts and potato salad—I can't cook underway, but there will be something special to drink. It's a surprise. I'll only need five minutes to have everything ready." She stretched out on the lee bunk, breathed deeply the clean sea air, and soon fell asleep listening to the murmur of water rushing past and the cry of a gull.

Fred reviewed his plan. He decided they were already far enough offshore, but he would wait for darkness. He wanted to be sure there were no witnesses. If he were to follow impulse, he would knock her on the head while she was sleeping, tie an anchor around her feet and drop her overboard—no witnesses—no corpus delecti. Or better yet, strangle her as he had often wanted to do. But he realized that would be stupid. If the body was never found it would look suspicious. Furthermore it might be impossible to collect on the policy. The insurance company could say there is no proof of death—she might be waiting for him in Rio. The body must be found. That means an autopsy, so there must be no bruise marks to arouse suspicions. Fred smiled. He knew how he was going to do it. It would be the perfect murder.

The sun sank into a nest of black cumulonimbus clouds, and the sky darkened. A cold front was approaching. The scene was filled with vague foreboding, but it suited Fred's purpose because before long a gray frontal mist would creep over the sea, dense enough to obscure the loom of Boston's city lights and even those of nearby Marblehead. Fred felt secure. No boats were near now, no one to see, and he was ready. He switched on the running lights, put on a windbreaker over his heavy wool sweater, and called to Doris. Electric currents were running up and down his spine. His every impulse urged him to get on with it. He began to tingle with excitement. Never before had he been so ecstatic—so exhilarated.

"Let's eat dinner in the cockpit," he said. "I have to keep watch and can't go below for long even with the autopilot on. But you better put on something warm, it's damned cold out here."

"All right, Fred. I'll do that." Doris sounded happy. "Dinner in five minutes."

"Doris, put on a life vest over your jacket. It will give you some additional warmth, and you'll be more comfortable." It was important for her body to be recovered.

"Yes, Dear."

Fred switched on the autopilot and went below to fetch a small teak table that mounted in the cockpit on the front of the binnacle and had a folding leg to steady it. He also turned on the radar before returning to the cockpit.

When the table was in place, Doris stood on the first step of the companionway ladder and handed things up to Fred. The last item was a surprise for her husband—an imported, polished sterling silver wine seau from France—filled with crushed ice and a bottle of champagne.

"Fred, Dear. Many happy returns. This is something I've been saving to give you for our 15th wedding anniversary. In case you forgot, it's tomorrow. I couldn't wait though, so pull the cork and let's drink a toast."

"Why Doris, you couldn't have pleased me more. It's just what I have always wanted. How thoughtful you are." Fred was enjoying this new role, and his performance was accomplished with the finesse of a seasoned thespian.

He raised his glass in toast and waited for Doris to click her glass to his. "Here's to us. Drink, for this day we shall drown all our sorrows."

"Oh, how poetic."

"I also decided to jump the gun," he said. "Here is a little present which I couldn't wait until tomorrow to give to you. I hope you like it." Fred took a small gift wrapped box from his pocket and handed it to Doris.

"Oh, Fred." Doris was overcome with emotion. "You remembered." She opened the package and found a small elegant presentation box inside and in it a platinum watch decorated with numerous small diamonds around its bezel. For a while, Doris was too overcome to speak, but finally managed, "You are the dearest, most thoughtful man in the world." Her eyes brimmed with tears. "You know, women don't forget something like this. I haven't been so happy in years. I'll treasure it and wear it till the day I die."

A broad grin spread across Fred's face. "I had it engraved. When the sun comes up, you'll be able to read, 'Doris on our 15th wedding anniversary—all my Love, Fred.' Wish I could have said more, but there's not room for another word. Let me put it on your wrist so we can see how it looks." Doris held out her hand.

Fred checked both visually and by radar for other craft, not just because of seaman's judgment but to be doubly sure they were alone…nobody close enough to see what would happen in the next few minutes. He saw nothing on radar except a few tiny, barely visible dots of light typical of returns from lobster traps. As an added precaution he switched off most of the cabin lights.

When they finished their dinner, Fred said, "Doris, while you clear the dishes, I'm going to feed Yappie these left over cold cuts. He's asleep in the forepeak isn't he? After that, we'll sit together quietly and enjoy our champagne. It should be just the right temperature now."

"Stay where you are Dear; I'll hand Yappie up to you." Doris took the empty plates and descended the companionway ladder to the galley. A moment later she handed up the little terrier.

Fred fed Yappie a few morsels; then, after a minute or two, picked him up, pitched him overboard, and hove-to, stopping the boat's way. He yelled, "DORIS, YAPPIE FELL OVERBOARD!"

Doris was in the cockpit in an instant despite her age and bulk. "OH MY GOD, FRED!"

"Don't panic Doris."

"OH, FRED. WHERE IS HE? WHERE IS HE?"

"Here, take this spot-lamp and find him. He's a little astern on the port side."

Doris began probing the surface of the sea with the 300 candle power light beam. Yappie was in a yelping frenzy of activity, and Doris quickly spotted him.

"THERE HE IS FRED. THERE HE IS. OH, THANK GOD!"

"Now just keep the light beam on him so we won't lose track of where he is, and he'll know where we are. I've stopped the boat. He'll swim to us. If not, I'll start the engine and go to him. Just catch his collar with the boat hook. It'll be very easy."

As Yappie reached the boat, Fred took the lamp from her, saying, "Here I'll hold the light. You'll need both hands to hook his collar." Doris leaned over the life lines, intent on rescuing the little dog. She was already almost off balance.

"Bye bye, Doris." He said it casually as he gave her the quick shove that sent her over the side. He knew she could not live more then twenty or thirty minutes, at the most, in water so cold—hypothermia kills fast. He glanced at his watch.

She came up, choking and coughing in the cold sea water and couldn't even scream. Doris looked up at him, her expression a mixture of bewilderment, heartbreak, and panic. Fred gave her his most charming smile and sat down on the cockpit coaming to light a cigarette as he watched her futile struggle against inevitable death.

Following the careful plan he had made, he tossed the spot-lamp overboard. Next he jettisoned the man-overboard buoy—all ocean going yachts were required to have, and to use, them in emergencies. A lot of good it would do her in such cold water. It carried the red and yellow "O" code flag. Attached to it by a line was a yellow horseshoe buoy with a strobe light, and a smoke flare. Fred had tampered with the battery in the light to disable it. For good measure, he threw overboard several life vests and kapok filled cushions. Yappie was still frantically paddling alongside, imploring Fred to rescue him in the only way he could—barking and scratching at the hull of the boat. Doris, also alongside, was just starting to go into shock from hypothermia.

Fred waited until Doris was almost unconscious, then went down into the cabin and called the Coast Guard on VHF radio. He pretended he was in a panic—reported his wife overboard. She was wearing a life jacket, he said, but he couldn't find her. They dispatched a helicopter immediately—asked his name, the name and description of his boat, home port, position, how many aboard, and other routine questions. He read latitude and longitude from his Loran receiver and reported his position.

"Turn on your masthead and spreader lights...turn on your EPIRB [emergency beacon] if you've got one...hand all sail except a close hauled mizzen...play a flashlight on it...hoist a radar reflector on your flag halyard." The instructions came by VHF radio from the Coast Guard helicopter. These actions would make it easier for them to find and identify his boat as rapidly as possible, despite poor and worsening visibility.

Always methodical, Fred looked at his navigation watch, glanced at the Loran's position window; then in his neat precise handwriting made an entry in the log, "0021 hours GMT—Doris overboard, Lat 42° 29.7' N, Long 70° 48.1' W." When he returned to the deck he saw that Doris was still struggling feebly alongside. He stowed the main and jib, did the other things requested, started the engine and prepared to depart the immediate area, leaving Doris to die all alone, tossed about on the icy black roughening sea. Probably the last thing she was able to see would have been Fred, looking down at her one last time, a grin on his face, and his final show of disdain as he bowed, raised his glass of champagne, and drank a last toast.

Fred stopped the engine about three or four hundred yards from the scene of the crime. The boat began to drift very slowly down wind. For a while he could still faintly hear Yappie's frantic barking and then another sound. Doris had found a whistle, its lanyard pinned to her life jacket, and was feebly blowing it. All became silent shortly after a patch of thick frontal mist advanced and obliterated the ghastly scene. Death was near. Fred poured another glass of champagne and waited.

It would be another fifteen minutes at least before the Coast Guard got there, so he lit another cigarette. He thought about the exciting future and reflected on events so far. Everything went exactly as planned...got her overboard without a struggle...no scratches nor bruises on either of them. He had another sip of champagne...not a care in the world. He felt as if a crushing weight had been lifted from his back.

Soon the helicopter hovered near his boat and he identified by VHF radio. It started an expanding squares search, using powerful Krypton flood lights, and four pairs of sharp eyes. They found Doris rather quickly. She had turned on the small waterproof flashlight pinned to her life vest and it glowed brightly—Fred had forgotten about that. Yappie, his head under water, was clasped in her arms. The helicopter reported the finding but told him his wife might be dead—they could not be certain; she would be recovered by the crew and rushed to a hospital. They asked the name of the marina and slip number where he kept his boat in Boston and told him to proceed there directly...said they would be waiting to fill out a report. Fred assumed the police would be there too. He acknowledged instructions in his best grief stricken voice.

He decided to return under power. Navigation would take less of his time if he didn't have to tack; also sail handling was hard, dangerous work in the heavy winds that were making up. The autopilot held Leprechaun precisely on course and freed Fred to go below and get out of the icy wind and rain for five minutes at a time. He could finish washing and stowing things in the galley where Doris had been working. Any disorder upset him deeply. He also took the precaution of checking the contents of Doris' purse and the pockets of all the clothes she had brought aboard. He wanted to be absolutely sure there was nothing incriminating and it turned out there wasn't. On the contrary, he did find a sentimental anniversary card she had been saving to give him the next day on which she had written something he considered stupid and maudlin.

When all was shipshape below, Fred returned to the cockpit. Wind-driven rain pelted him with stinging force now, and the seas were building fast. He had put on his foul weather gear and buckled on his safety harness. Leprechaun pitched and rolled, but battered her way through squall-driven head seas, steady on course.

There was plenty of time to go over in his mind the story he would tell the Coast Guard and the police. He tried to light a cigarette and managed to inhale deeply just once before the rain and spray put it out. Best not to offer an elaborate explanation, he decided. It might give the impression he planned in advance what to say. Better to concentrate on acting the role of a grief stricken husband, and let them ask questions.

He would just say that some dolphins were gamboling around the boat. Yappie got excited. They dove under the bow and then leapt high into the air ahead of the boat, as dolphins do. Yappie was out on the bow pulpit, and in his frenzy, he fell into the sea. Fred called Doris on deck. While he maneuvered to rescue the dog, she used the spotlight and boat-hook to try to hook his collar. The boat rolled unexpectedly and caught her off balance as she was leaning over the life lines—she fell overboard. The spotlight went over with her and sank. It was dark as pitch. Without the light he couldn't see her. He had been in the lighted cabin just before this happened, had lost his dark accommodation, and could see nothing. He threw the man-overboard buoy, life jackets, and cushions where he thought she might be and saw that the strobe light attached to the buoy did not activate...something wrong with it. He ran below to turn on the spreader lights and get a flashlight. They had already drifted apart when he came back on deck. She disappeared just like that. There was no trace of her, so he called the Coast Guard—nothing else to do. He did try to save the dog but found it already dead. That would be his story, and he'd stick to it. They'd probably buy it, and if they didn't there was no way they could prove he was lying. He took another sip of champagne.

When Fred entered the channel leading into Boston harbor, he had a nagging feeling something was wrong—that he had made a mistake somewhere along the way.

What was it?...damned well better think what it was...not much time left...soon be at the marina and they will be waiting for me. What was it? What was it?

Not until he was in the inner harbor did Fred realize what was bothering him. He had told Michelle he and Doris had not gotten along for years and were contemplating a divorce. Damn, what a stupid thing to say. He had said it to convince Michelle he would marry her. Now he'd have to stop her from telling anyone else, if she hadn't already done so. He grabbed the microphone of his VHF radio, called the Coastal Telephone station, gave his call letters, gave the name of his boat, and would then have given Michelle's phone number, but it suddenly occurred to him the channel might be guarded by the police, or by the US Coast Guard—and dozens, maybe hundreds of people, with scanners—as well as many yachtsmen and fishermen. He cancelled the call just in time. I'm getting rattled. I nearly made one hell of a blunder. I've got to get hold of myself.

It had stopped raining as he approached the dock, and Fred was able to make out a group of men waiting for him. One wore a police uniform, and except for two in civilian clothes, the rest were Coast Guard officers. He wondered if the civilians were reporters or police detectives.

Just before entering his slip, Fred rubbed some saltwater into his eyes to make them red and teary. He eased Leprechaun ahead carefully, then reversed for a moment to stop forward motion, put out fenders, and hove his bow and stern lines to the men on the dock—then the spring lines.

"Are you Mr. Anderson…Mr. Fred Anderson.?"

"Yes."

When all lines had been made fast, a Coast Guard officer said, "May we come aboard, Mr. Anderson? I have some information for you, and I also have a report I must fill out with your help."

"Of course." Fred's eyes were stinging from the salt. He wiped the tears away with a handkerchief.

"First I have some bad news for you. We couldn't save your wife. She was probably dead when we hoisted her aboard…hypothermia. Never regained consciousness. We flew her to a hospital but she was pronounced dead on arrival."

Fred realized with a shock that he had forgotten to follow up with the Coast Guard. An anxious husband would have done that. He knew they were wondering why he had shown no concern—even though they had all known at the time that she was almost certainly beyond help.

The Coast Guard officer sat with Fred in the cockpit, asking many questions as he filled out his report form. Fred gave the appearance of being at the point of a complete breakdown. Once or twice he sobbed and spoke incoherently. The Coast Guard officer did not seem suspicious; he treated Fred with respect and kindness. During this interrogation, other officers of that service inspected the boat, probably for compliance with safety regulations, Fred thought.

While this was going on, the two men in plainclothes and the police officer walked back and forth along the finger piers on both sides of the boat, using their flashlights to inspect the hull near the waterline. One had a camera and from time to time his electronic flash turned night into day for an increment of time as they photographed something that interested them. What the hell is going on? What have they found?

When the Coast Guardsmen finished their investigation and left, one of the plainclothesmen on the dock finally spoke up. "I'm Lieutenant Sullivan of the Boston Police Department." He pulled out his wallet and flipped it open to show his badge. This here's Mr. Jones and Officer Baker. He didn't bother to explain that Jones was an attorney from the D.A.'s office. "We'd like to come aboard, have a look around, and ask ya some questions if ya got no objection."

Fred knew he had the right to refuse, unless they had a search warrant, but to do so would antagonize them and make it seem he had something to hide; besides they could quickly get the necessary document. He was, at this point, almost paralyzed with fear but he nodded affirmatively, not trusting his voice, and gestured for them to come aboard.

Lt. Sullivan was a giant of a man who had started life as a professional heavy-weight boxer. He had a reputation for being fast but thorough, and true to his reputation he had already seen the body, and questioned the Coast Guard at length.

Fred instantly sensed the man's hostility and his barely restrained violent impulses. He had a queasy feeling in his stomach, and wondered if he looked convincingly grief stricken to those appraising gray eyes. He tried to meet the lieutenant's gaze but couldn't.

For what seemed a long time, the big man said nothing. He just sat staring at Fred and chewed on the unlighted stub of a cigar. His eyes bored and searched as if observing and memorizing every detail of Fred's appearance and behavior—trying to see right through him. All the while he drummed his fingers on the cockpit coaming. It was one of the worst moments Fred would have to endure. He could feel himself wither and wilt. His hands began to tremble, and he put them in the pockets of his wind breaker.

"OK. I'm gonna read yer rights. Now lissun carefully." Sullivan took out a pocket notebook and shined his flashlight on its pages. His voice was perfunctory—he had read the same words a thousand times.

"Ya have a right to remain silent. If ya give up the right to remain silent anything ya say can and will be used against ya in a court of lor. Ya have the right to speak with an attoiney an to have an attoiney with ya durin questionin'. If ya so desire and cannot afford one, an attoiney will be appointed for ya without charge before questionin'. Now d'ya understand that?" His voice was deep, loud, and harsh, and the effect was like rasping exposed nerve endings with a coarse file. There was no hint of empathy nor compassion.

Fred was almost in shock. He nodded. Decided to cooperate because he thought it was what an innocent man would do. His heart was racing and pounding. He was obviously a suspect. He had not expected this. Have I slipped up somewhere or is the detective just trying to rattle me? My God, I think they are going to book me for murder.

Instinct told Fred to act like he had nothing to hide. He sat, head in his hands, not looking at the detective…waiting for the first question…waiting like a prisoner before a firing squad for the command, "FIRE."

"I wanna know exactly what happened. Speak slow so I can take it down." The ballpoint pen in his big hand seemed to be the size of a match stick. "You're gonna sign the deposition when I get finished. Don't leave nothin' out and don't make no mistakes."

Fred rubbed his eyes to make them look redder. He tried to control his trembling hands. His plan, to volunteer nothing, was not going to work. The Lieutenant would not have it that way. Fred tried to keep his voice steady, but it was no use. He wondered if the Lieutenant could tell the difference between guilty fear and grief.

When he finished his story, there again was a long silence. Sullivan sat looking at him with a cold, unblinking stare which Fred would see in his nightmares for months. The lieutenant's eyes and his silence communicated more eloquently then words—You lying son-of-a-bitch.

"OK. Explain again why ya didn't pull yer wife out of the water," said Lt. Sullivan after the unnerving pause. "I wanna hear that part again with more details."

"Like I said. I couldn't find her. By the time I found a flashlight and got back on deck, we had drifted apart. The sea was rough. It's hard to find a person in the water at night when the sea has built up." Though it was chilly, it was cold fear that made Fred's whole body and voice quaver.

"Ya said earlier ya could'a got the dog but he was already dead?"

"Yes"

"How could ya find him?"

"The boat was dead in the water. He must have just paddled over to it."

"Maybe I don't get it. Are ya tellin me the dog was smarter then yer wife? He knew enough to paddle over to the boat but yer wife didn't? She just drifted off?"

"I don't know. I don't know how it happened. Maybe she passed out," Fred improvised, realizing he had walked right into a trap.

When the ordeal was finally over, Lieutenant Sullivan called Jones as witness, read his notes, and asked Fred if that was exactly what he said. He agreed it was, and the detective told him to sign the deposition. This done, Sullivan and Jones walked a short distance away and had a brief conversation sotto voce. Fred tried to hear it, but couldn't.

"Bill, why did you read him his rights? Can you actually be getting ready to book him? I can't believe it."

"Why the hell shouldn't I Mirandize him? Of course I'm gonna book the son-of-a-bitch. How can we do anything else with all the stuff we got on him?"

"Don't do it, Bill. You are heading for trouble. There were no witnesses. The D.A. will be madder than hell. You can't go against him."

Lt. Sullivan said nothing more, but stood for a while chewing his cigar butt ragged—clenching and unclenching a big fist. He then came back.

"Here's my card." He scribbled something on the back and handed it to Fred. "We ain't gonna hold ya, but don't leave town. If ya think of anything else, call me. On the back I wrote the morgue where they took yer wife. Ya can see her body in the mornin' if ya want, but after lunch they are gonna do a autopsy. We're gonna look yer boat over now. Yer free to go after that."

Fred looked at the card. It read, "Detective Lieutenant William L. Sullivan, Homicide Department." He realized he was under suspicion. The words "Homicide Department" left no doubt.

When at last he could leave, Fred went into the first phone booth he could find to call Michelle. To his great relief she had not heard about the "accident" yet and sounded profoundly shocked. Good. He wanted her to hear it first from him. Again he told his story, just as he told it to the police, affecting once more profound emotion.

"But Fred, why you go on zee boat weeth 'air?"

"Well, you know, I told you we were planning a divorce. She said she would only agree if we made one last attempt at a reconciliation. I had no choice. She suggested we take a short vacation cruise in Leprechaun so we could have a change of scene." Having said that, Fred realized he was being inconsistent: he had previously implied Doris agreed to a divorce without any conditions. Michelle did not appear to have noticed.

"Michelle, Darling. I love you so, and I don't want to see you dragged into this mess. The accident was a tragedy for poor Doris, and now all this may even threaten our happiness. Imagine how bad it would look if they knew of our relationship and knew Doris and I were not happy together. You haven't told anyone have you?"

"Mais non, Fred. Nobody. Not even Papa. And I weel not."

Fred sighed with relief and relaxed a bit. "Darling, I'm sure you will understand. For the time being you must not call me at home nor at the office. I'll call you. You do understand, don't you?"

"Mais oui, but of course I do. Don't worry Ma Cherie."

The funeral was a small and private one. They didn't have friends as most couples do. Except for Fred, there was only a next door neighbor and someone Doris had met at church. Fred once more had to pretend sorrow, but he didn't intend to keep it up longer then necessary.

That evening, Fred's home phone rang. It was Jack Doyle of Northeast Mutual Life Insurance Company. What could he possibly want? Fred had already notified his insurance agent of Doris' death. The man had come out promptly with a form called "Proof of Death—Statement of Beneficiary" which Fred had filled out and signed, stating the cause of death was accidental. When Fred could not provide a death certificate, the agent obligingly offered to pick one up for him to save him the trouble.

Now Doyle wanted to know if he could come by the house for a moment—he said it was important. Fred agreed, poured himself a stiff shot of vodka neat, and began to pace back and forth trying to anticipate what he might be asked. In only a minute or so the doorbell rang. Doyle had phoned from the cellular phone in his car when only a block away.

When Fred opened the door he was taken aback at Doyle's appearance and the suddenness of his arrival. The man was big, red faced, red haired, and looked as strong as a fighting bull, but despite some intangible menace in his glance, he seemed superficially polite enough.

"It was good of you to see me like this on such short notice. I understand how you must feel and I'll make it very brief."

"Yes, yes. That's perfectly all right. Please have a seat." Fred gestured toward the sofa and took a chair nearby.

"Mr. Anderson, I head the Claims Department of Northeast Mutual. There are some points I need to clarify about your wife's life insurance policy that names you sole beneficiary. As you know, the amount of coverage for loss of life is $1,000,000. We have already begun to process this claim, and I expect our agent will be able to bring you a check within two to three weeks. In addition, a double indemnity clause stipulates a further payment of $1,000,000 will be made if death is determined to have been accidental. But you will understand, I'm sure, we must do a routine investigation before we can make final payment. This will take slightly longer. And now, if you don't mind, I'd like you to tell me how this unfortunate accident occurred."

He wrote in a notebook as Fred spoke, and at no time did he reveal by word nor by expression whether he believed or disbelieved what Fred was telling him. He asked a number of probing questions but made no comment, nor did he again express sympathy. Fred was more then vaguely concerned by the time he left.

A few days later, Jack Doyle and Bill Sullivan of Homicide sat together in Bill's smoke filled office at police headquarters. You had only to look at Doyle to know he had something to do with law enforcement. In his younger days he had been on the force and had taken many an armed and dangerous criminal without thinking anything of it. Now, his red hair was graying, but he was as tough as ever, though he had been with Northeast Mutual Life Insurance Company for years.

Doyle got up and began to pace the floor. "Bill, not in over thirty years experience have I had such a strong hunch. The red light is flashing. I'm convinced that bastard killed his wife, and it looks like he is going to get by with it and collect a $2,000,000 double indemnity payoff as well, unless you can nail him for murder one."

"Yeah, I got the same hunch. You think he killed her, I think he killed her, but the son-of-a-bitch is clever. He did it miles offshore, after dark, and no witnesses around. We ain't got no real hard evidence that would stand up in a court of lor. I keep lookin' for the usual murder motives...the four L's: love, lust, lucre, an loathin'. Can't prove nothin. The D.A.'s last three murder cases was thrown out of court by ol' Judge Mercer for lack of sufficient evidence. It happens again an D.A. knows he'll be lookin for a job. Ol Mercer's hung up on criminal rights an to hell with the victim. The D.A. just don't wanna take no chances on no murder one indictment without no witnesses."

"Bill, I think he's making a serious mistake. It's true there's only circumstantial evidence. But, as Thoreau said, 'Some circumstantial evidence is very strong, as when you find a trout in the milk.'"

"Right. Why don't the guy tell that to the D.A.?"

Doyle had always suspected Sullivan grossly exaggerated his own ignorance and lack of culture to make others under estimate him and drop their guard. The ploy had become an ingrained habit. Now Doyle had no doubt about it.

"I think the D.A. could easily make murder one stick," Doyle continued. "I'll have a talk with him. Here's something interesting I learned. I spoke to the agent who sold the policies to the Andersons. Anderson let the policy on his own life lapse soon after buying it, but kept up the premiums on his wife's policy. This suggests he wasn't concerned about her protection. He renewed his own policy just days ago. I think that's when he decided to murder her, and he was afraid it would look bad if there was a policy on her life and not on his."

"He told our agent he let his own policy lapse because he had been doing a lot of travel on foreign airlines and wanted to use the money to buy maximum trip coverage from the policy vending machines they have in the airports. I've checked and found there was no change in the frequency of his air travel, and the companies selling insurance through airport vending machines have no record he ever bought a policy. He lied."

"Son-of-a-bitch." Sullivan made some notes in his file as he chewed on his cigar.

"Let's go over, once again, what you have, Bill."

"OK, first the helicopter pilot told him, when they found the body, his wife looked like maybe she was dead but they wasn't sure. They hadn't even picked up the body yet. He didn't at no time try to contact the Coast Guard after that to ask about her. That ain't the way no lovin husband acts."

"Right. I can't argue with that. What else?"

"We found a red mark on the hull like the letter "M" but not quite completed. Forensic Lab says it was made with lipstick same as hers. We also found lipstick on the tip of one of her fingers. My guess is she was tryin to tell us somethin and didn't have enough lipstick on her lips to finish what she started. Just a guess, but it could have been the start of the word M U R D E R."

"You could be right about that, Bill—in any case, it proves beyond any reasonable doubt she was alongside—not drifted away like he claimed. That's important. What else?"

"Well he says he couldn't find her, it bein night an all. But the helicopter crew spotted her right off because of the waterproof flashlight pinned to her life jacked, which she had turned on. How come he didn't see it?"

"I don't know about that one Bill…fog patches, choppy seas…easy to spot it from a helicopter…hard to see it from the deck of a boat, but we don't need it. We've already established proof she was along side—not drifted off."

"Yeah, maybe so. Well the next one here…. We found traces of lipstick on the whistle. Forensic Lab says it was the same kind on the body. So she was blowin' it. Why the hell didn't he hear that and find her?"

"I agree completely. He probably did hear it. But it might occur to the defense to argue she didn't discover the whistle until she was almost unconscious and couldn't blow it loud enough to be heard."

"Well then there's her fingernails…all broke off and the traces of bottom paint in 'em. It's more proof she was right alongside scratchin' at the hull. An her knuckles was all bruised real bad—from poundin' on th' boat I guess."

"Yes I think that's damned good evidence. The primitive human instinct is to claw one's way to safety when in a panic."

"Yeah, but the D.A. don't think that's enough. Then there's them scratch marks made by the dog's claws all around the waterline. The bastard could easily have fished him out of the drink if he wanted to."

"Right. It shows a cold lack of feeling, and again he lied. Said the dog was dead when he found him. The defense would of course say that this evidence is irrelevant—and the judge would sustain. You can't indict him for murdering the dog. Wish you could."

"Hell, I know that. I ain't that dumb." Cigar ashes cascaded down Sullivan's tie and shirt front. Now here's another thing. The battery in the strobe light…ya know the flashin' light attached to the man-overboard buoy. It was dead, an we found a short piece of wire on a seat in the main cabin. It had a cupla bends in it the same distance apart as the battery terminals. Looks like he might have run the strobe light battery down on purpose by shortin' it out. I sent th' wire to th' Forensic Lab and they said it was annealed. Ya know, that's a fancy word meanin it had been real hot just like ya'd expect if he used it to run the battery down."

"I'll bet that's what he did, Bill. If he and the victim had become separated, as he maintains, they would both have gone to the light flashing on the man-overboard buoy. He had to disable the strobe light to make plausible his contention he couldn't find her. He's not stupid."

"Yeah, but it don't help us none unless the forensic lab can prove the piece of wire was used to run the strobe's battery down. That needs more follow-up but it looks like good evidence. Oh, another thing I almost forgot, maybe he ain't so smart after all. We found where he logged the time an th' exact location where she went overboard, an yet th' helicopter reports they found him several hundred yards away from there. I had his Loran navigation equipment checked and found it right on. It agrees exactly with th' one in th' helicopter. Coast Guard says where they found him ain't where wind and current would a took him, so it looks like he done somthin real cold-blooded—I think he shoved her overboard and left th' scene on purpose—left her all alone to show her he didn't give a damn.

"I think there is enough evidence to get a conviction Bill, but I want to think about it some more before I talk to the DA. Are you sure there's nothing you've overlooked in the autopsy report?"

"Ain't nothin' there, Jack." Lt. Sullivan picked up the report in one hand and fumbled for his glasses with the other. He found them on the top of his head and read: "Cause of death hypothermia…time of death approximately 8:00 p.m.…no body bruises, scratches, or broken bones…no torn clothin', blood-alcohol level just a trace. Then there's that stuff about the hands an finger nails like we was just discussin.' Did ya see th' body though? She was almost old enough to be his mother and weighed a ton. It just don't figger." He relighted the cigar he had been chomping on.

"Nothing in her personal effects?"

"Well, there's th' watch. She was wearin' a watch inscribed on the back—somethin' sentimental about their 15th anniversary. Don't prove nothin'; I seen the same trick before. Took me a hell of a time to find the jeweler who sold it. He said Anderson come in, bought th' watch and wanted it inscribed right then an there. Had to have it right away. Normally this guy needs a day or two warnin' for inscriptions. Anybody should know that. Anderson give him fifty bucks for a rush job. Sounds like he wasn't thinkin' too far ahead, don't it? Oh, there's one last thing. We took th' contents of her purse and run a routine fingerprint check. Guess what. His prints was all over everything. He searched her purse…question is, when he done it, and why?

Doyle agreed and sighed. His face was creased with the strain of frustration. "God how I hate having to approve the payment of a double indemnity claim—and another thing—if he killed once he could kill again." He added reflectively, "You know Bill, I'll bet there is another woman somewhere. I'll tell you one thing, I'm not ever going to close the file on this bastard until we nail him. He'll make a bad mistake sooner or later—wait and see."

The following day, Doyle met with the D.A. His arguments did not persuade the man to risk another embarrassment in court. No matter how overwhelming the circumstantial evidence, there was no witness and he was adamant. Doyle had no choice. He approved the double indemnity claim.

Fred knew people at the office would talk and speculate if he married again right after Doris' death, especially if he married the young and beautiful Michelle. Fortunately for him, he was able to arrange a transfer. They put him in charge of the Newport, Rhode Island branch office. It was ideal. Nobody there knew of Doris' death. They didn't even know Doris.

He and Michelle began to meet again from time to time, usually at small country inns in the hinterland of Rhode Island. The feeling of privacy emboldened them. They decided to abandon all caution and get married without further delay. Michelle and "Papa" wanted a big wedding, with guests coming from Paris, but Fred would not agree so the ceremony was held in a charming little country church. The wedding took place almost three months to the day after Doris' death. It did not escape Doyle's notice. He had been watching for the other woman.

Papa gave a munificent dowry that astounded Fred—a check for far more than the double indemnity Fred had collected, as well as a Mercedes 500 SL. Fred had no idea the old man was so rich.

The Andersons selected a choice two-acre plot of beautifully wooded ground at the edge of the sea near Newport, and after working with an architect, had an elegant and dignified colonial home built. It was in a neighborhood of other charming colonials, set in historic surroundings. Mullioned windows gave on an ever changing panorama of maritime activity with verdant islands and headlands in the background. Michelle had superb taste and brilliant originality. She did the furnishing and decorating like few professionals could have done, and made their home a showplace. Fred's study had built-in book cases and book shelves floor to ceiling on every wall, in order to accommodate their combined collections, and even in the sun room there were more shelves of rare books that added warmth and refinement to the decor and displayed the literary pretensions of the occupants.

Michelle had always wanted to have a place called "Paradise," so Paradise it was. The taste and elegance of their home, Michelle's beauty, her warmth of personality, and her exotic charm soon elevated them high in the ranks of the social elite of Newport.

Fred lacked his wife's joi de vivre, but he was witty, urbane, and full of humor. Never was the monster in him apparent to anyone; however, on rare occasions, he sank into a laconic mood which Michelle was quick to discern, and with her characteristic wit and social grace she would make plausible excuses for their early departure, before others noticed. Prominent hostesses of the venerable colony vied with one another to entertain what they all perceived as a remarkably attractive couple.

Fred could now afford to retire and live like a country gentleman, collecting not only first editions but also those of the sixteenth century that at one time he could not have even dreamed of owning.

He had kept Leprechaun at their private dock, almost visible from the house, and sometimes, when in one of his rare dark moods, he sat alone in the cockpit and thought of that night. He had no regrets, but was nagged by the fear they were still after him and closing in. At other times, in another mood, it gave him pleasure to come there and remember how he had changed his life so completely; then there were days when he and Michelle would cruise in the indescribably beautiful yachting wonderland that has made Newport world famous.

If the lives of Michelle and Fred seemed idyllic to their friends, it was an illusion. Michelle was a very discreet person but one day she confided to her closest friend that she and Fred were compatible on only a physical and intellectual level, but not emotionally. She said he somehow shut her out, and she didn't really know him. She made the best of it, and devoted herself mainly to social activities and to raising money for various charities.

Aside from Fred's occasional melancholia his only other behavioral peculiarity had to do with police. Michelle noticed that whenever there was a police car or motorcycle behind their car, Fred seemed irrationally agitated—far beyond what one would expect if he only feared getting a traffic ticket; however, she would not let her mind dwell on a possible reason.

If life usually seemed idyllic to Fred, it was because he underestimated Jack Doyle. The man was tenacious, relentless, and everlastingly energetic. Jack, true to his word, had not closed the file on Fred. He, in fact, kept it at home and reviewed it thoughtfully from time to time so no detail was lost from memory. Every important event in the life of Fred Anderson eventually found its way into the file and much minutiae as well, usually with the help of Bill Sullivan who had impressive facilities at his command.

While still a young man on the force, Jack Doyle had talked Northeast Mutual Life Insurance Company into giving him a grant to complete his education, with the understanding that on graduation he would come back and head their Claims Investigation department. He took a degree in criminology at The University of California at Berkeley, with a minor in English Literature. When he returned to the Boston headquarters, as agreed, he soon found his work and educational background provided an endless supply of ideas for short stories. Doyle began writing detective fictions in his spare time. They were instant successes, and soon his stories were in great demand. Working nights and on weekends, he eventually went on to become a best selling novelist.

One evening, about a year and a half after Doris' death, Jack was reviewing the Anderson file and soon, through habit, began to write character sketches of Fred, Doris, and Michelle. It was the first thing the writer always did when starting a novel. Suddenly it hit him. He couldn't imagine why he had not thought of it before. He wanted to make something happen. All right. Why not write a novel about a man named Fred Anderson who murders his wife, Doris? The story could be told exactly as it probably happened. He'd give it the title, "Perfect Crime?" Then…an advance copy to Anderson, by registered mail, and see what he does.

Jack knew his publisher would balk at such an exposé, fearing a law suit, but Doyle was their best money maker, and this gave him considerable leverage. They had gotten by with exposés before and made big profits on some of them. If they didn't want to do it, he would find another publisher. If all else failed, he knew he could go to a vanity press and pay the cost of publication out of his own pocket.

Jack also knew that as a professional writer he had the imagination and the ability to enter the minds of his characters, think the way they would think, see the world through their eyes. He was convinced he could reconstruct the crime by asking himself what he would have done if he were Fred Anderson, with that man's motivations and his psychopathic lack of conscience.

Some months later the door chime at Paradise sounded and the maid went to see who was there. A moment later she found Fred reading beside the pool.

"It's the postman, Mr. Anderson. He has a package for you but says you must sign for it." Fred went to the door.

"Good morning Mr. Anderson, Sir." The postman's manner was obsequious. It always was when he delivered mail in these elegant neighborhoods. "Just sign here please, Sir."

"Are you sure it's for me? I'm not expecting a package."

"Oh, yes Sir. It's for you all right…from Boston, registered. Comes from a Jack Doyle."

Oh, my God. What could this be? He strode through the house trying unsuccessfully to tear the heavy wrapping off with his finger nails. In the study he found a letter opener and, with unsteady hands, cut the wrapping and withdrew the book from its packing.

The dust jacket was a beautiful example of graphic art, but its excellence was lost on Fred. It featured a large black and white photo of Leprechaun, and overprinted in a huge red stencil type-face was the title, "PERFECT CRIME?" Fred turned the color of marble—the color of death. He felt a slight nausea and a familiar fluttery feeling in his stomach. For a moment his knees felt as if they were paralyzed. He had never been so frightened in his life.

Michelle came into the room and ran to him in alarm saying, "Oh Cherie, what eez eet. You feel seek? Eez eet your 'art? No?"

Fred suddenly bolted like a cornered animal. "Get out of my way." He ran past Michelle knocking her roughly aside. The change in his behavior must have left her crushed and stunned. A moment later his car accelerated down their long driveway, and the squeal of a high speed skidding turn echoed throughout the house, as he blackened the highway with rubber.

When he found a secluded spot, Fred pulled off the road and began flipping through Doyle's book, looking for the most incriminating pages, and he soon found them. He couldn't believe it. There was a nearly exact account of what happened. Everything he said and did and thought. It was impossible but there it was…just as if the author had been with them on Leprechaun that day. His fear was like an iron hand squeezing his heart and his lungs. If they catch me I've had it, and they are looking for me right now. I've got to get out of the country fast. Brazil. Yes, that's the place. No extradition treaty with the USA. They'll be watching the airports here, but I can sail to Brazil in Leprechaun. I'll need money though.

In a frenzy born of total panic, Fred took what he thought was a desperate chance. He withdrew the entire amount of their savings account, expecting to feel a hand on his shoulder at any moment. There was only a little over $15,000. The rest of their fortune was in the brokerage account, and most of that was invested. He'd have to leave it.

Next Fred went to buy provisions for the voyage. He chose stores where he had never been before. That done, he thought about the many things he needed for such a voyage: charts, light lists, tide tables, Nautical Almanac, plotting sheets, Pilot Books Sailing Directions, and a dozen other things. No responsible navigator would embark on such a voyage without these, but Fred imagined time was running out, and in any case chart purchases would reveal his planned route. He decided to try to get by with only the world atlas he had aboard. He topped off the fuel and water tanks and got under way.

An hour later Leprechaun could have been seen standing out to sea on a southeasterly course. Within two hours, she was hull down on the horizon. Once in international waters, Fred began to relax a little.

Four days later, he saw his mistake, and it struck him like a sentence of death. A brightly polished brass plaque on the bulkhead in Leprechaun's main cabin caught his eye. Engraved on it were these words:

AN OLD SAILOR'S REMINDER
June, soon
July, if you try
August, if you must
September, remember
October, over

It meant that in June the hurricane season would be soon. You might sail hurricane waters in July, if you try, or even in August, if you must; but September should and would be remembered as a time to avoid at all cost the seas where those dreaded winds occur—which no craft can survive.

He had put to sea during mid-September. Realizing at last the danger he was in, he tuned in WWV and waited anxiously for the weather news which was transmitted to mariners at eight minutes past every hour. He heard then that one of the worst of those devastating killer-hurricanes had just cut a horrendous path of death and destruction through the Leeward and the Virgin Islands. It had then recurved and was now headed almost straight at him. The center was moving fast, and sustained winds were reaching 150 miles an hour.

The report ended with these words: "This is the fourth hurricane of the season. It has been named Doris."

WATERMELON

Monday, 6:10 p.m.

Well, here he comes. 6:10 p.m. Just like yesterday and the day before, and the day before that...know just what he'll say...what he'll do...sit in front of the TV watching sports by the hour. Isn't there more to life and love and marriage than this? Why do I feel this way?...isn't that I don't love Edward any more but...I don't know, after ten years...what's gone wrong any way?

"Hi Hon. Gosh it's good to be home. How was your day?" Edward embraced his wife briefly and gave her a quick peck on the cheek.

Wonder why she never says anything...doesn't even answer me...just shrugs. Bev is drifting away from me. God, I wish I knew how to communicate with her...don't want this to happen, but I don't know what to do...feel so damned helpless. What's eating her? Why the hell doesn't she tell me? Maybe it's my fault...can't seem to get across to her how I feel...still love her as much as when we first met back in high school...more. How long ago was it?...fifteen years?

Edward climbed the stairs stroking his scruffy red beard thoughtfully. He changed into some comfortable old clothes and went back downstairs, fixed a bourbon on the rocks and sat down to watch the TV news. Beverly didn't want a drink.

Oh hell, I don't give a damn about this news. Bev's all I care about. We used to be so happy when we were first married...didn't have much money.

Life on the little farm in Ohio seemed kind of hopeless but looking back, those were the days…the plans we made together…sure was tough though when we lost our first child and doctor said she couldn't have another. Thought, when uncle Hank died and left me a little capital, everything would be better…great for a change to be able to get some things for Bev she had always wanted. She was so damned poor all her life up 'til then.

Edward glanced at the antique brass lamp on the desk in the corner. How she had been thrilled when he gave her that. She had dreamed of having one for so long. It was the first time he had been able to give her something really nice.

Then the move here to "the valley" north of Hollywood. Was it good or bad? I wonder. Sure liked the job I got though, working as a mechanic in the Cadillac agency. Never will forget when I came home and told Bev I'd been promoted to head of the service department. We were so damned happy…went out to that fancy restaurant on Ventura Boulevard—the Wild Goose…celebrated with red wine and all…spilled mine on the tablecloth. Bev just laughed. She wouldn't do that now.

Edward turned to catch a glimpse of his wife in the kitchen. She was still as slim and shapely as the day they met—so pretty and well groomed. Her dark hair looked so soft. But Beverly's face bore the unmistakable marks of sadness and strain and he was not reassured.

And oh how we scrimped and saved…did without till it hurt. But we were happy. Then my small inheritance did well in the stock market—and that wild idea I had to get a bank loan and open my own Cadillac agency farther out in the valley where it was growing so fast. Damned near lost my shirt for a while but I was just plain lucky. It was wonderful then to be able at last to give Bev everything she had never had—make all her dreams come true.

But that's when she began to change. Yes, by God, that's just when it happened. Now we have everything anyone could want but we're not happy. What the hell's gone wrong?

Never tells me he loves me. Never hears a word I say. Just sits there in those disreputable old clothes watching TV…nothing but sports news…looks more like the gardener than the man of the house. If only he had some social ambition. Every day he meets some of the most famous people in the valley…movie stars…directors…writers…producers…artists…all of them important people. And every day he just comes home exactly at 6:10 and looks at TV. We don't know anybody who counts—not really. He won't make the effort...can't get him to go to the opera nor the symphony. A mule couldn't drag him to the art gallery. He's just a cultural ignoramus I guess, and yet.... Oh, I'd be so proud of him, if only I could be. He could still be handsome if only he'd shave off that unsightly beard. A tear started but she brushed it aside.

Trouble is Bev went on this cultural kick. Poor Bev. She grew up without hope...poor as Jobe's turkey. I think maybe she's just gone overboard now we have all this money...wants the one thing money can't buy—class. To her that means everything cultural. It's why she joined that damned art center. She never smiles anymore...had such a pretty smile...never laughs anymore. What I wouldn't give to hear her laugh again. How could I make her do it?...might change everything. Now she's gone and got herself appointed one of the judges of the art competition. Its ads are all over town. Bet those gals don't know the first thing about art.

Damn, that gives me an idea. Just for fun, why don't I enter the contest? They've never seen me...won't tell Bev. When she finds out maybe it'll make her laugh like she used to.

Wonder what he's smiling about. He hasn't smiled much lately...wish he would. I think it was his smile that made me fall in love with him...seems so long ago.

Tuesday, 6:10 p.m

There's his car...home right on the dot like always. Sometimes I think I'm going mad. Wish he didn't always come home at the same time every day and say the same thing when gets here.

"Hi, Hon. Gosh it's good be home. How was your day?"

Just as I expected...how many times have I heard that? He doesn't want to hear about my day. Well I won't say anything. Maybe I'm being bitchy...don't know why...have a lovely home...beautiful furniture...my own new Cadillac...expensive clothes...furs...jewelry. He doesn't chase after other women. Whatever I want I can buy...I should be happy, and yet....

After dinner Ed told Beverly he had to do some work on his car and would be out in the garage until late. He added, "Don't wait up Hon."

Edward pulled out the art supplies from the bag he had stashed in the trunk of his car. Is this ever going to be fun. Let's see now how do I set up this confounded easel. There we are. Well, if anything, this'll be different. I'll confuse the hell out of 'em. I'll paint on a coco fiber doormat instead of a canvas—a real inspiration if I do say so myself…leave it unpainted around the edges to let the mat show…maybe they'll think I'm sort of crazy and gifted like Picasso.

OK, let's start with a background. I'll make it white. Now what shall I paint that will get attention? I know, a big slice of watermelon. Red will catch the eye…bright green rind…lots of black seeds. Ed went back into the house and got a big lengthwise slice of it to use as a model.

I don't think I need these brushes…just squeeze the paint out of the tubes directly onto the mat and work it around with my fingers…hey, this is fun. Now some more over here, and here. Damn, that's pretty good. Let's see how it looks when I back off a bit. Hmmm, not bad…well, not too bad anyway. Now what next? Oh I know, a bright-eyed little boy with no shirt on, eating the melon. Got to capture the ecstasy.

Edward, was so focused in his determination to catch one of those moments in childhood, that most adults remember only dimly; he worked without any sense of the passing of time, until he glanced up and saw the big oak tree in his front yard making a dark lacy silhouette against a crimson dawn. He was at last able to make the face express what he wanted—the joy of life—a carefree, happy moment of childhood.

There by God…not bad at all. Maybe as good as some of the competition. Ed cleaned up, and put the finished painting in the trunk of his car. He hid the easel, and started to throw the rest of his supplies away but changed his mind. He had not enjoyed anything so much in a long time and felt a strong urge to take up painting as a hobby.

As he had used paint in a thick and lavish style it took a long time for it to dry but, when "Watermelon" was ready, he went to the Valley Art Gallery and entered it in the competition. First he took the precaution of phoning to be sure Bev was not there then he put on a beret and a cascading flamboyant silk bow tie for his entrance. His red beard enhanced the effect. He hoped he looked sufficiently Bohemian.

Ed filled out an entry card giving only his first name—"Edward" and left blank the spaces for his address and phone number, scrawling by way of explanation, "Will be here when award decision is announced and can identify myself at that time."

Only after he left did the ladies look at the card and wonder who the mysterious stranger was. He had piqued their curiosity. They hastened to cut the hemp cord and remove the brown paper wrapping, then they all gazed at Watermelon in stunned silence. When they turned to speak to him, he had vanished.

Beverly stood conscientiously before each of the several hundred entries...contemplating, weighing one against the other, asking herself what the artist was trying to say. When she came to 'Watermelon' she felt a breathtaking thrill of discovery. Her heart raced and she held her breath in astonishment as little currents of electricity played up and down her spine. She was instantly captivated. She knew there was no use looking at the rest, though of course she had to. This was it. This was the winner. It had to be. An authentic masterpiece...a modern primitive in a unique style. It seemed to have a strange quality that drew her eye repeatedly from all other paintings. Such bold use of color...such imagination...such composition, line, focus, harmony...such brilliant originality. It was vivid and powerful. She marked her secret selection and deposited her vote it in the ballot box where it would remain with others until the night of the awards.

Judgment day arrived. "Edward, I'm going out tonight. It's no use, I know, to expect you to go with me to the awards banquet of the Valley Art Center—such things don't interest you—but I'm one of the judges, you know. She said this looking in the big wall mirror in the hall, patting her hair as women always do at such times.

"OK Bev. Enjoy yourself. I'm going to watch a ball game on TV."

"There's a pizza in the fridge. You can heat it in the microwave for dinner."

"Ok, Hon. No problem. Have a good time."

As soon as Beverly left the house, Ed went to his car trunk for the elegantly cut tuxedo, made for him by an expensive tailor for this special occasion. He showered and shaved off the scruffy beard he had worn for years—he was tired of it anyhow. When ready he inspected himself in the mirror. The transformation astounded him. He would not have recognized himself. People used to say he looked like the actor Paul Newman. The resemblance was even more striking now. He smiled when he thought of the trick he would play at the agency the next day, pretending to be the famous actor, to see if he could fool his secretary.

At the Valley Art Gallery there were many people and it was easy for Ed to lose himself among the crowd. He was careful not to be seen by Beverly. Ed wandered around and found to his amazement he was intensely interested in the various art entries. They ran the gamut from the bizarre but colorful to some of the most elegant and masterful paintings he had ever seen. They fascinated him and added to the excitement he felt deep within. This affair had attracted top talent. It was to be expected in the entertainment capital of the World. Eventually Ed's curiosity drew him to a group of people. They seemed to be admiring one of the entries. Being tall he could see over heads and to his utter astonishment there hung 'Watermelon.' Ed began to chuckle and hastily ducked out through a door marked "MEN," where, unobserved, he had a good laugh. Looks like I might have some folks fooled anyway, he thought.

Eventually the amplified voice of the Master of Ceremonies asked all to gather around. Ed saw Bev up there on the podium with the MC and four important looking women—the other judges. On a small table in front of them was the little black ballot box. After introducing each of the women, the Master of Ceremonies opened the lid and, with much fanfare, he extracted the five ballots.

"Ladies and Gentlemen, it gives me the greatest possible pleasure to read our first judge's ballot for the award of the one thousand dollar Grand Prize in the Valley Art Center Competition:

"Ballot number one…'Watermelon,' painted by Edward…there's no last name given." The announcement was followed by thunderous applause and other sounds of approval. Probably the only surprised person was Ed. He was dumbfounded.

"Ballot number two…'Watermelon' again." More applause. Beverly smiled broadly. Her judgement was being vindicated and she felt a warm glow of self confidence.

"Ballot number three, four, and five…'Watermelon,' 'Watermelon,' and 'Watermelon.' The vote is unanimous. In my seven years as Master of Ceremonies of this annual event this has never happened before." The applause shook the exhibition hall. Beverly was beaming.

"And now Mr. Edward—no last name—please come forward and identify yourself, so I can award you the Grand Prize—this handsome silver cup and a check for one thousand dollars."

Ed, dazed and embarrassed, hesitantly made his way toward the judge's stand, his mind in a whirl of confused thoughts. He had no idea he might win—only hoped to be noticed, with a bit of luck. How did he fool them so? Or did he? Was it possible he had talent and didn't know it? Would Bev see the humor in the situation? That's all he cared about. He watched her face anxiously as he slowly mounted the steps, waiting for a look of recognition and hoping for the warm smile he longed to see.

The judges and the MC wore ceremonial smiles, like the one that remains when a professional portrait photographer says "Now smile" and then fiddles forever with camera adjustments before taking the picture. At first glimpse of the smooth shaven, tall, athletic looking stranger in the immaculately tailored tuxedo, Beverly thought of her husband. How like Edward he was, but so much more refined. As he mounted the stairs, their eyes met and Ed smiled at her—she looked so pretty.

In an instant she saw the truth.... Edward, beardless after five years of beard—dressed now with formal elegance as she had never seen him before. The smile faded from her lips and tears of humiliation flooded her eyes. He had made a fool of her. How could he be so cruel? She shot past him in a fury, only dimly aware of blurry faces and murmured remarks as she fled through the crowd. Ed tried to follow, but lost her. From the terrace overlooking the parking lot he saw her car flash past headed for the exit. He sprinted to his own car and sped after her, running every red light—thinking, my God, what have I done? I've really messed things up now. He caught up with her just as they reached home.

"Bev, Honey. Wait a minute. Let's talk. What's the matter Hon?"

"How could you humiliate me like that? How can I ever face my friends again? I'll be the laughing stock of all the women at the Art Center—just when I was starting to be accepted socially, you made a perfect fool of me. And in front of all those people—all the people who really matter."

Ed understood. He thought of his pathetic entry in the contest, his poor little painting on a cocoanut mat. She had taken it for a work of genius and it was just different. Oh my God what a shock—what an embarrassment for her.

"It was just a joke, Bev. I thought you would laugh. I just wanted to hear you laugh again Hon."

The phone rang and Ed picked it up. It was a man's voice, someone at the Art Center wanting to speak to Bev, but she wouldn't take the call. Ed pushed a button to amplify the caller's voice.

"This is Mr. Hamilton. I'm sorry, my wife can't come to the phone now. If you'd like to leave a message I'll see she gets it."

"Yes, I certainly do want to give her a message. I am Mr. de Vere of the Valley Art Center. I am Master of Ceremonies of the award committee. Mrs. Hamilton left so suddenly. She must have been taken ill. We are all so very worried about her."

"Well Mr. de Vere it is all my fault. I submitted the silly little painting done on a coconut fiber mat—"Watermelon." Put yourself in her place. She was one of the judges who chose it for the top award. Can you imagine how this embarrassed her? My wife didn't know I painted it. I feel terrible about this."

"You painted it?"

"Yes."

"You are Edward?"

"Yes. Edward Hamilton"

"Beverly is going to be very proud of you Mr. Hamilton. You have real talent. Thank God we found you. You can't imagine the stir you have caused." Beverly stopped crying and her mouth dropped open in astonishment.

"No, of course you couldn't know. 'Watermelon's' the sensation of the art show. Some men from news magazines have photographed it and they want your release for the editions due out in a few days. There is another photographer here from the *Los Angeles Examiner* who wants a picture of the artist and his wife for the Sunday supplement. A reporter with him wants an interview. There are also a number of people asking us to put on an exhibition of your other paintings. Quite a few have asked the price of watermelon. What shall I tell them?

"Hold the phone a moment, Mr. de Vere."

Edward looked uncertainly at his wife. "They must be crazy, Bev. What should we do?"

Beverly had stopped crying. She looked at the expression on Edward's handsome face and began to laugh—and it felt good. In an instant they were both doubled over with laughter—just like in the old days. Edward knew all was going to be OK now. She took the phone from him.

"Mr. de Vere, this is Beverly Hamilton. You were right. I was ill, but now I feel better than I have for a very long time. We'll be there in fifteen minutes, but in the meantime please make the announcement that 'Watermelon' is not for sale at any price. I could never part with it."

POOR OLD CHARLIE

When Dolores arrived at the hospital she expected the usual routine that she had followed since becoming a registered nurse. She liked nursing but there were times when one or two tedious patients made life difficult and unpleasant. This morning was to be one of those times, but so memorable that she would spend the rest of her life retelling the events that began that day.

The Head Nurse told her to report to Private Duty Registry.

"Dolores, I'm giving you a special assignment until further notice," she was told when she got there. "You are going to take care of a celebrity. He's in room 407—had his tonsils out yesterday morning."

Dolores nodded and walked on toward the elevator, not asking the name of the man. The famous did not impress her at all. She wondered why nursing assignments were being changed. What, she wondered, happened to the day nurse who had been taking care of the man since his operation.

This was Hollywood and the hospital was popular with movie stars, directors, producers, and with the lesser luminaries. Stunt men constituted the most frequent admissions from the studios but they were undemanding strong silent men types. Most troublesome were the temperamental prima donnas, male and female. As she walked down the long hall on the fourth floor, intuition told her that there was trouble ahead and it was probably of the male prima dona kind. This would be her first trial by fire as a nurse. Dolores was young and had only recently graduated as a registered nurse. She had noticed that, until that moment, celebrities had always been cared for by the more experienced nurses.

On entering room 407 she saw that her patient was a big, husky, rough looking individual with several days growth of beard, his hair was all awry, and his bridgework was in a glass of water beside him. He was thrashing around in bed in a wild frenzy. Violent patients sometimes throw things, so the first thing she did was move his bedside table beyond his easy reach.

"Oh my God, my throat's *killing* me. Lock that God damned door. I don't want anyone else in here," he growled rudely.

Now Dolores recognized her patient, mainly because of his voice which was familiar to every American at that time—Clark Gable. With his teeth out and in his present condition that was not easy.

Gable was strong-willed and spoiled rotten. It was 1939, and he was at the height of his popularity. *Gone With the Wind* had just been released, and it was a sensational success. The man was accustomed to having people jump at his every command.

Dolores' reply must have given America's top screen idol quite a shock. She said, "First of all, don't you ever use profanity again, or any foul language, in my presence. As for the door it will *not* be locked. That would be contrary to hospital regulations. It remains unlocked at all times. That is for your own protection."

"Listen Sister, I'm paying $150 dollars a day for this room and I don't give a damn what the rules are. You will do as I say. Now bring me some ice-water and shut up."

"Don't you try to bully me or I'll bring you nothing." Dolores glared at him. She was a refined and deeply religious girl. "I've asked you not to use language that offends me. I do not intend to put up with it. Unless you promise to treat me with respect, I'll do nothing for you. If you want water, ask me in a nice way."

Gable was taken aback. Nobody had talked to him like that since Mrs. Livsey, his fifth grade teacher. With all of the skill of a superb actor he made his face frighteningly forceful—at least it would have been if his teeth were in. It didn't work. Like Sampson without his beard, his power was gone.

Dolores started to laugh. She just couldn't help it. Finally she said, "Be good now and let's try to get along. But remember what I said about your language and don't try to give orders while you are under my care in this hospital. Stop behaving like a spoiled king." She brought him some water but put her soft, cool hand on his forehead before deciding whether to give it to him or not. "I want to take your temperature before I let you drink this water," she said.

"Give me that damned water and shut up."

Dolores pushed a thermometer between Gable's lips, picked up the pitcher of water and left the room with it.

It was hard for a man to stay angry at Dolores for long. She was, after all, what he had asked for. When he entered the hospital he was quite specific as to the sort of day nurse he wanted. She had to be, "a slim but shapely, good-looking blond, with perfect legs." The head nurse had tried to ignore this and had assigned the most experienced nurse available, but she was not Gable's type, and he had threatened to leave the hospital. That's how Dolores happened to be assigned to the case. She fit Gable's specifications exactly.

When Dolores returned to check the thermometer, she found her patient smiling. It was that dimpled smile well known to all women who flocked to see Gable whenever his name appeared on the marquee. He had put his teeth back in and combed his hair. Unshaven, he looked like a charming rogue and at the same time looked a bit pathetic and vulnerable. His way of alternating between brutality and gentleness was his trademark, and it was not acting. It was Gable.

From that moment on Dolores was conquered by his charm and the magic of his personality. Her heart melted. She could see then why he was tops at the box office. It was impossible for her not to smile—and her smile was a thing of beauty. She gave him the cold water he craved and entered his temperature on the chart.

"Queenie, when I'm feeling a bit better you and I are going to have a hell of a party right here in this room...a few of my friends...plenty of champagne. We'll have a ball. You'll see." He smiled again and looked at her with kind eyes. Gable was a man who had a nickname for everyone. It was part of his charm. He had decided that, from then on, Dolores was "Queenie." Perhaps he thought of it when she accused him of giving orders like a spoiled king, and then made it clear that she was in command as long as he was in the hospital.

He had instantly and easily captivated Dolores as soon as he decided to do it. If anyone knew how to handle women, it was Gable. He didn't turn on the charm just to get more out of her, although that was the result. He liked her, liked her looks, and liked the way she stood up to him.

Now Dolores couldn't do too much for him. She tried to shave him with his straight razor, but, after a nick or two, she gave up and held the mirror while he trimmed his famous moustache. She then ran down to get some ice cream to surprise him. She played his favorite records...played card games with him, read to him…talked to him.

She learned that his father was an itinerant oil field worker. Although Gable had grown up in the roughest of company and had lacked polish, early on he aspired to an acting career. He told her that he owed his success to his wives. Each had given him something of great importance. For example there was number one, Josephine Dillon, a dramatic coach. She had seen some possibilities in him and though she was 17 years older, they married. Gable still had nothing but praise for her—said she gave him class and taught him everything he knew about acting. His second wife, an heiress, brought him great wealth. Now he was married to his third wife, Carole Lombard, the love of his life. Contrary to what Dolores at first expected, it became clear to her that he didn't hold an exalted opinion of himself as an actor, and yet Dolores knew he had won an Academy award and was nominated for two more Oscars.

Almost every day so many flowers came from M.G.M. Studios, and from various friends and acquaintances, that not all could not be brought into the room. Gable exploded. "Queenie, get all those damned flowers out of here. What do I want with flowers? Give them to others in the hospital who like them, with my compliments. He remained agitated until they were distributed. No patient in the hospital was without flowers while he was there.

Although Carole Lombard, Gable's wife at the time, visited daily, Dolores hardly looked at her, and to this day has no clear recollection of the woman whose death was soon to cast a shadow over the rest of Gable's life.

The doctors kept Gable in the hospital longer than one might imagine, because a tonsillectomy is much harder on an adult than on a child, but finally they were ready to release him. Now he didn't want to go. He said he was actually enjoying himself too much to leave so soon…everything was so different from his usual routine, *and then there was Queenie.*

"I always wanted to have my appendix out," he informed his astonished doctors. "A man never can tell," he said, "when he might get appendicitis while on location in Africa or while hunting in the Yukon." This was the ideal time to have the operation and banish the threat forever. So the operation was performed and Gable stayed a week and a half longer.

There is no question but what there was a strong attraction between Gable and Queenie. Call it a flirtation, infatuation—perhaps love or a mutual fascination of some kind. Why else would a man have his appendix out just to prolong propinquity by less than two weeks? In any case they made the most of being together in that strange platonic relationship. No hanky panky—she was a devout Irish Roman Catholic.

Inevitably the day came when Gable was to be discharged from the hospital. He invited some of his cronies and film friends to a champagne party in his hospital room and there was much gaiety. Victor Fleming, director of *Gone With the Wind*, was there and so was Hattie McDaniel, the colored actress. Dolores tried to discreetly stay in the background but Gable wouldn't have it.

"Queenie, have you ever tasted champagne?" he asked.

"Never"

"Why not?

"Oh, I guess I never could afford it."

"Well this is your lucky day. Come over here and stay by me so I can keep your glass filled."

He watched with keen interest for her reaction to the first sip and was delighted when she approved, and soon accepted more. He made her the center of attention, and she glowed with appreciation for the approving glances directed her way. He did indeed make her feel like a queen.

They were both trying to be lighthearted but there was a wistfulness, a sadness, a regret that an unusual relationship was about to end and the reality of life would soon thrust a hard to define loss on their respective souls, leaving them somehow deprived.

Gable departed and Dolores found herself thinking of him much of the time...his sudden smile, his derisive laughter, his unexpected remarks and reactions, his humor, his magic charm. Then three days after leaving, he phoned.

"Queenie, I'm having some friends to dinner at my home Saturday night, and I want you and your Charlie to come."

"We couldn't do that, Rhett!" She had taken to calling him that. It fit, and he let her know he liked it—coming from her.

"Why not?" He sounded deeply disappointed.

"You would be embarrassed if we parked an old worn out car in front of your big mansion. And we would also be embarrassed in front of all those other guests...rich people with Deusenburgs, limousines and chauffeurs, and all that..... "

Dolores heard a roar of relieved laughter and Gable replied, "If that's all that's bothering you, you can park it out in back and nobody will see it."

It developed that she and Charlie were the only guests. Perhaps he had cancelled the other invitations thinking the rich and the famous might make them feel ill at ease. Perhaps he just preferred their company to those others.

They were to go many times to dine at the Gable mansion. Usually it was just Gable, Dolores, and Charlie. Sometimes Carole, his wife, was there. Charlie never enjoyed going. Probably that certain mutual attraction between Dolores and Gable made him jealous, though he never had the slightest reason to believe that anything untoward had ever taken place between them or ever would. But then there was more to it than that. Gable was a big, lusty, powerful man—a direct talking, no-nonsense, dashing, irreverent kind of person—a famous matinee idol who knew *everybody.* On the other hand, Charlie was a humble, hard working, young engineer; and he stood only five feet seven with his shoes on. It was true though that he was well proportioned and rather good looking in his own way—and was loved to some degree, if not adored, by Dolores. Maybe he felt somehow inadequate in the presence of Gable. In any case as time went on he told Dolores more and more frequently that he was "getting a little tired of this Gable thing."

One day, Gable called Dolores up at the hospital. He sounded excited, "Queenie, I've got it all set-up. I'm making a new picture and there is a small role in it for a nurse. I told casting to save that role for you. You're going to be in a picture with me. How do you like that?" He didn't tell her that he had told the script writers to write in the part for a nurse.

"I can't Rhett." Her voice conveyed deep regret.

"What do you mean you can't? It's all arranged."

"I'm six months pregnant."

Events moved fast after that. Gable's wife, Carole Lombard, was killed in a plane crash. He had been deeply devoted to her and was devastated. He joined the US Air Force as a gunner, saw action over Germany, and won the Air Medal for "exceptionally meritorious achievement." He and Dolores remained friends until his death in 1960. Charlie was always invited when they met, and went with Dolores, grumbling every step of the way.

Clark Gable had been dead 32 years when I met Dolores and Charlie for the first time. She was 84 and he 86. Time had been kind to them both, and I would not have thought her 60, if that. I could see immediately that she must have been a stunning beauty when she was young. Time never erases all.

Charlie was a dapper little man, well preserved and active for his age. I liked them both immediately, but I wondered if they had had a happy life together. There was no obvious evidence of affection between them but rather a suggestion of mild discord. Both were strong willed and stubborn—that much was certain. Something seemed to come between them...to divide them. At first I could not define it.

I had not known them long though, when Dolores casually mentioned knowing Clark Gable. Charlie sighed. I pressed her to tell me about him. Charlie sighed again even more audibly.

"Well...It all started in the summer of 1938 when...."

"It was the spring of 1939," said Charlie with the air of one who likes to get minor details right. Perhaps it was the engineer in him.

"It certainly was *not! I* ought to know. It was the same time my Mother came down with the flu." She said this with just a touch of indignation. After all, who should know better than she when it was her mother got the flu?

"We were living in North Hollywood at the time."

"What do you mean North Hollywood? We were living in Van Nuys."

"Keep quiet Charlie. You don't know what you are talking about. You never do."

"Alright. Frankly My Dear, I don't give a damn."

It suddenly occurred to me then, who Charlie reminded me of. It was Clark Gable himself. Yes that was it, Clark Gable. He wore a mustache that was trimmed precisely as Gable trimmed his own when playing Rhett Butler in *Gone With the Wind.* Charlie's hair was now snow white, which is why I had not at first noticed the connection. He had learned, probably subconsciously, to talk like Gable. I suppose something deep in his subconscious mind spoke to him and said, "If you can't lick 'em, join 'em," or "what has he got that I haven't got?" or something of the sort.

As Dolores told me this story her narration was punctuated occasionally by deep sighs from poor old Charlie. I wanted to say something to make him feel better.

"Well Charlie, you're quite a man. You can make the boast that you took Dolores away from Clark Gable."

Instantly Dolores set me straight. "Oh no he didn't! We were already married when I met Gable."

I saw then that she still carried a torch for the actor and would probably have been one of his five wives if she could have been—except she was married to Charlie, and she was a Roman Catholic. I wondered if she saw

Charlie as the frustration of her lifelong dreams. I imagined also that Charlie wondered the same thing, and tried to play the Gable role in her life, ill equipped though he was to do it. It was the best poor old Charlie could do.

IN VINO VERITAS

Strange horrors lurk in the minds of some people and remain carefully concealed—except after a few drinks. As Pliny the Elder said more than nineteen hundred years ago, "In vino veritas—In wine…truth."

I wish it had never happened, but it did, when I was living on my boat in Monte-Carlo. An old acquaintance from Sweden had an apartment nearby. Sven, a retired wine importer, kept in close contact with fellow countrymen in Monaco and enjoyed giving small dinner parties for a few good friends. He prided himself on his gourmet cooking skills and liked to have everything just so…the right mood music, a superior wine with each course, then after the cheese platter, coffee and a good cognac.

I always looked forward to these agreeable affairs…a change from eating alone aboard my sloop, Dolphin, or in the usual harbor restaurants, pleasant though they were.

Sven's twenty third floor terrace looked down on a spectacular 180 degree panorama that included nearly all 388 acres of the tiny principality. The floodlighted palace of the prince was at the far right, high on "the rock," facing the ancient quarter with its traces of Phoenician and Greek culture. The famous Casino of Monte-Carlo was closer and a bit to the left in a cluster of luxury hotels—the Sporting Club and public beach in the foreground. Cap Martin was off to the left, with Menton and the Italian frontier just beyond.

I'll never forget one occasion in particular. Sven had invited me to a dinner party and as the view was especially breathtaking that summer evening, I went out on his terrace to watch the sun go down. Gerda, another guest who had just arrived, also came out, I thought for the same reason. She was lighting a cigarette from the stub of another, and seemed a little unsteady on her feet. I wondered if she had had a drink or two already.

"Hi Gerda. Did you ever see anything so beautiful?"

"Well John, I guess I'm used to it," she replied in her accented English. "And besides I'm too tired to care."

Her reaction disappointed me. I sensed she wanted to talk, as usual, about the frustrations of her daily life, but that was not my idea of an appropriate nor uplifting topic. She had made a trip to Stockholm a month before and her mother, who was sick and blind, died during her visit. Since then Gerda had sunk deeply into depression.

"God, I wish I had a drink."

"I'll get something for you, if you like." I felt obliged to make the offer. "You're a Scotch-on-the-rocks drinker aren't you?"

"Make it a double Scotch—and go light on the rocks."

I returned in a few minutes with her drink. "Here's what you asked for, Gerda, but be careful—it may be too strong if you're exhausted."

"I can handle it."

"It could hit you pretty hard…better not drink all of it."

"You worry too much."

"Maybe, but we're also having wine with dinner and cognac after."

I handed her the drink and, as she was obviously not in a good mood, walked to the other side of the terrace, where for a moment I stood by the rail lost in thought. Gerda, a neat trim brunette, was not unattractive. She was probably in her early thirties and had not lost that comeliness frequently found in Scandinavian women. She had come to Monaco after completing her nurse's training, and though she had no trouble finding employment and living well, there was something pathetic about her that I could not quite define. Sven and I discussed her on one occasion. She had no men friends and we didn't think she would ever marry—not because of shyness—she was anything but shy. Sven's friendship with her was platonic and the two of them merely exchanged small favors occasionally.

I decided to try one more time to be sociable…to get her out of the dark inner world in which she had been living lately, and called out, "Gerda, just look at the crescent moon. It's starting to set. Isn't that a pretty shimmering pathway of light it casts on the sea?"

"Oh, I suppose it's OK, but if you were as tired as I am…. " She shrugged her shoulders.

"Have a sip of your drink and maybe you'll feel better. Look how blue the Mediterranean is and how crisp the horizon. Do you see the mountains of Corsica in the distance?" I pointed toward them. "Just imagine, they're seventy five miles away. The atmosphere is so clear tonight."

Gerda had been standing with her back to the view, lighting another cigarette. She turned briefly to look in the direction I had pointed, but made no comment. Instead, she turned away again, exhaled a cloud of smoke, tilted her head back and drained the last drops of her drink from the glass. An ice cube fell at her feet and skittered across the concrete deck.

I took a deep breath of salty sea air and began to wonder if she might have a mental problem. Since her recent trip home, her personality had changed. She had become withdrawn, according to Sven, and behaved as if the whole world were against her. Gerda had become a tragic figure, evidently drowning in a sea of self pity, and in miseries of her own imagining.

The red and gold afterglow faded almost into blackness, stars appeared one by one and soon the sky was filled with their fiery brightness. I glanced at Gerda. She appeared oblivious to it all...preoccupied with still another cigarette.

Lights were winking on in the city and aboard yachts that moved silently on a sea that now was black. It would have been nice to share this with someone, but Gerda had retreated into her own private world, shutting me out completely. I watched in awe the day's last scene, but she completely ignored it. Both of us stood in silence, and solitude.

Gerda finished her drink and became, for a brief time, noticeably less withdrawn. The change came with lightening swiftness and I wondered if it was it an unstable, manic mental process or an alcoholic reaction?

"Le dîner est servi—come and get it." It was Sven's, tongue-in-cheek call to dinner. As he said this, he opened the glass doors to the terrace creating an al fresco ambiance at the table. It was almost like dining under the stars. Candles on the table fluttered slightly in the night air and I heard a cork being pulled from a wine bottle. There is not another sound like it and oh, how it delights the wine lover and raises his expectations.

Lars, a retired writer, and his wife Elga, had arrived and we sat down to enjoy a pleasant evening of good food, good wine, and good conversation. Most Swedish people are fluent linguists and I have often admired their ability to shift effortlessly into my language, feeling themselves at no disadvantage whatsoever.

At first, conversation was light and pleasant. Sven, Lars and I swapped a few jokes and amusing stories, while Elga and Gerda chatted amiably. The wine flowed freely—a different one with each course.

"Do you feel more relaxed now, Gerda?" I inquired. She seemed to be, and I thought she would say she was.

"No. I'm still worn out. I haven't had more than three or four hours sleep out of twenty-four since I got back from Stockholm, and even that is broken into half hour naps scattered through the day and night. I can hardly keep my eyes open." She took out a pack of cigarettes and lighted one, not asking if anyone minded.

I should have known better than to ask how she felt. Why didn't I realize it would only get her started and ruin the rest of the evening?

"I'm not working at the hospital any more. I can make more money as a private nurse, taking care of patients in their own apartments. I have two now, and that's more than I can handle." By now, other conversations had ended and Gerda had everyone's attention.

"Most patients are either too old or they're terminally ill, and they should have been dead long ago. I have one woman who's dying of cancer. She has about two months to go. I keep her sedated. If I were in her place, I'd just jump off the terrace and it would all be over in a few seconds. If she doesn't want to do it, she should be put out of her misery." Gerda refilled her glass with red burgundy and drank it like water, obviously not appreciating its delicate balance.

Some of us shifted uneasily in our chairs and I'm sure we were all trying to think of some way to get the conversation on a lighter, happier subject. Gerda was ruining the party that Sven had spent all day preparing. Things were going to get worse if she didn't stop drinking.

"Gerda, please pass the wine. I'd like a bit more of that good Clos Vougeot." I said it though my glass was only half empty. I wanted to get the bottle away from her, but she ignored my request.

"Then there's that old Mrs. Philby," Gerda went on. "She's ninety five, filthy rich, and spoiled rotten. You should hear how she orders me around—the old bitch. Seems like the worse they are the longer they live. The only thing that keeps me going is that she could pop off any time now, and the sooner the better as far as I'm concerned."

I saw shock and strong disapproval in the faces around the table. "Why don't you leave her and find someone easier to be with?" I asked.

"You just don't do that in my profession. I'd never get another referral.

Why are you all looking at me like that? Haven't you ever heard of euthanasia? By God, that's something I believe in—I'll tell you that much. And the more I see of old Mrs. Philby, the more I'm in favor of it." Gerda was slurring her words badly now. Her face was flushed and there was an odd look in her eyes that made me wonder again if she was quite sane.

Someone said, "Gerda, surely you can't be serious. Are you saying the patient's consent is not even necessary? Are you saying that your patients should be put to sleep like stray cats and dogs, just because they are beyond an age you arbitrarily set as the limit?…or because they are rich and spoiled and order you around?…or because they only have two more months to live? Is that what you are saying?"

"That's exactly what I am saying."

Those around the table exchanged glances as if to say, "Did you hear what I heard?"

"Oh, come on now. We can't play God. Surely you can see that. Why if we were to accept your view, who do you say should be the one to…." Elga, watching Gerda's face, did not finish her question.

"I would do it. I tell you I wouldn't mind doing it at all. An injection or a pill and it's done. That's it—C'est fini."

Elga spoke again. "I don't believe it. You couldn't do that, Gerda." The reply this remark evoked cost Gerda the last of the few friends she had.

"Oh you don't believe me, huh?" Her face now twisted into an almost unrecognizable caricature of itself. I'll never forget her round staring eyes. "Well let me tell you something. I killed my own mother."

EVIL EYE

Most of us don't know what "jus sanguini" means. That included George Vasilis Kostandinou, who was born in San Francisco, California. He would learn the meaning eventually—the hard way.

Now George sat facing his father across the table. They were alone aboard the old man's fishing boat, Katina, a big purse seiner.

"So George, you don't wanna be a fisherman like yer father an' yer uncle Dimitris?"

"Dad, I'm sorry. Since I finished high school three years ago, I've tried hard to be a good fisherman. I've enjoyed working with you and Uncle Dimitris, but.... I don't know quite how to explain it. I have this urge to become an engineer or a research scientist. I know I can do it. I know I will make you proud of me. You'll see."

"Sure, George. I know. I'm proud of you already. I won't say I ain't disappointed though. All these years since I come over from the ol' country with Dimitris, I been tryin' to build the company, Giorgos Kostandinou & Son, up big and good for you and me. It was like a dream. Know what I mean?"

"What can I say? For a long time now I've wanted to tell you. I couldn't seem to find the right words nor the right time...didn't want to disappoint you."

They sat in silence for a while lost in thought. Katina, tied to the dock, tugged at her lines as if anxious to get under way. Finally Giorgos' weather-beaten face spread into a somewhat sad smile.

"That's all right George. Man has to do what he wants to do in life. You are man now. You got to decide things for yourself. I gonna send you to college like you want, but first you gotta do one thing for yer ol' man—go to the ol' country for a visit. See where you come from. Meet all the family you got there an' never seen. When you come back you do like you want. I'll help you. OK?" George felt a gratitude beyond his power to express.

On arrival at Athens airport George was delayed by formalities he did not understand. Not being an experienced traveler, he assumed it was normal and thought no more about it. Instead of just stamping his passport, a man there looked at it as if he had never seen one before. He looked just as hard at George, wrote something in the document, and stamped it. George was then led to a nearby office where he had to answer many questions. A man in Army uniform asked the names, dates and places of birth of both of his parents, where he would be staying in Greece, the purpose of his visit, the names and relationships of all other family members he intended to contact as well as their addresses. Eventually he was allowed to pass through.

Before putting his passport in his pocket George looked curiously at its sixth page where his entry into Greece was recorded. It bore an imprint of rectangular shape about the size of a large postage stamp. He correctly guessed the Greek words in it said "Athens Airport, May 17, 1977, entry"—however, across it in bold black ink were printed by hand three words: *ΥΠΟΧΡΕΩΣ ΣΤΡΑΤΙΩΤΙΚΗΣ ΘΗΤΕΙΑΣ.* George had never learned the Greek alphabet. It was something he would do in the next few days. At the moment, however, he didn't have the slightest idea what those words meant; despite a brief foreboding of trouble, he forgot about them.

There to meet him were his paternal grandparents, numerous aunts and some cousins—nobody from his mother's family, all of whom had been killed in World War II. Grandmother Kostandinou held a cardboard sign with "George" on it. She need not have bothered; he would have recognized her anyway by family resemblances. For Greeks they were unusually tall, as was he, his father, and his uncle. Grandfather had the same strong jaw, grandmother the same broad brow. They knew him on sight too. Probably his father had sent his photo when writing of the visit. The moment he appeared all began to shout his name. The children were jumping up and down in anticipation. George was glad he could understand them. Like most first generation Greek Americans, he was bilingual and could easily respond to the torrent of greetings and questions despite not being able to read the language. There was much laughter and he felt instantly at home—touched by the warmth of the welcome.

After collecting his luggage, the two carloads of family went to the modest apartment of the grandparents facing the harbor in Piraeus, the port of Athens. The same night there was a great celebration attended by more relatives than George knew he had, and family friends as well. There he met Christina. He knew from the moment he saw her he was in love—knew she would become his wife.

Christina was the daughter of the family doctor. She had been well educated and well brought up. She was so ladylike, so elegant, so graceful...she had such lovely hair, such dignity, posture, and bearing. Everything about her drove George crazy with admiration and desire. He thought she was the most beautiful girl he had ever seen. She had a gentle, kindly manner, she had wit, she had humor and oh, such eyes—they held him spellbound—clear, big and brown, warm and lovely. He longed to take her in his arms—hold her close. But he knew he must not betray his impatience.

George, until then, had felt strongly attracted to women, and at the same time a bit shy. Christina changed him in an instant into a determined, confident suitor. He sensed she was attracted to him when she offered to show him Athens. She had a natural charm, a warmth of personality. Christina drew people to her; she made them happy in her presence. Her detailed knowledge of Greek history was astonishing—the bronze age Minoan and Mycenaean civilizations, the Persian wars, the Peloponnesian wars, the Macedonian period, and the Roman period. She knew it all—explained it in terms that fascinated him. Christina made George proud of his Greek heritage and it pleased him to learn that Athens under Pericles was the first democracy. He dreamed of her when they were apart and only began to live once more when they were together again.

One moment they shared will live in his memory always. It was a warm, moonlit night. They were dining in the open air at a rooftop restaurant. It was near the foot of the Acropolis, and the Parthenon brilliantly flood lighted, seemed to be suspended in space above them in the dark night. George wondered what the ancient citizens of Athens would have said if they could have seen it the way he did. As he looked at Christina's face by flickering candlelight, she seemed to cast a spell over him. He wanted to ask her to marry him, and though she gave every sign of encouragement, he was too overcome with the magic of the moment to react.

The next day, proud though he was of his Greek heritage, he did have one moment of misgiving. He was in the city with Christina when they happened on a parade. George caught his first glimpse of Evzones, the members of the elite mountain infantry whose dress uniform looked, except for the slippers, exactly like a woman's ballet costume complete with tutu, a fluffy white skirt, long stockings, and little white vests. Their shoes were Albanian style with turned up tufted toes. George imagined what would happen if anyone tried to make the U.S. Marines put on such a uniform and the thought made him laugh out loud. Christina came to their defense though, saying, "Evzones are among the bravest, toughest fighting men in the world." George realized he had offended her national pride and was sorry he had laughed.

For lunch they went to a pleasant fish restaurant Christina knew at the edge of the harbor where the seafood was cooked over the coals as soon as it was brought in from the sea and served with a delightful retsina wine to complement it perfectly. They sat at a table under an umbrella. A big warm sun beat down from high in the sky on the colorful scene around them, making striking contrasts of light and shade.

"Christina, I see many fishing boats have big eyes painted on their bows to protect against the evil eye. In San Francisco some of our Greek Americans paint their boats the same way. I think it's mainly because of tradition though. Do these fishermen really worry about such things?"

"Well, George, some of them do. It's a deeply rooted superstition among us here. More so than among the Greek Americans I suppose. Many Greek people believe that some are born with the evil eye, and those who have it can bring terrible misfortune on others, even without intending to, just by looking at them."

George grinned. He leaned closer to her, making outlandish owl eyes. "Do you believe in the evil eye?"

"No. Of course not." Christina laughed. "It's only a silly superstition. Nobody with education should believe it anymore. Just in case though, I do carry this."

Christina opened her purse and took out a cat's eye. George had never seen one before. It was part of a mollusk shell found on some beaches in the South Pacific—round and about the size of a quarter, with markings on it like the eye of a cat.

"This is supposed to protect you from the evil eye." She smiled and George thought he had never seen such lovely white teeth. He wanted to kiss her then and there. "Here, keep it as a souvenir. When you look at it, think of me."

He held out his hand to accept the little talisman saying, "I don't need anything to make me think of you, but I do want this because it has belonged to you. I want everything you have ever touched. Most of all I want you. Christina, will you marry me?"

"I've been praying you would ask me. Oh, I'm so happy." She took his hand in hers. "If you think you will always love me as you do now, yes, George. Yes! Yes! Yes!"

George almost knocked over the table getting to her. He took her in his arms at last—they twirled in a tight embrace until one of her shoes flew off, and then sat down again, laughing.

On a sudden impulse, she picked a red poppy growing nearby and flattened it between the pages of the menu. "I'll press and keep this poppy always in memory of this moment." George was deeply touched.

Christina had just reached an age when, in Greece, young women of a certain class are introduced into society. The event begins when one of the most important matrons of the social world holds an afternoon tea party in the young women's honor. The social elite attend—it is reminiscent of coming out parties, at one time more in vogue in America than they are today. The day came for Christina. She dressed and groomed herself to make her best impression. Any faux pas at such a time could mar her social opportunities. It would not soon be forgotten.

At the all important tea party, everything went well for Christina until the hostess walked over to her with a cup of tea. The clumsy woman slipped on a rug and went sprawling. Tea went all over her dress, all over Christina, and of course all over the floor. Conversation stopped. Every eye was on the hostess. She got to her feet in a fury, pointed at poor Christina and hissed, "Evil eye! This girl has the evil eye!" A moment of shocked silence followed, then pandemonium. Some women averted their eyes and hastened from the room. Christina's social future seemed to be suddenly shattered.

She rushed out of the house, ran through the garden, tears streaming down her cheeks, dimming her vision. Humiliated and sobbing she finally found her way home and phoned her father who rushed back to give her a sedative. It was probably all he could think of to do. Christina's mother had died years before; never did she need her like now. After a few hours she opened her eyes and her father tried his best to console her.

"Don't take it so hard My Little One. It isn't the end of the world. It will all be forgotten one day."

"Oh, Papa. I was so humiliated, so embarrassed. I keep hearing 'evil eye…evil eye…evil eye.' "

It was two days before George could see Christina again. He had heard what happened and wanted more than anything to reassure her—to help her put it all in perspective.

"George," she said. "I am branded—how can I ever live this down? They all believe it now. Even those who say they don't believe in superstition aren't sure, so they won't have anything to do with me. There is nothing left for me here in my own country. The country I love so much." She dabbed at her eyes with a handkerchief and continued. "Even if there is someone who does not condemn me as an evil eye, they could never invite me to any gathering in their home because many other guests would not come."

"Christina, what nonsense! It's not as bad as you think. People will soon forget. You are just overwrought and over reacting. Besides, I'm taking you to live in America where it will all be just a funny story. What does it really matter?"

"But George, I thought I was not superstitious. Now I'm not sure. I keep thinking, what if I really do have the evil eye? I could wreck your life and I'd rather die than do that."

"Don't say such things. Do you want to make me angry? Here let's put it to a test if it will convince you once and for all. Look into my eyes." George held her close in his arms and gazed deeply into her eyes. "Now evil eyes do your worst. I dare you."

Having said this George kissed away her tears and left. When he arrived home his grandmother handed him a letter from the day's mail. The return address told him it came from the Greek Army. How odd he thought as he opened and read it. With some effort he understood its meaning:

It has come to our attention you were born in America of Greek parents. According to the legal principle known as jus sanguini, if your parents are Greek, you also are Greek with all of the privileges and obligations citizenship entails. Every Greek man is required to serve two years in the military. You will therefore report to the address on this letterhead for duty in the Army on 15 June, 1977.

George could not believe this. It was crazy. He was an American citizen. Greece was not his country. He hurried to the U.S. Embassy and asked to see the Ambassador but they told him it was not possible. He did manage to see the First Secretary, however and explained the problem.

"What the hell's going on? They can't do this to me. I'm an American citizen."

"You should not have come to Greece. They can do this and there is nothing we can do to prevent it. I'm sorry. It isn't the first time this has happened. Believe me; our intervention is useless despite the huge amount of aid we give to Greece. They are very sensitive where matters of national autonomy are concerned."

George's anger was now tinged with fear. If the U.S. Embassy could not help him, who could?

"In all fairness," the First Secretary continued, "our own government recognizes both 'jus soli' and 'jus sanguini'—two fundamental principles of international law. The first means the country of birth determines an individual's nationality. Suppose a foreign woman tourist or even an illegal alien gives birth to a child in the U.S.A. Her child can claim U.S. citizenship. More to the point, the second means blood determines nationality. For example, if an American woman gives birth in Athens, the child can have U.S. citizenship under the principle of jus sanguini."

George, who was pacing back and forth, was in no mood for a lecture. "Never mind what we do. Just tell me what Greece does."

"I'm coming to that." The First Secretary's tone of voice was pedantic and condescending. "I'm giving you the background. Let's not get ahead of the story." The man reminded George of an insufferable teacher he once had. "Greece follows jus sanguini to a degree we frankly find incomprehensible. You are Greek if you are of Greek blood, regardless of where you are born. Even if you are a fourth generation American but of Greek ancestry, Greece still considers you Greek and subject to its laws. You can vote in elections here and you can be drafted into the Greek army.

"All I want to do is go home. You are telling me they can keep me prisoner here?"

"Each country has its own laws concerning citizenship. Its right to make them is the essence of its sovereignty. Frequently another country's laws conflict with our own. We are in no position to tell other governments what they can and can't do, though we often would like to. The bottom line is: in America we follow our laws—in Greece they follow theirs. I'm sorry."

"It's the first time I ever heard any of this. Why in hell didn't the Department of State warn me when they issued my passport?" George hammered the Secretary's desk with his fist.

"Perhaps they should have." The Secretary busied himself polishing his glasses, not looking at George. "I suppose you have to chalk it up to human error. No use trying to pin the tail on the donkey now. It won't serve any purpose." The Secretary stood up, smiled mechanically and walked toward the door. George understood the meeting was over.

He left feeling angry and let down. He walked and thought. When he came to a park bench he sat down to collect his thoughts. One thing he was sure of—he would not serve in the Greek army. My God, he thought, when I tell Christina what has happened, she will for sure think she has the evil eye...can't leave Greece on any commercial transportation because of passport control...can't even cross any land frontier.... I'll bet it's why they wrote those words in my passport when I arrived in Athens. He looked again at the document and was now able to read "Subject to military duty." Now they tell me to report for duty on the 15th—I have four days, then they will come for me if I don't show up.

George went home and talked to his grandfather. "I'm not Greek. I won't serve in the Greek army."

"My dear boy, I'm so very sorry. You have to do what they say. There is no other way. Don't say you are not Greek—you are. You can make it even worse for yourself if you don't obey them. You could go to prison."

"Grandfather, I have a plan. It'll take more than four days to work out the details. I am not going to report on the 15th. When they come for me Christina's father must be here. He can say he is my doctor—tell them I'm running a high fever—coming down with something contagious. They will have to believe him. Maybe some red spots on my face would help. If he puts a quarantine sign on the house, they won't come back for a while. It will give me time to find a fisherman to take Christina and me out of the country. Will you help me?"

"You are asking me to put myself and others in our family at risk? You ask me to choose between you and my patriotic duty?"

George considered the old man's questions. "I'm sorry, Grandfather. You are right. No, I see it is wrong to ask such a thing. I had not considered the position I would be putting you and the doctor in. I can't do that; I won't do it."

George realized his plan to escape with Christina by fishing boat was too risky. He didn't like the way his grandfather was talking. If the police or the army put pressure on the old fellow, he might tell everything he knew. Furthermore George could never live with himself if he got either his family or Christina's father into trouble. He had to replan everything.

As much as he dreaded it, George knew it was time to tell Christina what was about to happen and involve her in an escape plan. He phoned to say he was coming to see her.

Maria, the elderly maid, answered his knock. From the way she looked at him, he knew Christina had told her of their engagement. The old lady had raised Christina like her own daughter from the age of ten when her mother died.

"Christina's father is not at home at this hour," she said, "so I can't ask you in. I'll tell her you are here and she can come out to talk to you."

"Ah. There you are my beautiful little butterfly. Feeling better now?"

"Oh yes, Darling. Much better." They embraced and kissed cheeks quickly. She introduced Maria. "I'm relieved to see you alive and well after looking into my evil eyes." Christina smiled as she tried to make light of the old superstition.

"Let's walk down to the little fish restaurant where I proposed to you and have a coffee. I have something to tell you. By the way, have you told your father yet?"

"Of course."

"What did he say? How did he react?"

Christina looked troubled. "Well, Darling, you have to understand. When I go, Papa will be all alone, so it is sad for him. It is even harder for him to bear knowing I will be going to America—out of his life. It is not as if I were marrying a local Greek man."

"I understand, but you will often come back for visits—I promise. Did he give his consent? Should I have asked for your hand in marriage? I don't even know if it is the custom here."

"Don't worry about it. My father knows customs are different in America. He understands. He wants me to be happy; what I want is the most important thing to him. Papa does want to tell you about my dowry though."

They reached the restaurant and sat at a table under a grape arbor at the edge of the sea. When the waiter started to approach, George held up two fingers and made signs imitating a coffee drinker. The boy smiled and nodded his understanding.

"Papa looks on the bright side of things. When I was accused of having the evil eye he was very angry. He knows how hard it will be for me to hold my head up in Athens now, at least for a while maybe a long while. Then when I told him about us he said, 'It is God's will. You see how He is watching over you? Now you will live in that wonderful country America where nobody will ever say evil eye again.' There were tears in his eyes when he said it. I know he was thinking how he would miss me." When she said this, tears welled in her own eyes. George squeezed her hand.

"Little butterfly, what would you say if I told you we must be married and off to America within three days?"

"In three days?"

"Yes, three days. Well, two or three—three at the most. There's no other way. You will understand when I tell you why."

The waiter brought their drinks. George took a sip of the strong coffee, explained the meaning of jus sanguini, and showed Christina what was written in his passport. A grave expression came over her face. He told of the letter he received ordering him to report for two years service in the army. George saw profound sadness and resignation in her eyes.

"Oh, My Darling, I knew it was all too good to be true. Now in spite of how crazy it sounds I have to face it—maybe I do have the evil eye. You got the letter right after you looked into my eyes."

"Don't be silly. That had nothing to do with it. The letter was mailed several days ago."

"Yes, but you have looked into my eyes every day."

"Oh, you little idiot. What am I going to do with you?" George made "little idiot" sound like a term of endearment, which it was.

"Darling, even if you are right, they will take you from me. There is no way to stop them."

Why was she so resigned to fate, he wondered—so ready to accept the will of the government? "It isn't going to happen. Trust me. Do exactly what I say. All will come out right." They held hands and stared silently at one another.

At the end of the day, George felt exhausted by the tension he had been under. He fell into a deep and troubled sleep, dreaming he was inducted into the Greek army. When he went to draw his uniform from the supply sergeant, he was handed a fluffy white ballerina's tutu and some Albanian style slippers with tufted turned up toes. He was an Evzone. In the dream, even the underwear issued to him was feminine, perfumed, and trimmed with lace. He was a guard at the tomb of the Greek Unknown Soldier where he had to pace back and forth looking like a ballerina while tourists took pictures and snickered. Finally the inevitable happened. A group of athletes he knew from high school came by with their cameras and recognized him. They hooted and hollered and he wanted to die of humiliation.

"Hey, George. Wait till they see these photos back home. They're not going to believe this—or are they?"

Under threat of severe penalty George was not able to say a word. All he could do was march back and forth on parade and execute a ridiculous high stepping about face at each end of his to and fro performance. He didn't even have bullets in his gun. If he did have he'd damned well make them dance, even if he got thrown behind bars for five years.

"Hey Georgie, how about showin' us your garter." His tormentors roared with laughter.

"Hey Georgie, Honey. What'cha doin' tonight…huh?"

When George finally opened his eyes, he found himself drenched in sweat. He got up, shaved, showered, and dressed. Skipping breakfast he left the house for the airport. There he inquired about charter flight possibilities. Someone directed him to a man with an office in the corner of a hangar.

"Are you Theofilos Vakirtzis?"

"Yeah."

"I want to arrange a flight for two persons to Izmir, Turkey. Can you handle it?"

"Yeah, I guess so. When?"

"Let's discuss money first. How much you charge?" George knew he was expected to haggle over price.

"170,000 drachmas."

"What? You must be crazy," George shouted, pretending his intelligence had been insulted. "130,000 drachmas—not one drachma more." Both men stood facing one another, inches apart

"145,000." yelled Theofilos, with tremendous lung power, drawing himself up to his full five feet six inches.

"140,000." replied George. Both had seen early on where demands and counter offers would converge, nevertheless it was necessary to complete the negotiation according to the custom of the country. Once price was agreed upon, the conversation now proceeded on less contentious terms.

"Let's say departure will be tonight or tomorrow night. Any problem?"

"Makes no difference to me."

"What do you estimate the flying time will be?"

"About an hour."

"Tell me. Do we have to clear passport control before we board your plane?"

"Of course,"said Theofilos. "First, you clear passport control, and then right behind the counter is a door. It leads out to the area in front of the hangars. I'll be by my plane waiting for you." He was getting suspicious now.

"Damn. This won't do." George looked desperate, and was. "I might as well level with you. You see, my fiancee and I are eloping. She is a well-known person—picture in the society section of the paper all the time. Her father is very powerful and dead against our marriage. He would reward anyone for a tip off and some people would be quick to take advantage. A snap of his fingers and the airport police would descend on us. We'd never get off the ground."

"Yeah? What's her name?"

"Think I'd tell you? I'm not stupid."

"Oh, I wasn't thinking what you think."

"OK." George thought otherwise but let it pass. "Tell me though, isn't there another way onto the field? How do you get there? You certainly don't go through passport control when you go to work."

"You're asking me to do something dishonest?"

"Do I have to repeat the question?"

"We have to discuss the price of the fare again. I can't fly you to Izmir for less than 300,000 drachmas."

George didn't want to haggle again. "OK 300,000 drachmas it is. You are taking all the money we were going to spend on our honeymoon." It wasn't so of course.

"Here's my card with my office and home phone numbers on it. Call me when you're ready to go. We will meet in the coffee shop of the departure lounge. I have a gate key. I'll get you in. Don't worry."

"One more thing, Theofilos. I don't know you, so I'm taking no chances. I'll pay you half the money when we are in the plane. I know Izmir airport. I've been there before." He was bluffing. "If you take us to any other place, the other half of the money goes overboard. Understand?"

Theofilos nodded.

Although it was not the kind of wedding Christina had always dreamed of, she and Maria improvised as best they could and the bride was a lovely sight. George was happy and proud—the Doctor sad and proud. The grandparents were present and George let them think he had reconciled himself to a two year hitch in the Greek army. No others were there except for Maria who shed the tears Christina's mother would have if she had been alive.

Christina hugged her father and they kissed on both cheeks. She promised to write often. She couldn't say goodbye. She and Maria hugged, cried, and then they were off. George had his fingers crossed. He had a nagging feeling he couldn't trust Theofilos. He couldn't say why—just a feeling.

At the airport Theofilos was sitting with a cup of coffee, waiting for them. He looked hard at Christina. It was obvious he didn't recognize her.

"OK, let's go." said George, not wanting to introduce Christina. It occurred to him he had not even introduced himself.

The little pilot led the way out of the building to a gate in the fence surrounding the hangar area. He unlocked it and they walked to the twin engined plane, George carrying their two suitcases and an oversized wallet.

Theofilos opened a compartment in the side of the fuselage, stowed the luggage, and all three climbed aboard. He held out his hand for the money and George took half of the fare from the wallet as agreed.

Ten minutes later they were airborne, on course for Izmir. George began to relax. He had taken the precaution of checking what the compass heading should be just in case Theofilos tried any tricks. The heading was correct. Suddenly the pilot reacted violently. He banked sharply to the left to head back in the direction they had come from saying, "My God! Now I know who she is. She's the girl with the evil eye. I saw her picture in the paper. I'm not flying across 175 miles of ocean with her." Christina was in despair. It was more than she could bear.

Acting quickly on instinct, George, who was sitting right behind the pilot, pulled a heavy fire extinguisher out of its holding clamp. He thumped the back of the pilot's head with it and said in a voice that nearly froze Theofilos' blood, "If you don't get back on course right now, I'm going to bash your skull in with this. I can fly this plane as well as you can and I'll just take over." It wasn't true. Fortunately the little Greek had no way of knowing that. He did as he was told and broke out in a cold sweat.

The plane was once again back on course. Though George remained vigilant, he felt he could relax again and said, "My Darling I can't wait to phone home. The folks will be so happy to hear we are married and on our way home. We'll have a second wedding—a big one. You'll have the white silk wedding dress you dreamed of. Dad will invite the whole Greek community of San Francisco. We'll have your father and Maria there."

"Oh, George. I'm so happy. I can't wait to meet your family—can't wait to see America. Although I've traveled all over Europe, San Francisco is the city I've always wanted to see."

In less then an hour they landed at Izmir. It would have been hard to tell who was the most thankful. After they left the plane, George noticed that Theofilos always faced away from Christina, avoiding eye contact. He wondered if the little pilot was trying to ward off the "evil eye." George handed him the rest of the money as promised. As Theofilos reached for it, he dropped a cat's eye he had been holding. He quickly picked it up with one hand and grabbed the money with the other, both actions at the same time, then crossed himself as he ran back to his plane. In an instant he had started the engines and was taxiing for take-off, ignoring the fact that he should have reported to Customs Control with his passengers.

George turned to Christina. "Come my wicked Little Evil Eye." He tried to look serious. "Let's go catch our flight to the good old U.S.A." They laughed, hugged, kissed and walked into their future arm-in-arm.

A LONELY MAN

Despite his millions, Jerry Reed was the loneliest man I ever knew and the most unhappy. He was married and loved his wife but she would not live with him. His children were grown and living their own lives and his dog "Wa-Wa" was dead. Having made an enormous fortune importing German cars into North America, he retired to spend his last years in Europe.

Jerry tried to use his money to increase his self esteem and to gain entré into illustrious circles. This was an obsession and I thought it suggested an odd combination of determination and insecurity. He often told me how much he spent, dropped the names of rich and famous acquaintances by the score, and constantly asked, "You know who *he* is don't you?" Usually I didn't and this habit of his annoyed me a bit.

Jerry was a small package—short, trim, graying and balding. When I first met him I thought he was drunk but I was wrong. He only talked that way. He confided that he had been a hopeless alcoholic at one time and that was why his wife had left him. Now he never touched a drop, or so he said. I think it was true. His slurred speech may have been the result of a mild stroke and I thought how difficult it must be for him to make friends among strangers who invariably thought he was plastered. He even tried joining the expensive and prestigious MonacoYacht Club but met there with icy Gallic reserve and silence.

He bought a chalet near Vaduz in Liechtenstein, a yacht in Greece which he almost never used, a home and business for his son in Zurich," and a villa in Cap Ferrat near one that had belonged to Somerset Maugham. For some reason never completely clear to me he didn't live in that lovely bit of heaven, with its sweeping bougainvillea framed view of Villefranche—one of the most beautiful and picturesque panoramas on the French Riviera.

Jerry chose to live instead on a yacht in the Riviera but his knowledge of such things was pathetic. He knew that the bow was the "pointy end" and that's all. Nevertheless he made inquiries and learned the whereabouts of the biggest yacht on the Riviera. Nothing less would do. Without making an appointment he went right over to what looked almost like an ocean liner, a little under 400 feet overall. She was tied up in the outer harbor at Antibes. Jerry marched up the gangway, in his inimitable way, and was intercepted on the fantail.

"I'm Jerry Reed," he announced as if you had to be stupid if you didn't knew who that was.

The Chief Stewart looked down his nose and said, "Monsieur has an appointment?"

"No but I want to see the owner.

"I regret Monsieur that he cannot be disturbed."

"You tell him I want to buy this yacht. If *you* don't and *I* do, I'll fire you."

How he managed to convince the steward that he was serious and not drunk I don't know. Probably he refused to leave the ship—that would have been in character for him.

It turned out that he was in luck, but only in a manner of speaking. The owner, a member of a family of brewing fame, was aboard and it just happened that although he was "not *anxious* to sell," the idea *had* occurred to him lately and he might consider a suitable offer.

"How much do you want for her?" asked Jerry, who was a man of action, not one who liked bargaining.

A figure was named. It sounded like the national debt when he told me, but he had replied, "I'll take her."

Jerry said later that it was not one of the best decisions he ever made. His wife never once set foot aboard. He had bought the big yacht to surprise her—thought she would love it—no other reason. He spent most of his time looking for personnel. French cooks in particular seemed unable to get along with French chief stewards, and neither could get along with anyone else. Every week or so one and then the other would pack up and walk off in a huff.

Just to keep the huge ship at the dock cost him a hundred and thirty thousand dollars the first year even after reducing the ship's normal compliment from fifty to a mere skeleton crew, and that was many years ago.

Jerry sank farther and farther into depression. One day he was sulking in the main saloon when his chief steward came in to announce a visitor.

"Monsieur Reed, Sir. There is a gentleman to see you."

"Tell him to go to hell."

"Very good Sir." The steward bowed and left. Five minutes later he passed through the main saloon again on his way somewhere.

"What did he want?" Jerry asked in his slurred diction, sounding as peevish as he could under the circumstances.

"He said he wanted to buy the yacht Sir," replied the steward in a casual tone of voice.

"You idiot. Why didn't you say so? Which way'd he go? What'd he look like? Come with me." Jerry dashed down the gangway, ran along the piers and all around the harbor. It was no use. The visitor had vanished like an apparition. In a rage he fired the steward, but hired him back when he started to leave. After all who else knew what the sought after man looked like?

"Did you finally catch up with him?" I asked.

"Yes, but not until the next day, after the sonova bitch had bought the second biggest yacht in the Riviera." Jerry said this without a trace of a smile. I don't think he ever saw the humor in the situation. Come to think of it, I don't recall that he ever smiled or laughed during the two years I knew him. If he did, I wasn't aware of it.

After a long and expensive delay, Jerry finally sold his big white elephant and bought a more appropriate yacht. With improved judgment the second time around, he found a 65 foot ketch which was quite luxurious, comfortable, and suitable in every way. To sail it he hired a crew of two Yugoslavians who spoke some French but no English. He knew neither of their languages so I never could understand how the three of them managed.

Jerry was not stimulating company but it intrigued me that a man with so much money could not find even a modicum of happiness. Then too there was something vulnerable and pathetic about him and I felt obliged to look in on him from time to time when I was passing through Beaulieu, where he tied up. He always seemed glad to see me, though I can't say my visits ever appeared to drag him up from the depths of despair.

I recall that on one visit I asked why he made no use of his fabulous villa near by at Cap Ferrat.

"I use it. That's where I make all my phone calls."

"Why don't you make them from your yacht?" I asked.

"I tried it and it didn't work."

This didn't make much sense to me but then nothing Jerry did made any sense. Instead of having the radio fixed—who in his right mind would buy a million dollar villa just to have a place to make phone calls? Perhaps he had bought the villa in the hope his wife would come back and live with him and, when she refused, he kept it as a symbol of hope.

Jerry called one of the Yugoslavs and made hand signals to indicate he wanted coffee for two. While sipping mine, I noticed a silver framed picture of a little white dog and asked him about it.

"That's Wa-Wa," he said, looking even sadder.

"Where did you get *that* name?" I asked.

" I was just two years old when I named my first dog Wa-Wa and since then I gave every one of them the same name."

"Jerry," I said, "how do you spend your time? Do you like to read?"

"No. Never. I get up at dawn every morning and go out to pick up cigarette butts before breakfast." His slurred speech was worse than usual. I sniffed the air for alcohol but didn't smell any.

"Say that again—what you do at dawn. I thought you said you picked up cigarette butts."

"That's what I said. Is there anything wrong with that?" he asked testily.

"I guess not, but why do you do it?"

"I get my exercise that way and I clean up the dock at the same time. It's more than these Frenchmen do. They just sit around, all dressed up, with bouquets of flowers all over the place—eat, and drink champagne. Most unfriendly bastards I have ever seen. They won't even talk to me. Nobody wants to be friends around here. Not one.

"Yes, I know what you mean. But what else do you do with your time?"

"Call up an old friend in San Francisco and talk to him most of the morning. He's in the hospital, dying."

"Gosh Jerry, you must have quite a phone bill."

"Oh no. Comes to only two or three thousand a month usually. It passes the time. Sometimes I call my wife. Sure wish she would come back for more than just an overnight visit once every six months. I get so fed up with this unfriendly place. Next week I'm taking my boat to Scorpios. Know that place? One of the Greek islands. It belongs to Onassis. Most beautiful place I have ever seen. I spend months there every year, a few weeks at a time."

"Oh really? You know Onassis then?" That surprised me, although he seemed to know almost everyone.

Jerry squirmed. "I don't *yet* but I figure sooner or later he will notice my yacht at anchor there and invite me ashore for lunch or something. Once

Ari—er Onassis that is—and Jackie had some guests that swam out to my boat. I invited 'em aboard for drinks but they were nobody you ever heard of."

There it was again. That need to rub elbows with the famous—that need to collect names to drop. I had heard this sort of remark many times before. One name Jerry especially liked to drop was Howard Hughes. He used it casually and apropos of nothing at all.

"Yeah," he would say, "it's like Howard said once, Howard Hughes that is...."

And his familiar variations would go on from there. Once I asked some probing questions and confirmed my suspicion that Jerry had seen Howard Hughes only once in a bar. Naturally he barged up and said, "Hello, I'm Jerry Reed." I suspect Hughes replied 'Oh Yeah?' I wish I could have overheard that conversation, if indeed there was one, between two of the world's most eccentric men.

The thing that hit Jerry the hardest was reaching 70. It was as if he had seen a ghost and that ghost was his own. I was driving through Beaulieu and decided to stop and say hello. That's when I learned it was his birthday. The psychological difference between 69 and 70 was more than immense. It was frightening. It was ominous. Before he was always in the doldrums but now he had sunk to a new low—a whole order of magnitude of hopeless melancholy beyond anything I had seen before. Was 70, to him, the end of the line, or was he upset by the prospect of spending the day alone, perhaps without even a phone call or a card from his wife, son, or daughter?

Whatever the reason, the change in him shocked me. I invited him to dinner and he accepted, but that dinner was no celebration. He sat in gloomy silence most of the time, ate little, and refused to be cheered up. Once he looked at me and said, "When I die you can have my yachts." I was stunned and didn't know what to make of that remark.

A few days later Jerry's boat was gone and the Captain of the Port told me he had sailed for Scorpios. Ah yes Scorpios—"the most beautiful island" he had ever seen. Well I hoped that Onassis would be kind this time and invite him to come ashore. It didn't happen though.

Jerry didn't return. The morning after anchoring off Scorpios, the Yugoslavs found him dead in his cabin, an open bottle of sleeping pills nearby. Beside him on his bunk were pictures of the people he loved...his wife and his beautiful daughter...none of the son who had been such a disappointment to him. And in his hand, it would have been the last thing he saw, was the little silver framed picture of Wa-Wa, perhaps the only one who really loved him.

JOHNYEE, I'M DYING

"I'm sorry Darling, I don't believe in ESP and I never will. It's all just superstition with no scientific evidence at all to support it—like old wives' tales." If I had said the world was flat I could not have aroused in my wife greater feelings of indignation. We were newlyweds then and as newlyweds do, we were struggling to understand, and to be understood.

"You are a clever man, Johnyee. I never confused you with an idiot, but you are wrong." Her accent was a charming blend of Russian and French. "Haven't you ever known what someone was theenking just by reading hees thoughts?"

"Well, yes—to some extent. You think I'm being stubborn and unreasonable. Right? I know it by deductive reasoning. That's all ESP ever is, whether you realize it or not."

"Nyet, nyet, nyet—you're wrong." She trilled her r's in such a delightful way when she said it. "Sometimes my bodyee ees all full of electricity, all full of dynameesm and I know so much about everybody eet geeves me zee cheeken peemples. Sometimes eet makes me sheever with all my bones. Why you laugh, Johnyee? Why you laugh? You shouldn't be so septical."

"Skeptical."

"Yes septical, that's what I said—septical." Her expressive face showed mild exasperation.

"OK, give me one example of your most recent ESP experience."

"Zat was yesterday. I was talking to Telma and Artur, I'm such a chattering box you know. And she said to me, 'Assia, guess who ees coming to veeseet Artur and me.' and I said, 'Your mother, father, and seester. Zey weell arrive tomorrow night by train.' Her eyes almost popped out of zer socks and Artur, eet nearly scared zee guts out of heem. Johnyee, why you laugh at me? I was right. You don't believe?"

"Of course I do. There is an explanation though that I once read about. Thelma probably told you before and then forgot she did. You forgot about it too, but stored it in your subconscious mind without realizing it."

"Oh, Johnyee. You should be more elastic. You are such a book wormer. If you would only beleeve, eet would work for you too. Sometimes you make me so mad I get all porcupined up."

"Believe me, I wish ESP were real. I learned today I'm soon to be transferred from Paris. Now is as good a time to break the news to you as any, although I'm not sure where we will move. I wish you or I had the power to divine it—my best guess is London." I saw sadness in her eyes and some tears. Paris was her home. She had lived there since she was "half past five." I knew to leave it would be almost more than she could bear.

"I felt it when you came home tonight, making a long sourpuss face. Eet weel be Madreed, Johnyee. You weel be transmuted to Madreed."

"Transferred."

"That's what I said. No? When I get sad maybe my words get all tweenkeled up."

"It's all right, My Darling. I love you anyway. And I love your 'twinkeled up' words too."

"Well, I don't know why you shouldn't."

Making one of her split second mood shifts she gave me a dazzling smile. It accentuated the high, aristocratic cheekbones of her lovely face—"chipmunk cheeks," I called them.

"It won't be Madrid, Darling; that much I feel sure of."

A month later I did get transmuted, er, transferred to Madrid, of all places. The year was 1955 and we found ourselves stunned by the unbelievable devastation left by the Spanish Civil War. There was no middle class. The masses barely existed in soul-killing poverty while a few fortunate ones lived like grand dukes on the loose.

We found an elegantly furnished apartment on the Avenida Castillana. I must say it was grand and spacious and we settled in to begin our new life in surroundings that combined unaccustomed opulence with a hundred year step back in time. Our maid, Maria, had not attended school a day in her life and spoke only Spanish. Assia considered it to be no problem and in a few days my little Russian was able to make herself understood with ease. In a month she was almost fluent in kitchen Spanish. Russians are irrepressible linguists. I struggled along with my high school Spanish, making only an increment of progress from one month to the next.

One inconvenience we could not live with was the lack of running hot water. In order to prepare a bath, Maria had to heat water on a huge black monster of a stove out of the distant past. It consumed vast amounts of kindling as well as coal by the shovel full.

Soon though, I was able to buy a small gas-fired water heater, the first on the market in Spain. The great day finally arrived when the ominous looking boiler, pipes, and valves were installed on our kitchen wall. It frightened our poor unlettered Maria who had never seen one before. We, however, were delighted at the prospect of again being blessed with the luxury of running hot water.

That evening, to celebrate running hot water, I took Assia to dinner at the fashionable Castillana Hilton Hotel. We were in the highest of spirits. To go with the main course, a tail-coated waiter served Spain's excellent Marque de Riscal wine, from the Rioja region, as a string ensemble played softly in the background. All was again right with our little world—or so it seemed.

Assia said she wanted to have another celebration party, in our own apartment, to entertain new-found friends and show off what was probably one of Madrid's first hot water heaters.

"OK. Good idea," I said. "Who'll we invite?" I took out my pocket notebook and pen. Assia loved to entertain. Making the guest list was part of the fun, and as we didn't know many people yet, it didn't take long.

"Anybody else?" I asked, after jotting down four names.

"Yes, zat nice old gentlemen from America and hees wife. What eez heez name? Oh, you know who I mean. He eez Professor of Butterflies at Columbia." I smiled and made a note. I didn't know then that one of us might have never attended another party.

The following morning I was at my office in the penthouse of a hotel in downtown Madrid, dictating to my secretary. In the middle of a sentence a feeling came over me I had never felt before, and have not felt since. There was no impression of specific words as I recall. Instead, I had an overpowering awareness of grave danger...an irresistible compulsion to get home as fast as I could...an emphatic sense of a catastrophe about to happen. I knew it was a matter of life or death.

In the middle of a sentence I left my astonished secretary and ran out of

the office,
saying, "Got to get home…finish this later." The elevator seemed to take forever to reach me. When it did, I paced back and forth in it like a caged animal during the agonizingly slow descent. Finally the door opened and I sprinted through a lobby filled with startled people who turned to stare. Fortunately my car was parked nearby.

Instead of going home my usual way, following principal streets through the center of the city—a horseshoe shaped route. I took a shortcut. It was half the distance, had far fewer stop lights and less trafic, but it took me through a part of town where I had never been before—an area of back alleys and narrow streets. There were donkeys, pushcarts, and children playing in the streets, nevertheless it was the fastest way and maybe the only way I could get home in time. I took chances. I ran every red light. I ignored police whistles. Oddly, not once did I ask myself why I was doing this. I concentrated only on getting to Assia as quickly as I could. I knew every second counted.

When I reached our apartment, a crowd was standing around a woman lying on the sidewalk. I got out of my car running, my heart beating wildly. It was Maria. What had happened? Where was Assia? Gawkers clogged the courtyard and surrounded our doorway. I knocked the curious aside like ten-pins in a bowling alley. In the apartment, to my profound relief, I found Assia in her wet bathrobe talking to the sereno—the keeper of the keys. She looked shaken, but glad to be alive. When she saw me she ran to my arms.

"Oh, Johnyee! You came. You heard me, and you came."

"What happened, Darling? Why are you all wet?"

"After you left for work I called Maria and said, 'Por favor, agua caliente.' I needed hot water for zee bath. Maria turned on zee gas, and zee water heater had no pilot light. She had to light eet weeth a match to get hot water. Zee man who made zee installation didn't tell her zat." [He didn't tell any of us "zat"].

I soon pieced together the story. Assia had waited about a half hour for the water to heat, then put on her robe and went to the tub. She opened the hot water faucet. Cold water came out. She let it run a while. It made no difference. Leaning over the tub to check the temperature, she became dizzy and fell into the icy water. Momentarily revived, she tried to get out. She felt faint and dizzy—fell back into the tub a second time. She suddenly realized she was being asphyxiated and struggled desperately now, knowing her chances were less with every passing second. She thought, Oh my God. I'm going to die. I'm going to pass out and drown.

She called, "Maria! Maria!" No answer. In desperation she had screamed, "Johnyee, I'm dying. Come home queek. Save me!"

Assia then managed to get a leg over the rim of the old fashioned tub. With one final, frantic effort she rolled out onto the floor. She was almost too weak to move. She had once been told that in such an emergency one should breathe the air closest to the floor. She crawled out of the bathroom, nose as far down as possible, and proceeded down the long, unlighted hallway leading to the kitchen in which the water heater was installed and where she expected to find Maria. Feeling her way in the dim light, she soon came to the unconscious maid. She tried to drag Maria, but couldn't...almost passed out trying. It occurred to her Maria might already be dead. Weak and desperate, Assia then crawled to the sitting room at the other end of the hallway. "Oh God, let Johnyee be coming," she prayed.

Using the drapery for support, she pulled herself to her feet. From the window she could see two maids, "chicas," who were shaking and beating carpets from a window across courtyard. Black spots started to cloud her vision. Her knees were turning to rubber. Everything began to whirl before her eyes and a buzzing sound came from inside her head. It grew louder. She tried to open the window. It wouldn't budge. She beat on the glass with one hand.

Not knowing the Spanish words, she called out in French,"Au secours!"—screaming like a "feeshmongrel," as she said later. The chicas heard her, but didn't understand and thought it all hilarious. About to lose consciousness, Assia took off a slipper and tried to break the glass with it. She couldn't. This sent the chicas into peals of laughter.

In Spain at the time, it was the custom for the sereno, to keep all keys. To enter your apartment you summoned him by clapping your hands. If not dozing, he came running and unlocked the courtyard gate as well as the door of your apartment for you. Our sereno knew a little French and when he finally heard the commotion, he quickly opened the apartment door, opened the windows, turned off the gas and water, warned away all smokers, and carried the insensible Maria out of the apartment. A moment later I arrived. Although Maria recovered completely, it didn't surprise us that she never again set foot in our apartment.

After this experience, do I believe in ESP? Don't "confuse me with an idiot." Wouldn't you?

FATE, YOU OLD DEVIL

Turks call it Kismet, Arabs call it Quismah, Hindus and Buddhists call it Karma—we call it Fate. Usually by common sense and uncommon hard work an intelligent person of western culture can put the odds in his favor and live a reasonably happy and prosperous life. Look around you though; it doesn't always happen that way.

Sometimes it seems there is no limit to the good fortune nor to the misfortune that can befall us in life. We may be blessed with one or cursed with the other, or we may be blessed and cursed at the same time. Though we exert our often feeble influence on events for better or for worse by the decisions we make, by our motivations, by our risk taking, and by other things we do or fail to do, some mysterious force appears to be the final arbiter.

Whenever I ponder this point, my thoughts invariably go back in time and I see myself again in Madrid, where I once lived. The company I worked for was represented there by a firm owned and run by Count Ricardo Martinez Cabrera, a man of great wealth and prestige—a grandee of Spain. His power and influence enabled him to form other important connections as well, one with an American manufacturer of jet fighter aircraft whose planes the count sold to the Spanish Air Force. Commissions from those sales alone would have made him a multi-millionaire, if he were not one already. He had, in addition, a steady yearly income of over a million dollars just from the sale of spare parts to support aircraft previously sold—a mere lagniappe compared to his other profits. I asked myself how a man could be so fortunate.

Many addressed him, according to the custom of the country, as "Excelentisimo Señor," but to my American ear, such forms of address always sounded pompous on the one hand, and smacking of servility and self-abasement on the other. I even avoided using "Señor el Conde" and instead called him "Count." It didn't seem to upset him, but probably only an American could have gotten by with it.

The count, a man of middle age, had dignity and presence out of proportion to his size. His neatly trimmed dark beard enhanced those qualities, and he always held himself rigidly straight. The Spanish are a proud and umbrageous people—especially the aristocracy. I found the count reserved, but friendly. Courtly, rather formal manners made him seem pleasantly anachronistic. He was a man of few words but was a good listener. His gray eyes never wandered when we were talking—an engaging trait.

His brother Miguel looked very much like him though taller and a few years younger. He had been a test pilot in the Spanish Air Force, but after nearly losing his life on three occasions, it seemed wise to change professions. He told me the birth of his second child finally made him consider his "mortality." It was natural he should join the count in business as sales manager. The ex-pilot was almost as responsible for the company's extraordinary success as his older brother. Miguel, an extrovert, had a spontaneous charm, as well as a Latin vivacity you couldn't help liking. We soon became good friends.

I was sorry though that I didn't know the count better. It came therefore as a pleasant surprise when he invited me to dinner at his casona—his estate in the country.

When Miguel learned of it he asked me to join him for lunch at the Jockey Club. I sensed he had something he wanted to tell me that wouldn't wait. I was never sure whether the count had put him up to this or whether it was his own idea.

At the Jockey Club, Miguel came right to the point. When our cocktails were served, he said, "John, my brother told me that he has invited you to dinner Sunday."

"Yes. I'm looking forward to the opportunity to know him better, and to meet his family."

"Good. Here in Spain we enjoy eating out and we do it often. When we want to entertain friends or business acquaintances, we usually take them to one of the many fine restaurants here in Madrid, or to the Golf Club. Only rarely do we invite them to dine at home, unless they are old friends. That is the custom of the country. I want to explain why this is especially true where my brother is concerned."

What can he be leading up to? I wondered.

"I'm, going to be very frank John and I count on your discretion. You see, it's Elena, the countess. She is not well. If she doesn't join you at the table, I don't want you to be offended. She does this to all of us—often. Sometimes she is quite abrupt. Ricardo is frequently forced to make excuses for her. We in the family are afraid she may have a mental problem, but it is not certain."

"Well, under the circumstances, it's kind of Ricardo to risk having me dine at home with his family. I feel doubly honored and I hope there is some logical explanation for the countess's behavior other than the one you think probable." This was the first hint that Fate had marked the count and his family for misfortune but nothing prepared me for what would happen.

"Yes, I hope so too. She is such a charming person when she is herself. It is just that we haven't seen her like that for quite some time. But If she is herself, I am sure you will like her instantly."

Having said this, Miguel's mood changed and he relaxed. He was a fun loving man who liked to laugh and had what seemed an endless stock of amusing stories.

The count lived about fifteen miles from Madrid's outskirts and, knowing I would probably have trouble finding the way, he was kind enough to pick me up at my apartment in the late afternoon of a beautiful, mid-summer Sunday. As we approached the huge casona, I saw it in the distance. We were already on his property, winding through hectares of fruit orchards and fields cultivated in vegetables. He explained this was a large land grant that had come into family possession through feudal tenure under King Philip II, 365 years before. Fire destroyed the original mansion, but it was rebuilt of quarried stone in 1755. Farther on I saw a veritable oasis of shade trees, and extensive gardens that provided the cut flowers for the casona. We passed tennis courts, a swimming pool, a shooting range, a stable for saddle horses with a paddock beside it, and circled a fountain that faced the main entrance. The road then led on to a large separate garage that held six or seven late model, expensive, passenger and sports cars.

The casona itself was imposing and splendid with its roof of Spanish tile the color of red earth. It had elegance and that hard to define mystique that the patina of time and two hundred years of noble residence imparts. My first impression on entering was of a magnificent, almost palatial, entry hall paved in marble parquetry of intricate design. On the walls I saw the count's ancestral bearings, and oil paintings of severe looking ancestors, in heavy gilt frames—some of them dressed in ruffles as they did in ancient times. The count indicated one by a respectful nod of his head and told me it was his great great grandfather. He seemed enthralled by the painting. I had the feeling that the proud, stern old aristocrat with penetrating eyes and frigid stare, was judging us—and we were not entirely to his liking. It occurred to me to wonder if a mere painting like this could have anything to do with the sometimes exaggerated pride and fierce sense of family honor that one finds among the Spanish nobility.

I recognized an immense tapestry as a Gobelin, imported from France perhaps by one of the ancestors now looking down at us in mute grandeur. On the left was a grand stairway with ornately carved newel posts. It swept up gracefully and majestically in a way that evoked in my mind visions of spacious and luxurious bedrooms, dressing rooms, morning rooms and sitting rooms.

The count opened a door on the right and said, "You might be interested in my guns and shooting trophies." We entered a room whose walls were paneled in polished oak. The mounted head of a cape buffalo looked down fiercely at us. It seemed as enraged in death as it must have been in its last moments of life. There was a panel of safari pictures, one of which showed the count, rifle in hand, standing by a slain African elephant…next to it a photo of the count with a black gun-bearer and a lion. Another picture showed the count with a Bengal tiger. I also saw a display of colorful prize ribbons and badges of various sorts—probably more than a hundred. Except for these things, shelves of gleaming silver trophy cups of every size covered the walls. Most were inscribed "First Prize."

"I noticed the shooting range as we passed it," I said, "but I had no idea you shot in competition."

"Oh Yes, I have been shooting in national and international matches, rifle and pistol, since I was seventeen. I won the World championship twice with the rifle and three times with the pistol. Last year I entered the International Skeet Competition and came off with a second. That explains these six cups." He indicated them with a wave of his hand.

Next, we went through an archway into the adjoining room. Gun racks and cabinets lined the four walls. Across one I saw a collection of American guns starting with an authentic muzzle loading Kentucky long rifle and a Maynard breech loading single shot Civil War gun. It ended with a Garand and a Thompson .45 Caliber machine gun from the Second World War—the kind issued to amphibious ships of the U.S. Navy. Another rack held a similar collection of British guns from the Ferguson breach-loading flintlock to present issue rifles and carbines. There were shotguns too, made by Purdy of London.

"I visited Purdy a few years ago," I said. "I remember that a haughty looking old gentleman with white hair, dressed in a morning coat and striped 'trousers' came to greet me. He stared at a point in space several feet above and to one side of my head, and asked, 'Would you like to be fitted for a firing piece, Sir?'"

The count smiled. "That would have been old Blakely. Did you order one?"

"I considered it until I heard the price—decided to buy a new car instead." I looked longingly at the Purdy collection that would have cost a small fortune.

He showed me the Remington M40XB with which he had won two internal rifle competitions and then the Winchester M70 that he used for thick-skinned dangerous game. It had bolt action and was similar to a Mauser, but was chambered for the massive 458 Magnum Winchester cartridge with 500 grain bullet.

"This is my most powerful rifle, he said. It is capable of deep penetration through bone and thick hide. To bring down an African elephant you have to go through two feet of bone to reach the brain. The main problem is that with over 5000 foot pounds of energy at the muzzle, it kicks like a mule. The recoil almost knocks me flat on my back when I fire it. Sometimes at first I'm not quite sure whether I have shot an elephant or have been trampled on by one." He smiled.

What an awesome weapon. For me it was a thrill just to hold an African big-game rifle and to imagine its devastating potential.

A glass top cabinet in the middle of the room displayed his extensive hand gun collection. He seemed more proud of a pistol with which his grandfather had won a duel than he was of the one he had used to win three international championships.

The count then led the way to a large sitting room and library comfortably furnished in superb taste...fine massive Spanish antique tables...cabinets of polished oak and maple. The old was blended with the modern for comfort and color. On the walls were some paintings by the French impressionists, a large pastoral scene by Constable, an El Greco, and a Velasquez. Large windows giving on the rose garden were open with the drapery drawn back to invite a flower scented, cooling breeze. In an adjoining room, servants were setting a large refectory table for dinner.

"John, I am going to have a campari soda before dinner. Would you like one too or do you prefer something else? A scotch and soda perhaps? Or a sherry?...Jerez as we call it here in Spain."

I was glad he had used my first name. Until then I had avoided using his, knowing that some criticize Americans for rushing into the more intimate form of address which Europeans usually reserve for old and established friends. Like most of my countrymen, I was more comfortable with first names. I knew and appreciated that he had done this out of deference to informal American customs. "Thank you Ricardo, Jerez please."

"I think I'll change my mind and join you. I have a particularly good Manzanilla I'd like you to try. As you probably know, we age Jerez in a solaria system that blends each year's vintage so that some fraction of it is as old as the solaria. My Manzanilla is quite old."

Just as he was pouring the slightly chilled, fine, dry, pale Jerez for me, his son Ernesto entered the room. When we were introduced, the young man flashed a quick and sincere smile that put me at ease immediately. Like his father he spoke perfect English and plainly welcomed the opportunity to use it. Ernesto was taller than his father, slender but strongly built. He had his father's dignity but also a spontaneous warmth of personality. His eyes were brown, not gray like his father's, and he had a lighter complexion than is common in Spain, which surprised me. I recall he had wavy brown hair, and his teeth were very white and even.

His father poured a Manzanilla for him saying with a smile, "I don't have to ask this one what he prefers to drink." Something in his glance suggested his immense pride in Ernesto.

"Ernesto," I said, "I'm glad we both appreciate a fine Jerez, but tell me more about yourself. Are you a gun enthusiast like your father?"

"No, Señor. I'm only an average shot I'm afraid. I don't have my father's sharp eyesight, his fine coordination, nor his steady hand. I'm a horseman. I like riding and jumping."

"He is being too modest," said his father. "Both he and Maria, my daughter, have won trophies in riding and jumping competitions. As for his shooting, I agree he is only a fair shot—just fair. Each person has within him the power to excel at something though, and that is what is important, don't you think? As for me, riding is something I like, but shooting is my passion."

Ricardo raised his glass and said, "I drink to your good health...Salud."

I acknowledged the toast, "Salud." It was an excellent Jerez and I said so.

We tend to take special note of things that, because of habit or training, interest us. It was the Count's hand that I watched with particular curiosity. It was the hand of a world champion pistol shot...dexterous and steady like no other. When he said "Salud," he looked me in the eye and held his wine glass rock steady at arm's length toward me—not the least trace of tremor. I had the impression he was sighting over the top of the glass. Perhaps he did it instinctively. For a moment I imagined what it would be like if he held a pistol instead of a wine glass. I would not like to be in his sights.

Just then a breathtakingly lovely young woman, about Ernesto's age, entered the room. We all stood up. "John, I would like to present my daughter, Maria."

I acknowledged the introduction and thought, the children and young adults in Spain are almost without exception, strikingly attractive. Maria, like her brother was tall, slender, and straight. Also like Ernesto, she was of fair complexion. Her eyes were big and brown, her hair dark though not black, and her features finely formed. Her English was perfect, as I expected it would be. They told me she was eighteen, but she had the poise of an older woman—a poise that suggested high intelligence. Ricardo must have read my thoughts. "My children are de buena madera—of good wood," he said proudly.

When the countess came in, I was at first curious, then relieved. I felt that I had already met her—she and her daughter looked almost exactly alike. She had aged so slightly and so gracefully it was hard to imagine she could be the mother. Dressed in elegant taste, she wore a beautiful pearl necklace that contrasted nicely with her dark dress. I found her most gracious and recalled what Miguel had said, "If all goes well, you will like her instantly." It was true.

A servant announced that dinner was served and we adjourned to the dining room. I still have vivid images in my mind of that pleasant occasion, undimmed by years. Maria sat on my right and I remember her lovely eyes, her warmth of personality, and her charm. In time words fade into oblivion; I have long ago forgotten most of what we said, but as frequent retelling reinforces memory, I have total recall of the following conversation.

"Are you a hunter like my father, Señor Riley, or do you prefer other sports?" she asked.

"Yes, I was raised with guns Maria and I like to hunt," I replied, "but your father is in a class by himself." The others at the table were listening. "More than any other sport though, I like sailing. Have you ever sailed a boat?"

Maria replied, "Oh no. I'm afraid I wouldn't know one end of a boat from the other."

I smiled and said, "Until you learn that fundamental, Maria, I advise you to let someone else take the helm."

She and the others laughed. "As for me," she said: "I love horses. Give me a horse to ride and to jump and I am in heaven. Ernesto is the same."

"Well," I said, "I wouldn't know one end of a horse from the other.

Her expression became lugubrious but her dark eyes sparkled as she restrained a smile, "Until you learn that fundamental, Señor Riley, I advise you to let someone else put the saddle on."

Her talent for tu quoque repartee showed a quick mind and a delightful sense of humor. At times though I thought I saw some fleeting sadness in her eyes. I sensed that something troubled her deeply.

"If I loved horses as much as I love boats, do you suppose I would be twice as happy as I am," I asked.

"It is an interesting question. I have often pondered—in your language do you say pondered? Yes? I have often pondered the same thing. Does happiness in life come from cultivating many interests and enthusiasms or from exploiting to the utmost the one we like best?" She said this pensively and I marveled at the depth and intelligence of this charming young señorita.

"I don't know, but many things fascinate me," I said. "I might even become interested in horses, given the time and the opportunity." A fragment of a poem by an obscure author passed through my mind. It seemed apropos so I said:

Give a man a horse he can ride,
Give a man a boat he can sail;
And his rank and wealth,
his strength and health
on sea nor shore shall fail

Maria looked at me in surprise. "Can you believe it? Of all the English poetry I have read, The Vine, by James Thomson is my favorite. How strange that you should think of it." After saying this, her mood changed suddenly and I felt I had in an instant lost contact with her. It was as if we had been talking by phone and the line was cut. "Oh if only Leif were here tonight," she said. "He is my fiancé."

Instantly I saw Ernesto's expression change. It was obvious he detested

Leif. Looking at the count and the countess I could not read their feelings. The Countess reached across the table, squeezed Maria's hand, and said, "Never mind my child, I know how you feel, but try to be happy tonight. All will be well."

After dinner Ernesto gave me this explanation. It was his sister's birthday party. Maria had of course invited Leif to attend. He knew, or should have known, what an important day it was for her—how she counted on his being there. He had simply said he was sorry he couldn't make it. No explanation...no flowers...no gift...no note and not even a phone call on that special day.

Ricardo tried to pretend they were not offended, but I knew the Spanish pride and their intense sensitivity. He explained, searching for a plausible excuse, that Leif was a brilliant young medical doctor from Sweden. He would soon be qualified to practice psychiatry in Spain and was working very hard to make it happen. "Sometimes his mind is only on his studies."

He told me Leif had been attracted to Spain and would make his career here. He had said he wanted to leave behind the long, cold, dark winters that depress many Swedes—winters that drive many to drink. Furthermore he had his fill of confiscatory taxes and socialism. Ricardo said Leif had a flair for languages and had become quite fluent in Spanish. I heard also he was an excellent horseman and had met Maria at a riding academy.

After dinner Maria's birthday presents were brought out. Her father gave her a riding crop, jodhpurs, and some superbly crafted riding boots made to her last by Lobb's of London. The countess gave her an Hermes scarf in gold and red colors, a suede jacket elegantly tailored by Balanciaga, and a smart black equestrienne's hat.

A shadow seemed to pass over us all. Even the weather changed. Ernesto and the count dashed to close the windows as a violent thunder storm struck in full fury. Lightning flashed, zigzagging its fire across the black sky and tumultuous thunder rent the air. It was as if two invisible titans were engaged in a stupendous struggle, hurling thunderbolts at each other.

Though Maria tried to act as if she were happy and carefree, her voice quavered slightly, suggesting that she was on the verge of tears. The ear splitting thunder made her hands tremble.

Ernesto did his best to revive his sister's spirits, presenting his gift last and with great fanfare. It was a lovely gold watch to be worn like a locket around her neck on a fine matching chain. An inscription that he had selected, probably after much deliberation, was engraved on the back. Maria seemed moved. Her eyes brimmed with tears when she read:

To my dear sister Maria,
from brother Ernesto 12 June, 1956
The time to be happy is now
The place to be happy is here

When I thought about the inscription I imagined it held a subtle message. Reading between the lines, I understood that something was indeed troubling his sister—casting a shadow over her happiness. It seemed a heartfelt but futile gesture on his part.

After Ernesto drove me home I found it hard to sleep. I kept reliving the events of that evening. Everything had impressed me deeply—especially Maria's bantering conversation. I could not forget her playful, teasing way of speaking nor the lightning quickness of her mind. In retrospect, I'm glad I had the opportunity to see her when I did.

During the next two months I traveled on business in Europe and Africa. On my return, I went to the office to see the count and Miguel, but found only Miguel there. Instead of the usual clatter of typewriters and those other sounds that successful commerce generates, I found instead a strange quiet. Miguel seemed depressed. Without elaborating, he said that Ricardo was at home. He invited me into his office, closed the door, beckoned me to a chair near him, and asked his secretary to hold all calls. He poured a cognac for me and one for himself, as a man will do when he has something unpleasant to say and feels the task beyond him unless he is fortified by alcohol. After these many years I can't repeat verbatim what Miguel said, so I will tell it in my words, true to the facts he gave me.

Ernesto hated Leif. It started when he found out Leif was living with a woman. It was not in him to be true to Maria nor anyone else. Ernesto kept it from his sister not wanting to break her heart.

Miguel said Leif was wrong for Maria…good looking, a fine horseman and all that, but icy cold. He thought the man's main concern was to find a woman who had money. He said anyone not blinded by love could see right through him.

There was one thing though that bothered Leif—he had convinced himself that Ernesto was a borderline schizophrenic. This seemed absurd. Ironically it had escaped his notice that the countess may indeed have had a serious mental problem.

A day or so after I was there for dinner, Leif came to the casona to see Maria. He and Ernesto had a violent argument. Ernesto knocked him down and they fought as if one would surely kill the other. It could have ended that way but Ricardo stopped it somehow.

After the fight, Leif went home and wrote an utterly heartless letter to Maria, in which he told her it was his "professional opinion" her brother was a schizophrenic. He said he "could not marry her with insanity in her family because it is hereditary." He wanted his "children to be perfect—not mental defectives like Ernesto." The engagement was off. She was to kindly send back his ring. Miguel showed the letter to me.

It was Maria's only love affair. She was inconsolable. The next day she left home without a word...rode off on her mare, Angel, to see her aunt who lived nearby. She tearfully told all that had happened, said good-bye and rode off again. That night Angel trotted home without her. The family was frantic. They phoned Miguel and he came immediately to join Ricardo and Ernesto. They looked for Maria all night in a violent downpour. The thunder and flashes of lightning frightened their horses and added to the futility of the search. With only flashlights to light their way, it was hopeless.

The next morning Maria's aunt called Ricardo by phone. She was hysterical. It took him some time to make out what she was saying. When he finally did, it almost killed him. She said she had found Maria's body. She had hanged herself from a tree on the property there. Saying nothing to the others, he dashed to his car and raced away, hoping and praying no doubt that there was some mistake or that he might arrive in time to save Maria, but when he saw her hanging like a slaughtered animal on a gambrel, he knew he was too late. She had been dead when Angel trotted home. Maria had dressed in her new jodhpurs and boots, her Balanciaga jacket, and her Hermes scarf. Around her neck was the engraved gold watch that Ernesto had given her. Her new equestrienne's hat lay in the mud where it had been knocked from her head by the rope. Since she was a little girl, she always wanted to look pretty—was always at her very best. She had dressed as she wanted to be buried.

But her body had hung in the wind and rain all night and was by then a pitiful sight. Her tumid eyes and tongue protruded hideously. Her face was bloated and purple. She was almost unrecognizable.

Ricardo cut her body down, carried her to his car, placed her gently on the front seat, and brought Maria home. Miguel said Ricardo would never get over the grief and shock as long as he lives.

When he arrived with Maria's body, Ernesto and Miguel were waiting in front of the casona for him. They had not known about Maria's death and had just finished organizing the servants into search parties. At the sight of his sister's pathetic body, Ernesto went from profound shock to almost insane rage. He and Maria had been very close. In a white heat of passion, he seized his father's big game rifle—the one used for elephants, ran to his Porsche and sped off in the direction of Madrid. Ricardo was still stunned by horror and grief and didn't react. Miguel knew that if Ernesto killed Leif, he would have to stand trial for murder. He had to stop him.

Ernesto drove his red Porsche like a madman—his uncle following close behind. They both took desperate chances, but Miguel had faster reactions and greater driving skill. He thought of the consequences if he failed to stop Ernesto. At least they had it in Leif's handwriting that in his professional opinion, Ernesto was schizophrenic. He could plead insanity. He probably would be sent to an asylum for the criminally insane, but that was unthinkable.

They were not more than two kilometers from the casona when a herd of milk cows being driven to pasture, temporarily blocked the way. A ditch on each side of the road left no possibility to go around them. Ernesto and Miguel slid to a stop just in time. Miguel jumped out, ran around to the passenger side and jerked the door open. Before Ernesto could stop him, he grabbed the box of ammunition from the seat and hurled it into an irrigation ditch. When Ernesto ran to get it, Miguel took the rifle and had time to lock it in the trunk of his car.

"Don't be an idiot," he said. "Do you want to be tried for murder? If you won't think of yourself, think of the family honor."

Ernesto was in such a fury he was almost incoherent. "I'll kill him," he said. "I'll blow that bastard to shreds. He doesn't deserve to live."

"Get hold of yourself Ernesto!" Miguel implored. "Do you want to disgrace our family? Do you think that is what Maria would want?"

Ernesto put his arms and head on the steering wheel and became very quiet.

Miguel could now talk and be heard. He told Ernesto. "You can challenge him to a duel. A duel is the only correct way to settle affairs involving the family honor. Blasting him with an elephant gun would only bring dishonor on us all."

I was with Miguel one hundred percent until he said this. Now he had shocked me. I had not realized that an outdated custom like dueling still survived. This vestige of knight errantry, however, didn't pass from the scene for at least another ten years.

After some time Ernesto finally said, "You are right Miguel. It is the only honorable way. I see that now."

Back at the casona, the countess had collapsed. She hadn't spoken a word since that day. The doctor called it "complete catatonia." She just sat in her bed and stared into space. We would never know now whether she had been having a mental problem before that, because the shock she suffered was enough to drive any mother insane.

Ricardo would be reminded of Maria every time he looked at his wife. The two were so much alike. As for Ernesto, he now lived under the sword of Damocles, wondering if he might go mad like his mother...or could this affliction skip a generation and affect his children.

They buried Maria in the family plot near the rose garden. She was laid to rest, dressed as she had wanted—jodhpurs, boots, suede jacket, and her new gold watch around her neck. Because she looked so bedraggled and pitiful after what the wind and rain and rope had done, they mercifully covered her body with rose petals and her face with her Hermes scarf. Angel with empty saddle stood by the grave. Maria would have wanted that. Leif didn't even send flowers. Nobody heard a word from him.

Ernesto did what any Spaniard of noble blood would do—must do—under the circumstances. He challenged Leif to a duel. Leif accepted and chose pistols. Ricardo wanted to duel Leif, but Ernesto had challenged first. The Spanish code of honor would not permit any substitution now, nor would Ernesto have allowed it. He was determined to uphold the family honor. Ricardo gave him a Colt .45 caliber M1911 National Match pistol—the special model with the 'NM' stamp, and match ammunition. The Spanish dueling code required that Ernesto offer an identical weapon to Leif, which his second did, but Leif refused it. Ricardo and Ernesto then spent two days on the shooting range next to the casona, practicing on a man-sized target placed at twenty paces. Ricardo showed Ernesto the fine points of dueling. It would be necessary to finish Leif with one shot. Each man would have only the one cartridge in his pistol. Ernesto could not have had a better coach and his shooting was much improved.

At the appointed time the duelists, their seconds, Ricardo, Miguel, and a few others arrived at the selected field. Everyone was astounded when Leif appeared dressed in an army camouflage jacket that would help him blend with the background. This was in shocking disregard of Spanish custom, but Ernesto chose not to object. The man was beneath contempt. Ernesto wore the traditional white shirt and dark pants. The shirt was of silk. It had been worn by his great grandfather in a successful duel that also involved the family honor.

When all was in readiness the two men took their places back to back. Each advanced ten paces and then they turned to face one another. Their arms were at their sides awaiting the word "disparen"—the command to fire. Ricardo was watching Leif intently. He whispered a prayer and crossed himself.

"DISPAREN!" Ernesto's 45 barked and his gun arm flew up from the powerful recoil. He had gotten his shot off first. Leif seemed startled. He appeared to jump back as if he were about to run, but he was obviously unhurt. Ricardo's hopes turned to fear, then horror. Leif took his time now. He was in no danger. He aimed carefully and deliberately. Ricardo murmured a prayer that Leif would just shoot to miss or to wound slightly. After a long pitiless pause allowing Ernesto, Ricardo, and Miguel time to suffer the agony of suspense, Leif squeezed off the one round, Ernesto reeled from the impact of the bullet and dropped to the ground.

They rushed to him, but he was beyond help. He had a bubbling, breathing, chest wound, and was gone in seconds. Coughing blood, the last thing he said before he died was, "Forgive me. I failed you Father. I failed Maria…failed the family."

Leif walked over to where Ernesto lay dead and spat contemptuously on the ground by his body. Ricardo went wild. In an instant he had Leif by the throat and tried to kill him with his bare hands. They had to restrain him. Leif the younger, stronger man might have beaten him senseless. As they held him, Ricardo challenged Leif to a duel and he accepted. Nobody could believe it. Leif calmly agreed to duel the man who had won the World Pistol Championship for the third time not six months before. He had seen the count's trophies. He had to know he couldn't win. To Miguel it could mean only one thing—Leif intended to skip the country, probably in a privately chartered plane.

Miguel was deeply affected by the tragedy. Ernesto had been like a son to him. He learned later that Leif had been trained by the Swedish army, decorated for marksmanship, and had shot in pistol competitions in Sweden.

The day before the second duel Miguel was of course with Ricardo who was honing his skills on the practice range. He had never seen such incredible shooting in his life, but he told Ricardo of his suspicion. To his great surprise Ricardo turned to him and said, "Oh, he won't run, he'll be there all right. You can bet everything you own on it." Miguel didn't know what to make of that, and Ricardo wouldn't explain.

On the appointed day they assembled at the same field where Ernesto had been killed. This time reporters were there, as well as a priest, and a police officer to be sure the Spanish dueling code was observed. To Miguel's astonishment Leif did show up, inappropriately dressed as before. He was stoical and abrasive, as usual, and didn't appear to be at all nervous. This man could not begin to outshoot Ricardo and he knew it. If he wasn't worried, why wasn't he? When Miguel saw this he was more than suspicious. He reasoned that Leif was an obvious psychopath who had killed without conscience and in doing so, had acquired an insatiable need to kill again. It occurred to him he might intend to fire before the command—even shoot Ricardo in the back when they were pacing away from each other. No, that was not likely. It would be a dueling code violation and he would be held accountable in court. Leif had something else in mind, Miguel thought. It occurred to him that he might have found a way to drug Ricardo, difficult as it might seem.

"How do you feel Ricardo?" he asked.

"Very well."

"Your eyesight is sharp and your hands are steady?"

"Yes."

Miguel was completely mystified. One thing he was sure of—Leif had a surprise for them—but what?

When the duel was about to take place, Ricardo handed an envelope to Miguel. "If I should lose the duel, you must open and read this letter immediately. But don't worry. I don't intend to lose." Miguel was even more puzzled and worried now.

The duelists took their places back to back. Each took ten paces and turned to face the other. Ordinarily Miguel would not be in the least worried, but under the circumstances he was. He looked at Leif's cold and confident face and shuddered. What surprise was he counting on? My God! It suddenly struck him—the ammunition. It had to be that...Leif had somehow tampered with the ammunition. He must have paid someone to plant defective cartridges. Yes…it had to be that…too late now.

The two men stood facing one another, hands at their sides. Ricardo was holding the same Colt .45 match pistol Ernesto had used—cocked, safety off, and one cartridge in the barrel.

"DISPAREN!" Almost at the very instant of the command, a shot rang out. Miguel was watching Leif intently. His head went back as if in haughty contempt, but there was now a neat red spot between his eyebrows like the bindi mark Hindu women wear on their foreheads. In that brief fraction of a second, Leif ceased to exist. His knees went limp and he fell heavily to the ground, his lifeless blue eyes staring at blackness…at nothing. Ricardo walked over to where he lay and spat on the ground. Oh, how he hated that man.

When Miguel told me this, I felt confused. "Miguel," I said, "I've done a bit of shooting with hand guns and there is one thing I don't understand. In this situation the knowledgeable shooter would go for a quick body shot. When life depends on one bullet finding its mark, and time is absolutely vital, to aim for a smaller target like the head, which could be easily missed, is not something one would do. Only an International Champion would attempt it, but why did he take that unnecessary chance?"

"John," Miguel replied, "I said the same thing. Ricardo told me to open the envelope I still held in my hand and read it. This is what I found." Miguel opened the drawer of his desk, found the letter and handed it to me. I read:

Querido estinado Condé Martinez Cabrera,
[translating now]

I own the best stocked gun shop in Zaragoza where I sell everything for sport shooting and for police needs. I have tried to reach you by phone. You didn't answer so I send you my news by this letter. Someone told me about the duel where your son was killed. He said now you have challenged the same man.

Be careful Sir. I think he may be the one who bought a bullet proof vest and camouflage jacket from me the day before your son was killed. This man had a foreign accent and I saw Madrid license plates on his car.
Your attentive and constant servant, who shakes your hand.
[Signature]

Attached to this letter was a note from Ricardo to Miguel.

As you see, Leif probably wore a bullet proof vest under his camouflage jacket during his duel with Ernesto. I thought Ernesto's bullet hit a vital area of his body and the impact seemed to knock him back slightly. I am almost certain he plans to use the same trick in his duel with me. I have two possible options:

1) I could call him on it—tell him I will demand proof he is not wearing body protection before I will duel with him...or

2) I can try for a head shot. That of course is considerably more difficult in rapid fire. If I miss his head I'll just have to stand there and let him shoot me as he did Ernesto.

If I select the first option, I am sure he will not duel and I will lose my chance to kill him. I have therefore no choice but to go with the second option. If I miss his head and he then kills me you will know by this letter the circumstances of my death. I know I can count on you to bring him to justice, for violation of the Spanish dueling code. They will try him for my murder and Ernesto's. One way or another, Miguel, we will avenge the family honor. If I miss, Dear Brother...Adios y vaya con Dios.

After Miguel read this letter they went over to Leif's body to examine carefully his camouflage jacket. Sure enough they found a bullet hole from Ernesto's shot. It hit the chest left of center and would have been fatal. The impact was what had caused Leif to suddenly turn and assume a new stance before firing the fatal shot. They unbuttoned the jacket and there was the bullet proof vest for all to see.

Ricardo had not been near the office since Maria's death. Miguel said he had become a recluse and he doubted if he would ever come to the city again. He just sat by his wife's bed...talked to her, and brought her a red rose every day, as he had always done. She was all he had left, but Miguel said, "She never moves and never speaks."

I gulped the last of my cognac, left the office lost in thought, and wandered along the Avenida Castillana, oblivious to people and to direction. In a park I found a bench and sat down to think.

"Ah, Fate, you old devil...."

"What would you say now Maria, now that your passion is no more, if you could only communicate?" I imagined she might reply about like this:

"Señor, I was a very foolish girl. I'm sorry for what I did. Now I can only hope that people will remember me as I once was.

'Let my voice ring out and over the earth
Through all the grief and strife,
With a golden joy in a silver mirth...'"

"But Maria—the last line of that quatrain is: *'Thank God for life.'"*

NO PHONE TOKEN

If only I could have glimpsed the future on one occasion, it might, in my opinion, have changed the lives of several people, prevented a serious tragedy, and frustrated an international intrigue.

My SAS flight from Stockholm touched down in Helsinki and I was soon inside the rather small wooden air terminal building which, in 1960, was all they had. In the baggage claim area was that distinct smell of fish oil they used to treat the wooden floor. But then my mind returned to the reason I had come to Helsinki and I reread a telex from Osmo that said, "Minister of Foreign Affairs wants to see you urgently on a confidential matter." I passed through customs and passport control and was glad to see the friendly, grinning face of big, jovial Osmo Oksanen, our distributor, who had come to meet me.

That afternoon, at the appointed time, we entered the Foreign Ministry, identified ourselves by passports, and were immediately taken to a private elevator that went directly to the office of the Foreign Minister, Martti Mikkela. He met the elevator and greeted us graciously.

Mr. Mikkela was about sixty years of age with white hair, a distinguished face, and kindly expression. He had the refined manners of an aristocrat. His suit was conservative gray, nicely tailored, with a white handkerchief in the breast pocket. I somehow felt I could trust him and liked him instantly.

From his spacious penthouse office atop a fifteen-story building, Mr. Mikkela could look out across the Gulf of Finland and see all the way to Tallinn, Estonia, fifty miles to the south. Numerous oil paintings of the sea and ships adorned the oak paneled walls and leather bound books contributed to the impression of taste and intellect. Some Persian rugs and fine old credenzas added to the tasteful decor. Mr. Mikkela dragged a chair over and we sat on a sofa facing him, with a teak coffee table between us.

I was impatient to hear about the mysterious matter that had brought us together, but Mr. Mikkela was in no hurry. He politely offered drinks

"Cognac? Scotch? Sherry?" In Finland one is offered alcohol of every description at all hours of the day.

Osmo and I declined, but accepted coffee when finally it was offered. The Minister was careful of the finer points of etiquette and formal behavior, but his gestures of hospitality were obviously sincere. I sensed, however, that he enjoyed chatting amiably with us over a coffee more than he looked forward to discussing the business at hand.

After the second coffee, having delayed all he could, he began by giving a short resumé of recent Finnish history. He referred to the Russo-Finnish Continuation War and Finland's final defeat in 1944. He then explained how the terms of the armistice had put Finland under some measure of U.S.S.R. influence. Since then, he had often been "obliged to do things for the Communists" he would rather not do. He sighed, and finally got to the point.

"Mr. Riley, would your company be willing to sell to Finland, for transfer to the Russians, technical manuals for every piece of equipment you make for the television industry?"

I was astounded. It was unthinkable—an outrageous request. Russia did not have television at that time. The company I worked for had spent over $100 million developing this product line and the Russians wanted to buy all that technology just for the trivial price of the manuals. I didn't have to think about it.

"No. Certainly not," I replied without hesitation.

Mr. Mikkela seemed pleased and relieved. He had done what he had to do, with evident reluctance.

"I'll convey your reply to the Russians. Let me just say, you have answered exactly as I expected and hoped you would. Make no mistake; however, they will pursue every other channel available to them to obtain a set of those manuals. In my opinion, this is only act one of the drama."

I sensed he was trying to tell me something in the obscure and subtle language of diplomacy, but I did not understand it as a warning—until it was too late.

Soon I was home in Geneva. It was nice to be back. We had our office on the second floor of a building on a small island in the Rhone River, accessible by bridges to the left and right banks. It was a charming spot. I could look out on a medieval stone tower across a narrow street—like a clock tower, but supporting an ancient sundial on it's south facing wall. At ground level there was a tiny restaurant, cozy and convenient for a coffee, snack, or lunch. When I thought to listen I could hear the Rhone River rushing past nearby. On one bank was the fashionable Hotel du Rhone, popular with Arab sheiks, well heeled tourists, and business men on expense accounts.

We needed another European engineer to do installation and maintenance work to support the TV station line of equipment that I was selling in Europe. I had run an ad in several London papers and now had some applicants to interview. The most qualified candidate was a tall, cadaverous-looking man of sallow complexion from London named Kevin Livingston (not his real name) whose restless brown eyes were always looking somewhere else. He looked like a stereotypical undertaker, but was a 30 year old graduate engineer, educated in a good university near London where, upon graduation, he had worked for several electronic companies. His references were excellent. Instinctively I disliked him, but the need was urgent and qualified men were hard to find. He said his father was English, his mother Swiss, and he was trilingual—fluent as a native in French, and his German was also very good, though of Schwyzerdutsch dialect. He had been raised in Switzerland and England, but his British English betrayed no trace of foreign accent. Like many people who are fluent in both French and English, he had the habit of embellishing one language with apt words or phrases from the other. As we were an international company, language ability was a definite asset. I soon had the impression, however, that he was not completely trustworthy. Whenever I asked a question that he didn't want to answer, I noticed he invariably switched to French and gave an evasive answer. Kevin, when asked if he saw himself as British or Swiss, replied, "I never thought of it in those terms before. I guess it doesn't matter much one way or the other." He evidently did not feel that he owed loyalty to any nation.

Unfortunately he was the only applicant technically qualified, so against almost overpowering instinct I hired him. It was the biggest mistake of my business career. Three days after he reported for work, I arrived at the office to find one complete set of TV technical manuals missing. They had been there the previous day at closing time. I called Kevin into my office.

"Kevin," I said, "I can understand that you are keen on learning our product line, and that's fine, but you must not take home the entire set, all 53, of the technical manuals at the same time for study." His long face assumed a perplexed expression. "I agree that you need to study them, but keep only one at a time. Bring the rest back immediately."

"I haven't taken any manuals home," he replied, avoiding eye contact—a touch of righteousness in his voice.

I was stunned. Immediately I thought of my meeting in Helsinki with Mr. Mikkela. If I had only had the wisdom to see it, he was trying to tell me what the Russians would do. They wanted those manuals, and what they wanted they usually got. These technical books were strictly proprietary. They represented at least 400 man-years of brilliant research and development effort.

A Swiss secretary, who had arrived first that morning, had found the door locked as usual. The last man to leave the previous night, was certain he had locked the door. All employees, including Kevin, had keys. The suspicion naturally fell on him, because the theft occurred only three days after he reported for work, while the others had been employed for over two years. Still it could have been the work of a foreign agent—an outsider.

My first impulse was to fire him. However, I immediately phoned Jason Bennet, Managing Director of our International Division, and told him what had happened. He got the company's Security Officer, a man named Blake, on the phone in a three-way conference call. Blake was ex-CIA. We had no hard proof of Kevin's guilt, only circumstantial evidence and instinct.

We decided to retain Kevin, for the time being, but watch him carefully.

"Don't let him know he is under suspicion," Blake said. "He might make another move. He may try to get certain production know-how or get away with some key component parts. Always check his movements when he is traveling. If he deviates, in any way, from travel plans you give him, I want to know the details. Expect him to make a play for advancement as soon as he thinks he can. Send me a copy of companies where he has worked and his references. I want to know about everyone who has known him or should have known him. I'll contact CIA and INTERPOL. Don't discuss this with anyone and keep me informed."

I called Kevin to my office again and pretended to have concluded that it was an outside job—undoubtedly the work of a Russian agent.

"Well," I said, "there's nothing we can do about it now. The horse is out of the barn."

His only comment, while looking down at the floor was, "I say, that's most disturbing."

Emily, Kevin's wife, and Annie, his four year-old daughter, arrived a few days later, and I could not have been more surprised when I met them. She was at least fifteen years older than Kevin and looked like a poor, old, worn-out charwoman. She was shabbily dressed and overweight. Her graying mousy hair dangled in wisps and gave the impression that it was never combed or brushed. There were pronounced bags under Emily's watery blue eyes, and she clearly held herself in low esteem. She acknowledged our introduction in a barely audible voice and seemed embarrassed by the impression she knew she made. I did not expect that a man like Kevin, with his dour personality and somber appearance, would attract a wife who was a paragon of loveliness and charm, but even so, I was shocked. It was impossible to imagine how poor Emily could ever have attracted any man. She must have been very different when they married. I also could never understand how this couple could have produced "Little Annie." The whole office fell in love with her at first sight. She had a spontaneous smile for everyone and boundless enthusiasm. Everything interested and delighted her. Annie was full of talk, and one had the strange feeling that she had almost adult intelligence. She stole our hearts away. There must have been more to Emily than met the eye. She had to be a remarkable mother, judging by Annie.

When the Livingstons were settled, Kevin began to travel on business, following schedules I made for him. Without being obvious, I carefully verified that he was where he was supposed to be each day, checking discretely through third parties. For a number of weeks there were no problems, and I had been getting back reports indicating satisfaction with his work. A day came, however, when he cut short a scheduled visit, did not check into the hotel reserved for him, and submitted a falsified report. I passed this on to Blake in Corporate Security, but let Kevin get by with it as Blake had instructed. It might have had something to do with the profiles of foreign operatives. This marked the beginning of a new chain of events leading swiftly to tragedy.

Shortly after Kevin left on his next trip, Emily came into the office. Her eyes were red and puffy from crying. Annie was with her, big eyed and quiet. I learned that Kevin had gone on a one-week trip leaving no money for food. I advanced Emily what she needed and tried to reassure Annie, but I could not change either of their pathetic expressions of concern. The same thing happened again two weeks later.

"Kevin" I said, the moment he got back, "this has to stop. If it happens once more I'm going to have to let you go."

"I'm sorry. I just had a lot on my mind and completely forgot to leave money." He stood with his back to me, looking out the window. That was all he said.

After that, things got much worse. Kevin left on another trip and Emily, holding Annie by the hand, came in again red eyed and weeping. We were all shocked to see that she had ugly bruises on her face and arms. She said she slipped and fell down the stairs. Nobody believed it.

"Do you need money?" I asked.

"No," she said, "I just felt I had to see and talk a moment to an English-speaking person." Annie said nothing but looked up at me as if she might burst into tears at any moment. I of course assumed Kevin had beaten Emily but something told me that if I accused him, she would deny it.

When it happened again, I asked to have a talk with the unfortunate woman.

"Emily, I'm concerned about your being so unhappy here. It's always hard at first to adjust to a new country, especially when you have to learn another language. I'm afraid also that it's not easy to make friends among the Swiss." I was groping for words to encourage her to confide in me. "I know you are having these problems, but is there anything else you want to tell me? Please let me help you if I can."

"I'll be all right. Yes, I miss England, but I'll be all right. I just wanted to come into the office to hear a few words of English." Tears welled in her eyes again. Her voice was faint and quavering. My heart went out to her, but she would not confide in me.

I noticed ugly new bruises. This time she had been hit in the eye. It was swollen almost shut and had turned blue-black. She said that, in the dark, she had run into something. Well, if she wouldn't confide in me maybe my English secretary could win her confidence. I called her in.

"Mary, Emily is feeling a bit low. Why don't you take her across the way and offer her a coffee. Have a long talk with her. I know she is lonesome and would appreciate it." It was mid-afternoon so I suggested she take the rest of the day off, slipped her some money and whispered, "Take Emily and Annie out to dinner if you don't have other plans, and try to find out if Kevin is beating her."

That night I phoned Mary at her apartment and asked if she had been able to confirm my suspicions.

"If you're asking for a woman's intuition, the answer is yes. I don't have the slightest doubt that Kevin is beating her, but I couldn't get her to say it."

While Kevin was away this time I received a letter from my boss in the States saying: "I was flabbergasted to get the enclosed letter from the new man you hired a few months ago. Please handle it any way you see fit, but I don't think he should be working for us."

I read the attached letter, "…and I must inform you that I am by far the best man to run the department. I suggest therefore that it would be in the best interest of the company if I be appointed Manager at the earliest possible moment." It was my turn to be flabbergasted.

I called Blake again and brought him up to date. His comment was, "Just what I expected. This guy really fits the profile."

"I'd like to fire the bastard," I said. I can't stand the sight of him anymore, and he is causing me too many problems."

"I don't blame you. Well, we still have not been able to turn up any hard evidence, and it looks like we won't be able to. OK. Go ahead. Give him the ax."

The next time Kevin returned to Geneva, I called him in and handed him the letter he had written to the home office. He showed no emotion.

"OK, I guess I'm fired. I can't say I blame you." He shrugged his shoulders.

"Here is your final paycheck." I handed an envelop to him. "Clean out your desk today, turn in your key when you leave, and don't come back."

He did come back, however—the very next morning—and sat down in my office facing me.

"Emily died last night." His voice was as matter-of-fact as if he were announcing the time of day. It betrayed no feeling, nor did he appear to have shed any tears.

"My God! How did it happen?" I already suspected he had killed her.
He said, "I woke up about four a.m. and she was making strange sounds." He gave a realistic imitation of the death rattle and it chilled me to the marrow of my bones. "I could see that she was dying, so I just pulled up a chair and waited." I pictured him lighting a cigarette and glancing at the evening paper as he "waited." "She died about ten minutes later. There will be a service for her in this church just over here." He pointed out my window to one on the river bank. "Please tell everyone in the office they are welcome to attend. Ten a.m. tomorrow." With absolutely no trace of sentiment, and, not waiting for any condolences from me, he got up and walked out.

Appalled, I asked Mary to pass the word in the office. The clatter of typewriters ceased. One of the women went over to get "Little Annie" who had nobody now to care for her properly.

Later that day, three of the men in the office came to talk with me confidentially.

"John, I don't know what you think, but we are convinced Kevin murdered his wife," one man said. "We think he beat her to death."

"I think so too, damn it," I replied, "but I don't see any way to prove it—unless an autopsy would turn up something—or unless Annie was a witness. The testimony of a child that age might not be accepted in court. It would be terrible to put her through such a thing, especially if we are wrong, and we could be. The others nodded agreement. "In any case," I said, "I plan to go to the police tomorrow right after the service and tell them that I think they should investigate Emily's death. I'm going to suggest an autopsy and an inquest. It would be a good idea if you all came with me and backed up my suggestion. Are you willing?" All said they were.

I sat alone for some time thinking. If Kevin was a Russian agent....If Emily found out. . . .. If there was a hysterical confrontation.... She was badly beaten. She came into the office covered with bruises and crying. It happened twice. She almost leveled with us, but couldn't quite turn her husband in. Next she probably found out that Kevin had tried to double-cross me and had been fired and there was still another violent confrontation. She might have said, "I've had all I can take. I'm going to tell everything."...another beating...a blood clot formed and worked its way to her brain, and she died of an embolism or was deliberately smothered with a pillow to keep from waking Annie. He would have called the doctor only after she was dead. The man pronounced her dead officially. Kevin would have put on a convincing act for the doctor...no doubt seemed overwhelmed by grief...explained that she had an accident...fell down the stairs...Doctor signed death warrant..."cause of death accidental."

The final shock came when we assembled for the service. Kevin and the little girl looked so pathetic. I wondered if Annie would ever again be like she was. Kevin stood with his head tilted curiously to the left and seemed to be making a brave attempt to carry on. These thoughts passed through my mind: maybe I'm completely wrong. Maybe the man is just one of those who can't express his feelings. Who knows how he could be suffering inside? For a moment I felt deeply sorry for him.

As the service started the minister began with this explanation: "We have this casket before us to symbolize the tragic death of Emily Livingstone. I should explain before starting, that this is a memorial service, not a funeral.

Emily is not with us here today. Her body has been cremated."

Damn, damn, damn, I thought. *He has had her cremated to destroy all evidence of his brutality. This man is a cold blooded killer. He murdered his wife. Beat her to death.* My mind was not on the service after that. Now there is no evidence at all. Nothing for the police to investigate. No point in going to them.

None of us expected to see nor hear from Kevin again, but one morning about six months later, in he walked with a stunning young Swiss woman on his arm. She was elegantly dressed in an obviously haute couture, white silk dress with black polka dots. We hardly recognized him. He was expensively dressed in superb taste—houndstooth sports coat, dark gray woolen slacks, and white tailor-made shirt with hand embroidered monogram. He walked with bearing and assurance. Like an actor playing a new role, he had miraculously changed his personality, his demeanor, and his whole being. I would not have recognized him. Now if you tried to appraise him by his appearance you might say, "A man of fashion and leisure with plenty of money, savoir faire, a bit of a dandy, but in good taste and able to carry it off."

The girl on his arm was charming, educated, and poised. I'd say she was about in her mid-twenties. She appeared radiantly happy after two weeks of marriage and was evidently quite in love with him. He was obviously proud to have won such a prize, although one felt he would be the last to deny that he himself was something of a prize too.

The new Mrs.Livingston mentioned casually that they were just passing through on their way to Biarritz in their new BMW and Kevin wanted to stop in, say hello, and introduce her—show her off more likely. Clearly Kevin had come into money. I wondered if he married it or if maybe he was paid off by the Russians for one of the most valuable coups in the history of commercial espionage...or maybe he had taken out an insurance policy on Emily's life before murdering her...quite possibly all three.

I took Kevin by the elbow and drew him somewhat aside saying, "I'm glad you dropped by. There is something I very much want to ask you. Do you mind stepping into my office for just a moment?" Under the circumstances a man with a guilty conscience might have considered this ominous.

"No, not at all," he said genially. "Glad to."

He followed me into my office. I closed the door, waived him to a chair, and sat behind my desk. Kevin seemed to be casual and friendly, like an old school chum one meets unexpectedly after not seeing him for some time. I studied him for just a moment and could not see the slightest indication of unease. He was poised and supremely confident. He crossed his legs, lit a cigarette, inhaled deeply, and sent a cloud of blue smoke my way as he returned a silver cigarette case to his pocket.

"Well?" he said, returning my gaze for a brief moment, a slightly defiant smile now on his lips.

I had been surprised by his visit and had not had much time to think through the best way to approach the subject I had in mind, but in another minute he might have been gone, and I probably would never see him again.

"Tell me, how is Annie? All of us around here miss her. It always brightened our day when she came into the office with Emily."

"Oh she's fine, I guess. I gave her to my mother to raise. She's in Burgdorf, a small village in the Bernese Oberland."

Surprised, I said, "But don't you miss her?"

"Oh sure, but—well you know how it is. Life goes on. I'll visit there a week every summer."

"Have you got a picture of her in your wallet?"

"No, I never carry those things around."

"That was tragic…about your wife I mean. Uh, there's something that has bothered me since her death, but at the time I thought it would be awkward to bring it up. You were in mourning. Let's see, it's been what?…six months now since it happened, and you obviously have adjusted very well."

He nodded "yes," took another drag on the cigarette and held it before him as if thoughtfully preoccupied by the length of its ash. I shoved an ash tray his way. Was he deliberately avoiding eye contact now?

"What exactly did she die of?" I said at last.

"I'm not sure. She had a fall the day before and hit her head. That probably had something to do with it."

"When Emily was dying, I have always wondered why you just sat in a chair 'waiting for her to die,' as you said you did. Why didn't you phone for a doctor? That's what I would have done—what almost anyone would have done."

He seemed ready for this and I had the feeling that he had rehearsed an answer to what must have seemed to him the inevitable question.

"Well I could see that she was dying and figured it was no use to call a doctor because she would be dead before he could get there, and I thought she would want me with her when the end came. Besides we didn't have a phone in the apartment." I wondered how he could know with such certainty that she would be dead in a few minutes.

"You could have gone next door to a neighbor."

"It was four o'clock in the morning. I didn't want to disturb anyone." He was looking out the window as if at something far away.

"If a doctor might save her life, what difference would it make if you had to disturb someone? But wait a minute Kevin, I remember now, there was a public phone in your building just down the hall from your apartment. You could have called from there."

He got up, took a final drag from his cigarette and carefully extinguished it in the ashtray, still avoiding eye contact. Kevin slowly ground the stub around for a moment until there was no part of it still aglow. "Pas de jeton," he said finally, shifting into French and shrugging his shoulders. "No phone token."

YOU ONLY LIVE ONCE

I had gone to Rome on business. It was my habit in those days to explore on foot whatever city I was in and I particularly enjoyed doing this in that fascinating ancient city, which is so rich in history and atmosphere that you could never see it all. One evening I came to the picturesque Trastevere district and as I had been walking for some time I was glad to sit down at one of Fabrizio's sidewalk tables. It was time to have an *aperitivo* before dinner.

As I enjoyed my compari soda my thoughts drifted idly from one thing to another—calling up images in my mind. Perhaps it was a man in the street selling communist newspapers that brought visions of Stalin, Lenin, and others of that persuasion, including a man named Walt Williamson. As my mind wandered from association to association I began, for the first time in ages, to think of Walt.

I hadn't seen him for at least three years—not since he had left the company under mysterious circumstances. Nobody seemed to know why he had departed, but he made many of us happy when he did.

Walt had irritated everyone and wrecked the morale of the office. He was a cocky young know-it-all recently graduated from an Ivy League college. His father was evidently a wealthy and very influential man who obviously had considerable influence with someone high in our corporate management. On the strength of that he suddenly appeared on the scene, and nobody knew specifically who he reported to. He began traveling to African countries that were a part of my territory but did not key me for copies of his reports. Though totally unqualified by experience, he I learned, was strongly critical of me before we ever met. He had decided that ours was to be a relationship of uncompromising antagonism. When I thought of him I always had the vague impression that I was watching a play on the world's stage and suddenly an actor appeared who was not in the cast, one bent on destroying, for no apparent reason, the entire production. He just didn't fit in. Unfortunately, in American corporate life, one encounters this kind of person and this kind of circumstance from time to time.

Through the grapevine I learned that in each country he visited, he sought out the most influential individual without regard for reputation, and forged some sort of personal alliance with him, company policy be damned. After months of exasperating rumors concerning this ruthlessly ambitious young new-comer, he finally arrived unannounced one day at the European regional office in Geneva.

Aside from that natural look of villainy all have whose credentials are so inadmissible, he looked thoroughly presentable. Walt was about medium height and he was always immaculately dressed with not a hair out of place. If you didn't know him and could therefore appraise him objectively would you say he had more than average good looks, but he came across as cold and arrogant, and he repelled people. What I remember most about him was icy cold blue eyes and the extraordinary symmetry of his features. He seldom smiled but when he did it had nothing to do with humor nor with pleasantness, but everything to do with the self-satisfied image he projected. At those times you noticed that his teeth were even and like his other features precisely formed. One could easily imagine him as an impostor coming from outer space, shaped in an alien mold to exacting mathematical standards but too flawless to pass as a real earthling.

To be qualified for his job, he should have been an engineer but was not. In all fairness though, he had a first rate mind, but his intelligence was not guided by experience, not guided by morality, and not guided by wisdom. He made me aware as no one had before, that we humans are animals and some among us are dangerous predators.

One day when several of us went to lunch together he attached himself to our group. During the meal, this know-it-all regaled us with his political insight as if "casting pearls of wisdom at the feet of the swine." Every idea he expressed was straight communist party line.

"So you are a communist?" I finally asked.

"Well, let's say that I'm *pink,*" he conceded.

"From that," I said, "I infer you *are* one."

He offered no denial but turned his cold defiant eyes on me and displayed his even white teeth as if to say, "So what are you going to do about it?"

This shocked us all. Some of us had security clearances and we didn't want any contact with the radical left nor were we comfortable that he was in our office where he might be able to overhear possibly sensitive information. I felt obliged to report to the home office that I thought him a security risk and learned that, at the same time, he had written his unknown mentor, high in the corporation, to say that I should be fired for political reasons.

One day, as suddenly as Walt came, he departed. Nobody knew what happened to him. The home office announced that he had left of his own volition, but then they always said that whether someone left voluntarily or was fired. At the time I thought my "security risk" report might have been heeded. I tend to forget people I don't like, but in Walt's case I made an exception. Strangely these were the memories that were going through my mind as I sat sipping my aperativo.

"Well I'll be damned, imagine bumping into you here." This remark directed at me by a passerby on the sidewalk interrupted my reverie. I looked up and there he was—Walt Williamson, of all people. Uninvited he took a seat at my table.

"Hello Walt. When did they let *you* out?" My opinion of him remained unchanged but, for some reason, we tend to "play the game" as they say, especially when meeting someone unexpectedly after a long time, and under quite improbable circumstances. In any case I try not to let my feelings get in the way of my curiosity.

He took a chair across from me and beckoned to a waiter.

"Who are you working for now?" I asked.

"John, you are looking at a man of leisure. I haven't worked since I left the company three years ago." I could detect no trace of his former ill-will. On the contrary he seemed friendly and glad to see me. This made me all the more curious.

"Did you inherit a fortune?" I asked. It was the only explanation that occurred to me.

Walt laughed. "Oh no, nothing like that." The waiter came and Walt gave his drink order, "Americano."

"You'll find it hard to believe, but due to a rare coincidence I had an almost unbelievable stroke of luck. Tell you what...if you are free for dinner why don't you come home with me, meet my wife and join us for dinner? I'll tell you my story...I'll tell you how I made a million dollars in fifteen minutes."

I was uncomfortable with this suggestion and replied, "Look Walt, I don't know what you have been up to and I don't think I want to know."

He grinned. "Would it make any difference if I told you that it was all completely legal? Would it also help if I told you that I am no longer interested in the politics of the radical left? I'm a capitalist now. Furthermore, I'm a happily married man and a father—quite respectable, believe me." The waiter arrived with his drink and set it down.

"Well then, if you don't think it would inconvenience your wife to set another place at the table on such short notice...."

"No problem at all. I'll just give her a call and let her know we'll be there in half an hour. She'll be happy to have another American to talk to for a change." He sipped some of his Americano and went inside to use the phone.

While Walt was telephoning I was preoccupied with my thoughts. How could anyone make an honest million dollars in fifteen minutes? Can't wait to hear how he did it...remarkable how the man seems to have changed...nothing like he used to be...actually pleasant company now...I'll let bygones be bygones. As I took care of the check, an old idiom came to mind: "Even beneath the ice, the river still flows." Maybe Walt is human after all.

He returned smiling and seemed to be looking forward to the evening. "No problems," he said. "Let's go." We left Fabrizio's and he led the way to his car, a low red Porsche. We stooped and removed our hats to get in.

"When I got my money," he said, "this was the first thing I bought. You only live once." I had heard Walt use those same words before and I wondered if they expressed his philosophy of life, or if they were offered in justification of his extravagant taste.

Driving home he said he would wait to tell me the story of his financial windfall after dinner—not that it would take much time but there were papers that he wanted to show me at the same time. As we shot through the streets of Rome, I avoided distracting him with questions, thinking it safer to let him concentrate on traffic. Driving in Rome combines the concepts of Russian roulette and gladiatorial combat. People there delight in playing chicken and vie with one another to exhibit machismo as if nothing else mattered. Clearly Walt believed that when you are in Rome you should drive as the Romans do. Nevertheless I learned some things from fragmentary comments. He had married about three years before, had a little girl now aged two, a poodle named Fifi, and a penthouse apartment in the Parioli district.

When we arrived, I found Walt's wife-to-be charming. Some people you feel you have known always the moment you meet them. Barbara was such a person and she was slender and lovely. For a few minutes she brought in little Janie who was just at that cutest of all ages. It seemed to me that Walt must have found happiness. If he had undergone a complete change of character, perhaps it was because he now had much of what he wanted out of life. Providence had to have mellowed him and given him a new perspective.

After another cocktail and an appetizing dinner of salad, steak, and red wine from the Chianti Mountains of Tuscany, Walt told me, with obvious relish, the story of how he became a millionaire in fifteen minutes. He had been on his way back to Geneva from Tripoli, Libya, and decided to break his trip with a short stop in the French Riviera—Cannes to be exact. After dinner he went to the Carlton hotel bar for a drink or two as was his habit. Standing next to him were two dejected looking Americans who had evidently decided to seek solace in alcohol for some reason.

"Well, you can't win 'em all," said one. "I sure thought we'd make that sale though."

"Yea, and there goes a nice chunk of bonus," said the other.

These words piqued Walt's curiosity and he began to eavesdrop. The two men had been drinking a bit, but were not drunk by any means—just at the stage where they had become careless about who heard them. Soon Walt understood that they worked for a major American aircraft manufacturer. They had come to Europe expecting to sell a jumbo-jet passenger plane to an airline there. To their surprise they had lost to a competitor, and were on the way home empty handed.

Walt was nothing if not an opportunist. He immediately thought of old Hassene in Tripoli who was married to the cousin of King Idris. This was before the coup by Quadahfi. Hassene had bragged to Walt just the day before, that he could sell anything to the Libyan government.

Walt spoke up: "Excuse me. I don't want you to think I have been deliberately listening to your conversation, but I couldn't help overhearing your problem. You may be glad I did. I have powerful connections in a certain country, which for the moment I won't divulge, but I think there is a strong probability that I can produce a buyer for the plane you were trying to sell. What would you say to that?"

When he recovered from the shock, one of the Americans said, "We're talking about a plane that costs over $22 million."

"What commission do you propose to pay?"

"Five percent"

"Nothing doing—I require ten percent. You can adjust the price if you need to, but it's ten percent off the top or no dice."

"Well, sure. If we can up the sales price we can pay that amount. I don't see any problem there."

Walt nodded. He took a gold ball-point pen from his pocket and an envelope to write on and said: "My name, by the way, is Walt Williamson. Now what would be the exact sale price and availability for delivery of this aircraft...say FOB Rome?" He jotted down the reply. "And now let me have a copy of the basic specifications—cruising speed, fuel consumption, runway requirements, how many passengers and crew...things like that. Then, I'll make a phone call, and I think I can give you a yes or no." The Americans were flabbergasted.

A few minutes later, Walt got through to old Hassene from the privacy of his hotel room. He explained the deal and asked the old influence peddler if he thought he could get the government to buy the plane. After a moment's pause, the answer was, "Yes, in sha' Allah," [Allah willing]. I need seven percent and you can have three—that's...let's see...$660,000 for you."

"It's no deal Hassene. I set this up. It's $1 Million for me or the deal's off. You'll get the same, plus over two hundred K to use for baksheesh [the usual bribes]. You agree to that and I'll be there tomorrow with the two men."

After a pause Hassene said, "Well, OK Walt. I didn't think you'd go for three percent but I have big expenses. You know what I mean. I had to try. Call me back as soon as you can confirm your flight."

"So that's how it happened John. They signed the contract the next day. It's almost unbelievable isn't it? You don't have to take my word for this though." He reached into his inner coat pocket and handed me a bank receipt showing that $250 thousand had been transferred to his Italian bank. Attached was a letter from the sender confirming what he had told me. This was the fourth and final payment of his $1 million finder's fee—now paid in full.

I handed it back. No doubt about it, his improbable story was fully documented. As far as I could see the deal might be legal. Morally it was not completely clear though, in two respects. For one thing, it depended on whether Libya needed a $22 million passenger plane – perhaps it did—or whether the poor people of that country would have to foot the bill for a white elephant, to enrich a few. Also his contract of employment would have stipulated, as mine did, that he would work full time for the company. He had no doubt accepted and cashed salary and expense checks during the period in question. A good lawyer could probably make something of the point that he had acted not as a private individual but as the company's agent when he negotiated that deal. It is not quite clear to me that equity would have been served by that turn of events. In any case it was time to get back to my hotel, the Hassler.

I never saw or heard from Walt again.

Unable to fall asleep that night I reviewed the events of the day. What was the significance of the double coincidence – meeting Walt by chance on the streets of one of the world's largest cities?—doing so just when I was thinking of him for the first time in three year?

Few would have recognized and seized the opportunity that Walt saw immediately. He was bold but I hope not too bold. I hope he didn't deposit his profit in a Swiss numbered account and fail to declare it as income. My guess is that he didn't and as Aristophanes said several hundred years B.C.:

He works and blows the coals
And has plenty of other irons in the fire

THE OLD SEA DOG

Entering a strange harbor, without local knowledge, without GPS, without Loran and without radar can be a humbling experience if night is coming on and there is a heavy fog. A prudent seaman might sail off shore, away from the dangers, and heave-to for another try at first light when conditions might be better. But Stanley was more stubborn than prudent and didn't know enough to be humble. He liked to refer to himself as a "master navigator" though in fact he knew almost nothing about the practical aspects of piloting.

But here he was off a rockbound coast near Canso, Nova Scotia in exactly that predicament. Oh, how he wanted to make port and get in out of the cold damp fog, brew a pot of coffee, eat a hot meal, and climb into the sack. The trouble was he couldn't find any of the entrance buoys that were out there in the fog somewhere.

This had not been his problem a few months earlier when he had sailed at nearly hull speed right into one which he could not see because it was behind his genoa. On that occasion he ripped out some planking just above the waterline and would have sunk except the sea was calm.

Now, it didn't occur to Stanley to shut off his engine and listen to the fog horns, whistle buoys, bell buoys, as well as various signals from boats and ships, nor did it occur to him that his depth sounder could give him a line of position. Instead he guessed at his position, set a course for the harbor entrance and motor sailed blithely on. Unfortunately he was not even close to where he thought he was nor had he corrected for a strong current setting his little yawl well off course.

Suddenly he heard what sounded like surf and before he could react there were rocks to the right of him and rocks to the left of him with seas breaking over them. In seconds he left the hazards astern but now Stanley was scared out of his wits and shaking uncontrollably. Afraid of more rocks, he shut off the engine and hove to. Now he remembered the depth sounder and as he found only twenty feet of water beneath his keel, he heaved the anchor overboard.

Having done this he looked again at his chart. There were not supposed to have been any rocks on the course he imagined he was sailing. Either the chart was wrong, he decided, or he wasn't where he thought he was. He preferred to think the chart was wrong. If that was not the case, the chart showed so many rocks and shoals along the shore he could be almost anywhere.

He went back to the cockpit shivering from the cold and shaking from fear. The wind and seas were building now. Stanley scampered back into the cabin again and looked at the barometer. It was dropping. My God, I wonder if a gale is making up, he thought. Here I am lost in the fog and surrounded by rocks. What must I do? Stanley didn't have enough anchor rode for a scope of more than about four to one and though he was not sure of it, he thought his Danforth anchor was slowly dragging on what must be a rock bottom. By the way the water was rushing past; he knew he was in a strong current. He could hear the seas pounding on rocks all around him in the fog. Stanley was desperate now. He could lose his boat. More to the point he could lose his life. He was not a religious man but not knowing what else to do he tried praying.

He fully expected he was going to drag down on one of the many rocks that must be all around him. His boat would be splintered into matchwood in seconds and he knew he would not survive long in that icy water. In ten or fifteen minutes, hypothermia would cause him to lose consciousness. He was so frightened he could no longer think.

But what was that sound? Was he imagining it? No. There it was again. The sound of someone rowing a dory. "HELLO-OO" shouted Stanley. "HELLO-OO."

"WOOF" came the gruff reply of a big dog and out of the dimly lighted fog appeared a dory rowed by an ancient lobsterman. It was piled high with lobster traps and in the bow stood a big black Labrador.

"God Almighty, am I ever glad to see you. Do you know where we are?"

"Yep"

"Where?"

"You lost young feller?"

"Well," Stanley, because he was Stanley, tried to save face. "I think there is an error in my chart."

"What's yer draft?"

"Four and a half feet."

"Foller me then. I'm headin back to port" The dory hove along side now and Stanley tossed a line to the old man so they would not become separated in the fog. The lobsterman stared straight ahead with sightless eyes as he felt for the line. Stanley stared in disbelief as he realized his rescuer was blind.

"How can you navigate in this fog?" Stanley asked. What he was thinking was *How can you navigate at all?*

"Fog or no fog. It's all the same to me. I been blind for years. It's my dog, Bosun here, who is the navigator. He can smell and he can hear. Fog don't bother him none. Knows where all of my traps are. Knows his way back to port in any weather. He don't get lost like a damned stupid land lubber."

To the monotonous sound of the oars working in oar-locks and the idling engine of Stanley's boat, the little procession threaded its way through the maze of rocks and shoals and into the safety of the harbor—Bosun, standing in the bow of the dory, sniffing the air and cocking his ears to catch familiar sounds—woofing from time to time. A very humiliated and chastised Stanley slumped in the cockpit of his little yawl and followed silently along.

Stanley stopped calling himself a "master mariner." He likes to see himself now as an "old sea dog."

PROFESSOR NUTZ

With winter coming on, the professor has been beset by two problems. For one thing his feet get cold at night. The other problem is that his workload has increased to the point that he is finding it inconvenient to do his yoga exercise—standing on his head for an hour every morning. Yet that is essential to his creativity.

These two problems have led to his latest invention. He realized that increasing the blood supply to his feet would make them warm and increasing the blood supply to his head would give him the same effect as standing on his head.

In a flash of inspiration, a moment of sudden insight, he had the answer. He invented the "centrifugal bed." This required careful design though. The bed had to spin fast enough to get his feet warm but not fast enough to give him varicose veins at one end and apoplexy at the other.

Playing a hunch he also investigated clockwise versus counter-clockwise rotation. It turned out that counterclockwise rotation was the answer. It helped him unwind at the end of the day. He is left handed though. If you are not left-handed, you must go around clockwise. Fortunately Mrs. Nutz is right-handed and her bed goes around the other way. This is good because when they get up in the morning, he staggers to one side and she to the other, so they can hold each other up.

An additional feature of the centrifugal bed is that in the summer without blankets, professor and Mrs. Nutz are pleasantly cooled in the breezes stirred up by the rotating beds, but as a result of all that blood circulating in their heads, both have become so smart they can't stand each other.

One of the professor's hobbies is the game of darts at which he excels. He finds it an additional challenge to throw an occasional dart at the target from his rotating bed. Is it any wonder that nothing happens when they ring for the maid?

BEHIND THE FRONT DOOR

When I was about to put my key in the door, it opened and there stood Assia with my slippers in one hand and a dry Martini for me in the other.

"Welcome home, Jonyee. Geev me zee beeg kees. Zee dinner ees almost redyee."

"But Darling, how do you always know when I'm here? Come on now—tell me. This is driving me crazy. How can you possibly know?"

"Jonyee Darlink, I've told you. I feel you. I always feel you."

I looked at my wife carefully for some clue that would tell me if this was another of those impish tricks she loved to play. Or could she be serious? It was impossible to tell. Her face wore an expression that suggested both amusement and unaffected innocence. This had been going on ever since our recent marriage.

She was, to me, the most exciting, most lovely, most exotic creature I had ever seen. The daughter of a white Russian countess and a Colonel in the Don Cossacks…the embodiment of charm and mystery. Though raised in Paris from the age of "half past five," her accent was unmistakably Russian. Tzarist Russian heritage gave her a passion for ceremony, jewelry, and elegant things. From Paris she had acquired that chic for which the French of a certain class are noted. Assia had the perfect figure of an haut couture mannequin—in fact she had been just that. Brown eyes that seemed to sparkle and high cheek bones emphasized the warmth and charm of her smile, which was like no other. Her bearing was that of the true Russian aristocrat, and that she was, but she had one more thing—ESP.

At that time, I was still skeptical of such things. Educated as an engineer, I put my faith in what I could see, hear, smell, touch, weigh, and measure.

ESP and "old wives' tales" were all the same to me.

Assia though, considered ESP a self-evident fact of life. To her, it was just another one of the senses. For me to argue otherwise would have been as futile as if a blind person were to say that there was no such thing as sight, or a deaf person sound. One might just as well try to tell her that God didn't exist, when she knew better.

On the other hand, my Little Pixie loved to play pranks on me. How could I be sure that these, apparently valid demonstrations of a power beyond my understanding, were not just another of her little tricks? I decided to find out.

We lived in Geneva at that time and my office was not far from our apartment. Sometimes I walked home, and at other times, took my car. When I drove at the end of the day I always parked in the garage under our apartment building and took the elevator to the third floor. If I walked, I also took the same elevator. The elevator! That was it! The elevator. I can't hear it from inside our apartment, but I'll bet she can. She can hear the elevator! But how does she know I am the one in it and how does she know exactly, to the split second, when I am about to enter the apartment? I examined the door carefully. The keyhole of our apartment door was not the kind a person could see through.

Now if she stood on the terrace, leaned far out and looked down the street, she might be able to see my car approach the entrance of the underground parking level, or see me on the sidewalk if I walked. If she heard the elevator stop at our floor two or three minutes later, it was logical that I was on it. Then she probably counted a certain number of seconds to allow me time to walk from the elevator to the front door. So that was how she did it. I felt better now. I wouldn't lie awake thinking about it. I now knew the trick.

The next evening I must have had a smile on my face going home. I had made my plans carefully. ESP—Hah, nonsense. I put the car in the garage. In about two minutes she would be expecting the elevator to stop on our floor, so I didn't use it. Instead, I walked up the several flights of stairs, taking my time, and took off my shoes well before reaching our floor. She mustn't hear my footsteps. Not a sound did I make, tip-toeing in my stocking feet on the marble floor. So far so good, but maybe there was a crack of light under the door as seen from inside. My feet would make a shadow that she would be able to see when I approached it. All right, there isn't going to be a shadow.

Instead of going directly from the stairs to the door I went like a burglar on cat's feet in quite another direction, then shoes-in-hand, I edged quietly along with my back to the wall. It would have been embarrassing if I had been seen by any of the neighbors, but I was lucky. I moved ever so slowly along one wall to another, turned the corner and continued in absolute silence until I reached the edge of my door, but kept well off to one side where I couldn't cast a shadow that she might see under the door.

I congratulated myself that I had a completely logical mind free from all superstition—a mind that worked in an orderly fashion—reasoning step by step until inevitably it got to the answer.

I had my key all ready now, certain of triumph. I reached out from my awkward position beside the door. Before the key touched the lock, the door swung open and there was Assia with my dry Martini and my slippers.

"Welcome home, Jonyee Darlink. Geev me zee beeg kees." The pixie smile that always made my heart go pit-a-pat faded slowly to an expression of astonishment. "Why zee shoes are off Jonyee?"

THE CUPPA JO

People who have not been in naval combat owe it to those who have fought and died for them to try just once to understand what it is like. Any writer who tries to convey it will find his eloquence challenged. Words can't make you smell the blood and burning flesh, nor hear the screaming and sobbing of the wounded and dying.

This is my story of only one of the many hundreds of Kamikaze attacks that made life aboard our ships a living hell in the final days of WW-2. It is also the story of how a cup of coffee saved my life. In combat, life or death often depends on some seemingly insignificant coincidence, an act of God, a yet unknown sense, or just plain luck.

The wartime navy ran on coffee. It kept us awake and alert. We were often at GQ, expecting to attack the Japanese or be attacked by them, sometimes averaging no more than a few hours of sleep a night for weeks at a time. Fresh coffee was usually made at the beginning of every four hour watch—at GQ, not even that often. The first man to find the Silex empty would throw in more ground coffee and water. Pressed for time, he was always more concerned with effect than flavor. The coffee got stronger, more bitter, and more vile with every hour that passed so that by about six bells (the third hour of the watch), if I had a cup, I always thought of Socrates drinking the hemlock. In the WW-2 navy we called it "a cuppa jo." Six months before the incident I am about to relate, I finally sworn it off altogether and was determined to never again drink another cup of navy coffee.

The following happened on Wednesday, the 13th of December, 1944 when I was a Lieutenant, E (L)-T, (Electronic Technical Officer) on the staff of

Rear Admiral Arthur D. Struble, USN, a remarkable man. He commanded Task Group 78.3 for the amphibious landings at Mindoro in the Philippines and our flagship was the light cruiser USS Nashville, CL-43.

Departing San Pedro Bay, Leyte the previous day we steamed at the best speed the task group could make. Kamikaze attacks, which inflicted heavy losses, came only in the daytime, so it was especially important to clear the most hazardous areas at night to the extent that it was possible.

Some other ships with us were: U.S.S. Hall, Paul Hamilton, Howarth, Pringle, Stevens, Dashiell, Fletcher, O'Bannon, Hopewell, Radford, Lavallette, Philips, Halford, Bush, and many landing craft.

At dawn, I showered and put on a freshly laundered uniform. Word had been passed ordering everyone to do this. The ship's doctor said it would reduce the danger of serious infection if we were wounded. After a quick breakfast, I went to the CIC (the Combat Information Center, where the surface and air-search radars were located—where all combat information was sent for plotting and analysis).

I was not yet on the watch schedule nor assigned a GQ station (general quarters, battle station), but that was where I had always been at GQ and I needed to show the radar operators an operating technique that would be new to them. I thought this was probably the only way we would have even the slightest hope of detecting Kamikaze planes approaching low over terrain. When they were high and over the sea, we saw them quickly and easily on radar, but a plane coming in very low over land could usually slip by unnoticed because its echo as seen on the "PPI" (plan position indicator) was obscured by massive returns from the terrain. Now, unfortunately, we often had land masses all around, so timely detection either by radar operated in the usual way, or by lookouts, was highly improbable.

Often we were unavoidably within one or two miles of land and at such times a suicide plane could crash on our deck roughly 30 seconds after first becoming visible to either the lookouts or the radar operators. If the men were momentarily distracted there would be almost no warning at all. As we could not avoid going through straits and near island groups, we had to accept the risk and the consequences, and this, above all else, was my greatest concern.

A new experimental search technique using the "A scope" might increase the warning time to a few minutes. That might make the difference between life and death. I was starting to explain this procedure to the operators when someone told me that the Chief of Staff wanted to see me up on the flag bridge "on the double."

The panoramic view from that elevated position was something I will never forget. Located above the bridge, the flag bridge, with no deck over it to obstruct visibility, was high above the sea. There were perhaps thirty officers and enlisted men there and in gun tubs or on lookout platforms near by.

The day was one of breathtaking splendor. White cotton ball clouds dotted a cobalt sky creating dazzling contrast. When the sea is deep it takes on the indigo hue of ink, and the sky that day seemed a more vivid blue than usual. Brilliant sunlight sparkled on a moderate sea and all around us I saw our immense task group. One had the false illusion of irresistible power and the deceptive impression of invulnerability. On every ship men were scanning the skies with 7 x 50 binoculars while others sat by their AA (anti-aircraft) guns. Our flagship was in a protected position well inside the destroyer screen.

The beauty of it all could lead one to imagine we were on a pleasure cruise to some tropical paradise. The men in the gun tubs and lookouts on elevated platforms, oblivious to hazard, exchanged high spirited banter.

Near by, I noticed Cdr. Beech, the Staff Communications Officer. I liked him. He had come up through the ranks from enlisted man in a rapid series of promotions. Beech had been on one of the battle wagons sunk at Pearl Harbor. He had shown exceptional initiative and bravery under fire. A big, powerful man with impressive presence, he knew his job thoroughly and radiated competence and self-confidence. He was a born leader and a pleasant shipmate, we all liked him—it was impossible not to.

"Good morning Mr. Beech…beautiful day isn't it?"

"Yep. Couldn't be nicer. Did the Chief of Staff send for you?"

"Yes, he did," I replied. "Otherwise I'd be in the CIC. Ought to be there right now. Don't like it when we are this close to land. Look, we'll soon have that island close abeam to starboard."

"Well, there are plenty of lookouts and gunners. Maybe too many. I see not only the regular watch, but also some off-duty men who have come up to bask in the sun and enjoy the view. I don't like to say anything, not being in the ship's company, but there is always the possibility they will distract one another. A lookout alone can concentrate on his job. Two together are apt to talk, argue, and forget why they are there."

"I hadn't thought of it like that, but now you mention it, I must say I agree. Besides some are needlessly exposed in case of enemy action. By the way, do you know why the Chief of Staff wants to see me?"

"I think he is going to assign you to a battle station up here."

"WHAT! OH NO! My GQ station has always been CIC. The Admiral wouldn't want it any other way."

"I don't know what he has in mind," said Beech, "but we'll soon find out; here he comes now."

The Chief of Staff, whose rank was Captain, USN, came slowly up the last few steps to the flag bridge. When I had met him for the first time, three months earlier, he had seemed quite genial, but the Admiral was present then. When he was not around the Chief of Staff "did a 180" and became decidedly disagreeable with all junior officers. Toward Admiral Struble, he behaved with sycophantic subservience. Beech and I saluted him. "Good morning, Sir," we said. He returned our salutes with a perfunctory reflex gesture.

"Mr. Riley, I sent for you to give you your GQ station. I want you up here with me on the flag bridge."

Even this late in the war, those of us who had been trained as radar technical officers occasionally had serious problems with some of the older officers who had no real knowledge of radar nor faith in it and would not let us do our job. Here was another one. I think that, because these older men didn't understand how radar worked, they resented junior officers who did—especially reservists. They went out of their way to underrate its capability. I hoped the enemy was making the same mistake.

"Sir, with all due respect," I said, "I'm the Staff Radar Officer. I was trained in radar and CIC. I wrote the radar annex in the Op Plan for this operation. I know a new radar search technique that is not yet used on this ship, but there has been no opportunity until now to train the operators. When you sent for me I was just starting to do that." I spoke fast, expecting to be cut off before I could finish. "I would like to be in the CIC right now doing that. The Admiral himself assigned me to that GQ station in all previous operations. May I ask you to reconsider?"

I saw both shock and fury in the Chief of Staff's eyes and looked first at him and then at Cdr. Beech, hoping for some discreet support.

"Mister," the Chief of Staff replied, "I don't care what you have done in the past. I'm telling you what you are going to do from now on. It is a job that has to be done. It has to, because I say it has to. Is that clear?"

What could I say? Would Beech dare to comment? After a moment's hesitation, the commander spoke up.

"Lieutenant, sometimes we have to carry out orders that may not make sense to us, but it is not for us to judge whether they do or don't. That is the responsibility of the senior officer."

His reply was ingenuous; it held a multiplicity of meaning and he had chosen his words carefully: "orders that may not make sense to us" and "the responsibility of the senior officer." Couched in terms of utmost respect, he said what I could not have. There was the subtle suggestion that neither he nor I saw the logic of the orders, but if they proved to be a mistake, the Chief of Staff would bear the full responsibility. He had discreetly planted a seed of doubt.

The Chief of Staff hesitated now. I hoped he was trying to think of a way to back down without losing face.

On a sudden impulse I said, "Sir. May I suggest that the three of us go down to the wardroom, have a cup of coffee, and discuss this?" A glance at Cdr. Beech told me he was all for it. The captain, momentarily undecided, finally said gruffly, "No, I'm staying here. You go on if you want to, but right after that I want you back here."

Good, that would give him time to mull things over. I assumed he also did not want to be seen fraternizing with a junior officer.

Beech had already taken several steps toward the ladder, but now he looked at me and said, "Well, I guess I'll stay here too." What choice did he have? If he had left the Chief of Staff to go with me, his position would have been a bit too clear.

I went down the ladder. The wardroom was just below the main deck and forward of the quarterdeck—not far away. Alone there, I found a Silex and poured a hot "cuppa jo," asking myself why I was drinking the coffee I disliked so, but I did feel an irresistible urge to do just that, even if the coffee was bad—and it was. I cannot say I had any sense of impending disaster.

I drank the steaming hot brew as fast as I could get it down without burning my mouth. Just when I put the empty cup on the green baize table cover, there was an ear shattering explosion and concussion. The ship shuddered under the impact and I knew that massive damage had been done. The blast had blown the crystal out of my watch and I was spattered with blood and tiny flakes of flesh that had been blown through the passageways of the ship, but I was unharmed. As I had not heard gunfire nor a GQ alarm before the explosion, I thought we had been torpedoed. We had not. It was a Kamikaze.

If it had been seen in time, every AA gun on our ship and on ships near us would have been in action.

Carrying two 63 kg bombs, and with nearly full tanks of aviation fuel, the plane, a Zero, had crashed on our port quarterdeck – the deck above me and about 30 yards aft. There had been numerous rounds of ready box ammunition near each of our three 5-inch gun batteries that were on both the port and starboard quarterdecks, and more by the twin 40 mm mounts. Most of that ammunition exploded at once along with the two bombs. These simultaneous explosions riddled bulkheads the length of the ship. Much of the rest exploded while the damage control detail was trying to extinguish the inferno of burning aviation fuel. Flames spread instantly from foremast to mainmast and leapt as high as the signal bridge. Another fire roared in the #2 fireroom uptakes (third deck), and our ship was marked by billowing black smoke that towered hundreds of feet, making us a likely target for another attack. Soon, 50 caliber Japanese ammunition from the Zero joined the cacophony of ammunition explosions in the fire.

In an instant, 323 men had been either killed outright, mortally wounded, severely burned or mangled, out of a crew of about 1100. Four were never found.

When the explosion occurred, I ran aft to mount the ladder to the CIC, just forward of the quarter deck, but met a wall of flame. The door to the CIC was tightly dogged—the men inside trapped by burning fuel. A human torch, a gasoline soaked officer or CPO with his left leg blown off at the hip, stood for a moment above me clutching a rail for support, and then pitched headfirst down the ladder and lay dead at my feet, flames consuming his body. I don't recall that this man screamed in agony. I think he must have, yet I had the impression of silence. Perhaps I had been temporarily deafened by the blast. Did he kill himself deliberately to end his torment or did he try to use the leg that was no longer there?

The forward exit from the wardroom was unblocked and through it I reached the main deck to make my way aft toward the flag bridge where I had been only minutes before. The first thing I saw, coming on deck, was a piece of aircraft marked with the red sun of Japan. It had been blown almost to the bow of the ship.

I will never forget stepping over the headless body of a seaman. Only his neck and right ear remained attached to the corpse—then near him, the legless body of another. I slipped in pools of blood and stopped once to administer morphine to a dying man using one of several syrettes I carried for such emergencies. His eyes were burned out and his flesh cooked. It hung from his bones like torn gray rags yet he was still conscious...whimpering, suffering, certainly aware of impending death, and perhaps thinking of loved ones he would never see again. I stopped once to take refuge behind a barbette while burning ammunition blew up. Near the quarterdeck in the midst of flames that leapt as high as a four story building, was a dead man on hands and knees—his body in the process of cremation. I recall wondering how he could remain in that improbable position. His hair and clothing had been burned or blasted off. Pressure had built up inside his body, making him look like a fat pig being roasted.

The damage control detail was already at work hosing down a munitions locker covered by burning fuel. It had taken them only two minutes to get there. I saw gloved men already in the gun tubs with the dead, throwing 40 mm ammunition into the sea. It was too hot to touch and might have exploded in their hands. They had been superbly trained. In emergencies like this men do what they have been taught to do and appear to conquer fear completely. The fire was out in 20 minutes. Until then, the ammunition locker could have blown at any instant.

On reaching the flag bridge I found that everyone who had been there was dead. Not just dead. Some were literally blown to bits. Bulkheads, rails, stanchions—everything was covered with a scum that minutes before had been muscle, organs, and brain tissue. Blood was everywhere, slippery like oil, its odor salty and nauseating.

I saw that the men in the gun tubs and the lookouts on platforms aloft had all been killed by concussion. Most lay with arms hanging down, and as the ship rolled, their arms all swung in unison like pendulums marking time, but the time they marked was the eternity of death. The limpness of the dead is profoundly distinctive. I knew at a glance there was no need to check for vital signs.

On the flag bridge, heads, pieces of heads, eye-balls, intestines, severed feet still in shoes, arms, hands, and torsos, slipped and slid in blood which surged like a red tide as the ship slowly rolled this way and that on the beautiful blue sea. Above, puffy white clouds like cotton balls drifted silently over the scene of tragedy and horror and the sun sparkled on the calm sea.

THE PROMISE

I was only a boy during the great depression, but I still have vivid memories of that era when everything went wrong—when people were bewildered and desperate. Panic and despair was everywhere. In some areas unemployment reached 38 percent. There were soup kitchens, bread lines, mortgage foreclosures, bank failures, and daily suicides. Human judgment and behavior became erratic. Hopes and dreams gave way to forlorn reality, and the world seemed to have gone completely mad.

Things that diverted people were odd by today's standards. One curious phenomenon, a symptom of the times, can be seen in retrospect as mass hysteria. Hoping to win a prize of perhaps two hundred dollars, people took to flagpole sitting, and to "dance-a-thons" in which couples danced night and day, holding one another up until they finally fainted or both dropped from exhaustion. These things became compulsions. People were like lemmings rushing to the sea. It was a time of bizarre stunts. I remember frequent fatal trips over Niagara Falls in barrels. The common denominator was not publicity, but the need for money. People were hungry, depressed...without hope. Many would risk even their lives for a pittance and were prepared to pay the forfeit if fate gave them the thumbs down gesture. Some seemed as resigned to destiny as the Roman gladiators whose last words were, "Caesar, we who are about to die salute you." such was the cavalier attitude toward life, and death, in those days.

Recently I was going through some letters and ran across one from an old friend, Don Sanders. He was reminiscing about something that happened to him in those appalling days when he was a professional stage magician, contortionist, and hypnotist. Though he was one of the best, he never should have tried to perform the stunt that almost killed Houdini. Here is his remarkable story as he told it to me:

"I was a young man then, trying to find money for college. Though not as badly off as most, I was not untouched by the prevailing mood. I tried by various means to augment my small income by moonlighting, occasionally performing at cocktail parties given by the wealthy. A spectacular but dangerous act brought me about three hundred dollars for each performance in a time when that was the cost of a new car, but Russian roulette would have been safer.

"Money was not my only incentive. On these occasions I could forget reality for a few hours and dream that I too was rich and successful like those who watched my performances; this contact with the affluent made my humdrum existence easier to bear and kept alive my hope for a better life someday.

"My friends encouraged me, telling me I had everything it took to be a winner—'brains, ambition, charm.' They were most kind. One said I had 'style;' another 'distinctive bearing and a strong will.' Well I don't know about that. It was nice to hear, but I'm afraid it all went to my head. The well-meant encouragement made me take desperate chances."

Having read this far, I put the letter down for a moment as my mind dredged up images from the distant past. I could still picture the Don I knew long ago. He was nineteen then, of medium height, slim and dark haired. His face was strong featured like the ones we see today in Marlborough cigarette ads and his hands were those of a professional magician, nimble and dexterous. He practiced the magician's art of palming so persistently that it became a mannerism. Cards or balls of paper constantly went back and forth between his hands and then vanished, only to be plucked from some unexpected place. Like most professional performers he was a born actor, but what set him apart was his determination to be perfect. He was my role model then. I tried to imitate his style and his slight-of-hand tricks but just could not do it. Something brought me back from my reveries and I continued reading.

"When I allowed myself to be chained and padlocked hand and foot, then locked in a steel coffin like Houdini and sunk to the bottom of a swimming pool, my life depended on flawless performance. Although, as in all magic acts, I used deception, it was an extremely dangerous performance because things could so easily go wrong. Even if they didn't, all of the skill, speed, and dexterity I could muster, under the most difficult of conditions, was required to avoid being drowned.

"The coffin was black and made of heavy steel with a number of holes in the sides so it would sink quickly to the bottom nearly filled with water. When it settled on the bottom, there remained only a small pocket of trapped air under the convex lid, sufficient for a few lungfuls. This gave me time to locate a hidden key and open the padlocks that bound the chains on my hands and feet. That was the hardest thing to do. It required endless practice and concentration. Even in daylight and with unlimited time, it is difficult, almost impossible, in the cramped confines of a coffin with my arms locked behind me. I also had to retrieve a concealed wrench and quickly dismantle four locking mechanisms that sealed the lid on the coffin (they were, of course, designed to be operated only from the outside). But all of this had to be done in dim light, while holding my breath under water. Submerged, there was no way I could communicate with the outside world if anything went wrong.

"I spent many hours practicing and perfecting my escape, timing it to the second. I counted on freeing myself without needing more air than the little that would be trapped under the coffin lid. I had to breathe a little of that trapped air, then work under water at frantic speed, then rise again and again to gulp a little more air, until able to escape.

"On the fateful evening, I drove up to Jimmy 'Ace' Laboda's Longhorn Dude Ranch in my old black second-hand Hudson with my coffin on the roof and parked among the Packard Straight-Eights, Pierce Arrows, and a Dusenburg or two. I presented an engraved invitation card and was admitted to the cocktail and dinner party. The host and owner was a notorious man of obscure connections, indebted to gambling, bootlegging, and tax evasion for his fortune. Everyone knew he had served time in San Quentin prison. He had been indicted once on a murder charge—one that had to do with a motiveless thrill killing, but the judge dismissed the case for lack of sufficient evidence.

"I read nothing ominous in Laboda's dark shifty eyes, though the slovenly appearance of the man repelled me. It's a disturbing thought that among us are some who may seem reasonably normal and sane by conventional standards, but at the same time they lack any trace of human empathy. Experts tell us that despite hideous warps in their personalities, psychopathic killers often evade detection even by trained professionals. They are not insane, but simply can not relate to any other living creature. They have no conscience. They never know love, remorse, nor pity. They might, on a whim of the moment, decide to cut your throat just, to watch you die. Perhaps you have known one without realizing it. Psychiatrists call them psychopaths—'beasts in human form.' [No doubt Laboda was one].

"When I arrived, I was at first introduced as a guest. I wore a rented tuxedo; a tux was the custom in those days. To keep my mind clear, I drank only black coffee instead of bootleg liquor. Mingling with the others, I tried to be a good listener, and to hold my own in the articulate and witty repartee of that rich, sophisticated society. Say, you should have seen the opulence of the décor, those bejeweled, expensively gowned and coiffed women and successful, prominent men. And somewhere in the background I could hear Gershwin hits coming softly from a Steinway concert grand.

"In one side of the vast reception room was a stone fireplace big enough to roast an entire ox if the occasion demanded. Two-inch thick, tender, top sirloin steaks and appetizing pork spareribs were being roasted; their juices dripping on the red-hot coals—making sizzling sounds. Tantalizingly aromatic smoke drifted through the room, making the hungry guests salivate in anticipation.

"I was so impressed! All of this excited me then as much as the thought of the money I would get. I could almost forget that outside those walls the Great Depression of the 1930's was still a devastating, soul-killing reality.

"From the immense picture windows I watched the last gold and crimson hues of sunset blending into the deep blue of early night. Still visible was the wild landscape of pine-covered hills and flat planes that seemed to stretch to infinity—out where the coyotes and wolves howled, antelopes roamed, and where hawks, buzzards, road-runners and rattlesnakes competed for precarious existence...and only the fittest survived. Only the fittest survived—odd, how the thought kept recurring that night.

"The guests lingered over their dinners, their coffee, and their after dinner drinks, until Laboda got so fidgety he chewed the end of his cigar ragged. Finally he threw it down, spat on the potted palm beside him, and, unable to restrain the impulse any longer, jumped to his feet to make the announcement—his voice shrill and animated. The scar on his left cheek had turned blood red.

"'Ladies and Gents, I got a special treat for you tonight. The famous magician and contortionist, Don Sanders, is about to perform his death defyin' act. Only other man ever tried this stunt was Houdini and he almost got hisself killed doin' it.' I would, he explained, be chained and padlocked hand and foot and placed in a steel coffin with lid locked on and sunk to the bottom of the swimming pool…'An he's gonna try ta escape.' In tones one might expect at a lynching he shouted, 'Follow me.'

"Ace led the guests through sliding glass doors to the atrium. Around the large irregularly shaped pool, its water black as the night which enveloped it, was a spacious patio with potted palms, cocktail tables, chairs, and benches, all dimly illuminated by candles. The pool lights had been turned off to enhance the macabre effect and the black coffin was near the edge of the pool, resting on two saw horses. I stood by it, dressed now in Levi's and a white shirt. All guests were ready. Feigning nonchalance and a bravado I didn't feel, I bowed to the audience. I was then securely chained and padlocked hand and foot by a grinning Laboda, and lifted into the coffin. Guests were invited to verify that the locking handles for the coffin lid could be operated only from the outside.

"'Don't forget to turn on the pool lights before you throw the coffin into the water, Mr. Laboda. That's very important.' Those were almost my last words.

"'Oh, sure, Kid. You can count on me.'

"'I sure hope so,' I said.

"The lid was then locked in place and I heard the strains of the Funeral March. It irritated me. I resented having him ham up my act, but it was Laboda's idea and the man had pigheadedly insisted on it.

"The host, aided by several of the guests, hefted the heavy load and carried it to the edge of the pool where, as I learned later, Laboda tripped or slipped, or so he made it appear, causing the coffin to tumble into the pool on its side. It sank like a rock.

"For a moment I again stopped reading Don's letter as I pictured the surface of the black water roiled by the sinking coffin and big bubbles rising from the depths of the pool leaving smaller ones and white foam swirling for a brief instant. After a momentary 'blub blub blub' there would have been silence, as concentric ripples spread over the dark surface and subsided to deathly stillness. I could imagine Laboda with a smile on his face. Captivated by the suspense, I read on.

"The coffin had gone to the bottom just as it entered the water—on its side. Because of this, it filled completely with water almost instantly. There was no pocket of trapped air. It had bubbled out through the side holes that were now on top. This would not have happened had the coffin settled right side up as I intended. It was completely dark inside the coffin; Ace, that son-of-a-bitch, had not turned on the pool lights. Adding to the hopelessness of the situation, the water was ice cold. It was supposed to have been warm following my careful instructions. I suddenly realized the man was trying to kill me.

"All of these things caused a desperate emergency. I thought I had just minutes to live. To survive without any trapped air I would have to accomplish my escape in about four minutes with only one lungful of air. I had never been able to hold my breath longer than that. The escape, on the other hand, had taken me almost five minutes in repeated practice sessions.

"Grasping frantically with scrabbling fingers I found that the concealed key for the padlocks had been dislodged during the sideways impact. Where was it? There were only a few places I could search in hope of finding it due to the cramped space and because my hands were chained behind my back, and I was lying on them. The heavy chains cut my circulation. Ice cold water was making me numb all over, and I felt helpless in the terrifying total darkness.

"Every moment counted and it took several seconds to find the key, which by the merest chance had fallen within my reach. I had not counted on having to search for the keys and now must somehow make up the lost time—more than make it up. My fingers were quivering from fear as I set to work on the padlocks—first to free my hands: that was the hardest. I was rapidly losing my dexterity now because the intensely cold water numbed my fingers. My all-important sense of touch was going fast, for the same reason. It took me a little longer than planned to free my hands.

"I didn't think I would be able to hold my breath more than another thirty seconds. Would that be enough?...if not, then what? I would either involuntarily gasp for breath and fill my lungs with water or I would lose consciousness and drown. What a way to die. For a moment I had a desperate but futile urge to try to attract somehow the attention of those who were casually sipping their cocktails and waiting expectantly just a few feet above me. My lungs ached. They felt as if they were about to burst. In the deathly silence of my dark watery tomb I could distinctly hear the thumping of my heart, feel my blood coursing through my upper body and throbbing in my head. *My God where is the wrench now? It isn't here where I hid it...dislodged same as the key...let's see it would have fallen down to the right...I think I feel it...my hands are so cold and numb it is hard to be sure...my lungs are bursting... Oh God give me the strength to open these lid locks in time... please God... help me to get out of here and I promise to be good for the rest of my life.*

"Working frantically I unlocked the two catches on the left side of the coffin with the wrench, but my weight and that of the heavy steel coffin was bearing down on the remaining two lock handles on the right side and this caused them to seize. If I could just exert enough force with the wrench I might still be able to budge them. Summoning all of my remaining strength I finally freed the third of the four locks, but now I was shaking from the fatigue that oxygen deprivation induces—chilled to the bone by the terrible cold. The exertion had used nearly all of the small amount of oxygen remaining in my lungs. I was starting to feel weak and dizzy, and a morbid feeling of hopelessness settled over me. I nearly gave up.

"Only one more lock to go, but the task now seemed impossible. I felt overwhelmed by the certainty of doom. If there had been any light where I was, I would have seen black spots forming before my eyes and getting larger by the second—a prelude to total blackout and the end. It occurred to me that maybe I should just breathe the water into my lungs and get it over with. But somehow I found the strength and determination for one more try. I fought the temptation to give up with renewed desperation, again fervently imploring God's help as most men do when all else fails. I made what I knew would be my final try—one last superhuman effort such as men have been known to make when life itself depends on the outcome. A clicking sound told me the lid was free. A push with my feet. The lid was off. Free at last, dear God...free at last.

"Rising quickly from the depths I saw what appeared to be a bright light above the water. I fought my way up to it and found a full moon, high, resplendent and frosty looking, in the cool dry atmosphere. It was the most beautiful thing I had ever seen. I reached the surface gasping and spluttering, just before I would have blacked out...heart pounding...shaking convulsively. I gulped air in ecstasy—deep lungfuls of exquisite fresh air. The sound of clapping from some of the pool side revelers reached me. They didn't know they had seen a near miracle—not just a clever trick, and attributed my apparent distress to showmanship.

"During the applause I clung, nearly exhausted, to the pool ladder, grateful to be alive. I thought how irrelevant the Depression seemed; how little a pocketful of money mattered to me now.

"A guest, more perceptive and kind than the rest, came to help me from the water, and as I climbed out I heard a man musing in undertones to himself in the shadows nearby, 'Jeez, I didn't think he could do it.' It was the voice of Jimmy Laboda—otherwise known as 'Ace.'"

SHUT UP BERNADINE

A few years ago when I was living in Monte Carlo, I was fortunate to become acquainted with William B. Mason, Brigadier General, United States Marine Corps. (Retired). I had been able to do him a small favor and he stopped by my apartment to thank me.

I opened the door there stood Bill, a smiling gregarious man of short but sturdy build who almost overwhelmed me with a torrent of words. Most of us speak in sentences but Bill spoke in lungfuls pausing only when he had to breathe again. I invited him in and we had a sherry together while enjoying the view from my 23rd floor terrace It was one of those clear days when we could see almost to Corsica.

In our first brief conversation, I learned enough about him to want to know more. His father, a Baptist missionary, took him from North Carolina to live in China when he was a very young boy. It was just the two of them. His mother had died and there were no brothers or sisters. He grew up bilingual in English and Chinese—Shanghai dialect. His ambition from earliest years was to become an officer in the US Marine Corps. and to have a command of his own When he couldn't wangle an appointment to the Naval Academy in the usual way, because of foreign residence, he joined the Navy as an ordinary seaman, took the competitive examinations, and with two or three others, finally got to Annapolis the hard way. (Several men each year are admitted from the enlisted ranks). He said he was sent back to China again, and then to Japan, and something about being a code breaker in Naval Intelligence during WW 2.

Bill was a chef by hobby and I a gourmet by inclination. We became instant friends and he said: "John I cook the best Chinese food you ever tasted. You can't get it as good in any restaurant. How about coming to dinner with Bernadine and me at our villa next Wednesday at 1900 hours?"

I was free that night and delighted to accept.

Wednesday I arrived at the gate of his villa promptly, with my best pair of chop sticks in the breast pocket of my blue blazer. His villa was near Cannes on some high ground overlooking the sea from a distance of about a mile. From a cul-de-sac street one saw only a high wooden grape stake fence covered with wine red bougainvillea and the setting sun shed its last rays on this colorful scene as I approached. Unable to find the catch on the gate I sounded a ship's bell mounted nearby. Someone came running—evidently a Chinaman I thought judging by the sing song intonations of the language I heard through the fence.

When the gate swung open Bill greeted me. "Hi John, Welcome. Welcome. Come on in the house and meet Bernadine. What would you like to drink? How about a Compari Soda? That's what we're having. Say, you are really going to enjoy this dinner. I cooked Szechwan style tonight. You like it hot and spicy? Gosh I should have asked you before. Some don't like it hot. I could have cooked Mandarin or Cantonese style just as easily." Again the familiar gushing of words—several questions but no pauses for answers, typical of Bill's ebullient style.

His way of speaking reminded me of Hugh Herbert, a character actor long gone now, but it was a warm welcome, enthusiastic and sincere. I felt very welcome and looked forward to the dinner and the company with keen anticipation.

As we walked toward the villa I said, "Bill, I thought I heard a Chinaman a moment ago."

He laughed: "I guess that was me John. I was just in the kitchen reading a recipe in Chinese and I was thinking in that language and got stuck in it. Sorry. Bernadine tells me I do that all the time. If it's not Chinese it's some other language."

I soon found that this was indeed the case, and disconcertingly it also happened in German, Japanese, Italian, French, Spanish, and Portuguese—the languages of all the countries where he had lived. I soon became convinced that Bill was quite unaware he was doing this until it was brought to his attention each time. This was not an affectation; it was a mannerism that was deeply rooted. When he slipped into *German,* his voice dropped an octave as his speech took on the guttural character of that language.

We came to a turning in the path and emerged from the trees and tall bushes. The villa came into full view on the other side of an expanse of lawn. It had a roof of red Spanish tile, white washed walls and a cool Mediterranean charm but was not large nor as sumptuous as the word "villa" probably leads some to imagine. Colorful annuals added charm and informality and there was a spice garden that had just been watered. A pleasant fragrance arose from the warm damp earth and the pungent aroma of a spice I couldn't identify. The glow of a lamp in a window seemed to beckon us to enter.

Bill showed me around the villa and then as he began to mix some cocktails, the clicking of high heels on tile echoed from the walls in a nearby hall. I turned to see a tall slender auburn haired woman, about 15 years younger than Bill. Her smile of welcome told me instantly that we would become good friends.

"John this is Bernadine. She worked in Naval Intelligence at the Navy Department in Washington during the war. We met there and got married, but I had to go to sea on a special assignment the next day and didn't get back for six months. C'est la vie, c'est la vie—eh?" All this was uttered in his high pitched voice and effusive style.

"Good evening Bernadine, and who is this?" I said indicating the Siamese cat in her arms.

"Oh excuse me for not introducing him John, this is King—The King of Siam, you know." The King looked at me condescendingly.

Bernadine's hair was the color of an Irish setter. She wore it long and it tumbled gracefully down her back. I saw that she had the fair complexion of an authentic red head but eyes that were hazel, an unusual but attractive combination. I could imagine her as a successful actress. At this stage of her life, though many men would comment that, "She must have been a beautiful woman," not "She is a beautiful woman." Others, with kinder eyes, would note that when a woman has been a raving beauty, some vestiges of that always remain.

Dinner was superb. Bill served the hot Szechwanese cuisine with a white wine—a fine chilled Pouilly-Fuissé—something no doubt unheard of in China, but the wine complemented the food perfectly without masking the delicate nuances of flavor. After a lengthy mock serious argument, we at last laughingly agreed that the wine had dignity, breeding, and honesty—this in the grandiloquent tradition of the French who in all seriousness attribute human qualities to wine.

During the meal I encouraged Bill to tell me more about his life, because his unusual background and association with wartime intelligence fascinated me. I hoped some things could now be told without violating national security regulations.

He started with his graduation from the Naval Academy, At this time, it's the custom to ask newly commissioned Ensigns to state their preference for duty. Some think it's also the custom to not grant them the duty they requested. Bill for example wanted to transfer to the Marine Corps and have a command, but he was told, "Chink," (the nickname given him by classmates), "You can be a Marine but you might as well get used to one thing. You are never going to have a command. You are going to spend the rest of your career in Naval Intelligence as a language officer. People with your gift for languages are too hard to find." Bill was crushed. He wanted his own command—his dream since boyhood.

The Navy sent the young bachelor officer in mufti to live in Peking, as it was called in those days, posing as an eccentric American millionaire. Bill did not have to pretend. He *was* "eccentric." He had a mansion there with twelve servants and was ordered to avoid all contact with occidentals. He steeped himself in Chinese culture, learned to be fluent in the basic dialects of the country including the three varieties of Mandarin plus Hunan, Hweichow, Wu, and Fuchow and I don't know what else. He traveled extensively, memorized over 20,000 calligraphic characters, studied the history of all the dynasties, the ancient art, had Chinese girl friends, mingled socially at all levels of society, and studied Confucianism, Taoism, and Buddhism. I decided Bill had to be either a genius or an idiot savant.

After five years they brought him back to the Navy Department in Washington D.C. and were pleased to find that he had practically turned into a venerable, cultured, Mandarin aristocrat. He was told: "Good. You've done well Chink. Anyone who can do what you've done also can learn Japanese."

I won't elaborate but off he went to Japan and he learned to speak, read, and write the Japanese language like a native and returned to Honolulu just before the bombing of Pearl Harbor. His lengthy preparation paid off. During the war, Bill helped to break Japanese naval codes and that helped shorten the war. Well that was all very interesting for him, but what he *really* wanted to do was to command men.

By this time we were like three old friends. We enjoyed one another, we told stories, and we laughed. I was fascinated.

Then it happened. Bernadine began to tell me something interesting and

Bill nearly brought the roof down shouting, "SHUT UP BERNADINE! CAN'T YOU SEE I'M TALKING TO JOHN?" This seemed to satisfy some deeply felt need in him. Needless to say I was shocked. In an instant Bernadine jumped up and flew from the room like a soul foreordained to damnation, tears streaming down her cheeks.

"I'm just as much John's friend as you are," she bawled. "I don't know why I'm not permitted to talk to him too." I felt so sorry for her.

Bernadine sulked and cried in the other room projecting her suffering through the walls and the thin door. As if by tacit agreement and after the prescribed amount of time Bill heaved a deep sigh, got up wearily, eyes turned upward as if imploring the Almighty to sustain him, and he went to fetch poor Bernadine.

She came back to the table red eyed, dabbing the mascara from her cheeks with a hanky, and Bill said, "all right Bernadine, now *you* can talk to John. I'll just sit here." He said this in soothing tones as if to conciliate a child or person of unsound mind, but he glanced in my direction, rolled his eyes and wiggled his eyebrows.

The scene had again changed abruptly. The King of Siam came cautiously down from some high point of refuge perhaps the chandelier or the valence over the window and hopped up on Bernadine's lap again. He fixed Bill and me, each in turn, with his big round accusing blue eyes. Bernadine began where she had left off, then gradually regained confidence. But soon Bill looked at Bernadine like Oliver Hardy looks at Stanly Laurel and in stentorian tones shouted, "THAT WASN'T HOW IT HAPPENED AT ALL BERNADINE." Again in a flash Bernadine streaked out of the room bawling at the top of her lungs.

I don't know a lot about psychology but I like to try to speculate on the events of that evening. See if you agree with me. I got the definite Impression that they were locked in a strange psychological dependance and also that both were born thespians. I believe they each acted compulsively and derived some satisfaction from their performances. I have little doubt that they "perform" in this manner every time they have guests for dinner and that they know in advance that this will be so.

Where Bill was concerned I see an additional factor. He wanted from the very early childhood to be a fighting Marine and to command men. Fate had cast him in heroic mold, but he had been assigned to Naval Intelligence his entire career. During all these years he didn't have a single chance to command anyone except maybe a WAVE yeoman second class. The pressure built up with every passing year.

I believe he would have explained his behavior about like this:
"What did they do to me? They promoted me to Brigadier General and retired me. That's something like giving a man a posthumous decoration. It's too late to be of any damned use. Not once did I have a chance to give someone an order as a Brigadier General in the US Marine Corps. Nobody is afraid of a retired officer, not even if I am a General. It is intolerable…unthinkable. It is an *outrage.* What is a man to do in a situation like this? If I can't shout a few orders at my wife, who *can* I shout them at? Why can't women be more understanding?"

A week later my phone rang. I picked it up and heard: "Nay ho Maaa!…" Then another voice, Bernadine's, cut in on the extension and said, "Bill you are in Chinese again. Get back into English."

"Oh yes. Sorry John, I did it again didn't I? Oh well…anyway John, I was just reading an ancient recipe I got in Manchuria long ago, for duck as it was prepared there in the T'ang dynasty. It sounds fantastic, and since Bernadine and I enjoyed it so much when you came to dinner, we wanted to know if you would be free to come again tomorrow night at the same time?"

I was more amused than surprised or embarrassed and I like a well cast, well acted comedy as much as anyone. It beats TV anytime. And besides I liked Bill and Bernadine…ancient Manchurian duck recipe—Mmmm.

THE DREAM THAT WASN'T

"Sir. Sir. Wake up Sir. We are serving breakfast now." The stewardess touched my shoulder, then pulled down the tray support from the back of the seat in front of me and placed my tray on it. I had boarded the flight before 5 a.m. and had fallen into a profound sleep even before the plane got off the ground.

Instantly I was awake now, but the dream I had been having was indelibly fixed in my mind. I knew that what I saw in it occurred exactly as it was revealed to me. Even today the impression is as distinct as it was then.

"There has been a helicopter crash," I said, without considering how it sounded to others. "There were two men aboard. It fell straight down like a rock and crashed in the middle of the freeway, but did not burst into flames." I looked at my watch and made a note of the time as I always do when something unusual happens.

The stewardess looked as if she didn't know quite what to say. "Coffee or tea?" she asked.

My mind was on the tragic accident I'd just seen. Two men were almost certainly dead: I doubted that anybody could survive a crash like that. The decision, "coffee or tea," seemed unimportant. She had to repeat the question. I had seen many men die during World War-2 but I was prepared for it then. This was so unexpected.

"You did have a bad dream didn't you?"

I looked at the man who had spoken to me. He was a husky, genial looking middle-aged fellow. Here was someone willing to listen. Two others moved away to find other seats.

"It was like a dream," I said, anxious to talk to anyone who would hear me out, "but different from any dream I ever had before. It was so vivid. It was real. I was there. I know it really happened. I saw it happen. It was more than a dream." He looked as if he believed me, but I knew he didn't. How could he? Probably just polite.

I was on a flight out of Rochester, New York. The first stop would be Chicago's O'Hare airport, where I would change flights for Albuquerque, and then change again for San Francisco, my destination.

"Do you live in Rochester?" he asked. He probably wanted to change the subject, but how could I talk about anything else?

"Let me tell you what has just happened. I'm not crazy. It really happened. I'm sorry if I keep repeating myself… I don't understand why I do that, but I can't seem to stop. It was like a dream, but different I tell you. Different from any one I ever had before because here I am awake now and I can't shake it off. I can't just say, 'Oh I had a bad dream' and forget it.'"

My fellow passenger seemed more interested now. He sat there staring at me, holding his cup of coffee but forgetting to sip. "Tell me all you can remember."

"When we can get the news, you will see I'm right. It is as if I was actually there when it happened." I was struggling to convey a feeling that was unique in my experience. I wanted to share it with someone but didn't know how. I could neither express myself convincingly nor stop trying. I groped for words and they eluded me. Probably that's why I kept repeating myself.

"Where do you think…I mean where did the accident happen?"

"I don't know. It was daytime—in the morning I think—clear sunny day. I was walking beside a broad highway, not a lot of cars. I can still see it distinctly. There were many traffic lanes. On my right was a large body of water. I believe it was salt water. I had that impression: maybe I smelled salt in the air. But it was flat calm so it must have been inland water, perhaps a bay."

He was listening now with apparent interest. My conviction and my intensity seemed to get through to him. "Along the shore were many small sail boats. I am a sailor myself, so I stopped occasionally to talk."

The stewardess came and took away our trays after which we could turn enough to make conversation less awkward.

"Well, as I was talking to one of the boaters, I heard that characteristic whup-whup sound of a helicopter. I turned and there it was. We both watched it from then on. It passed about 500 feet to the right of me going in the direction I had been walking, evidently following the highway. Its altitude was between one and two hundred feet. I wondered then why it made a complete circle to the left and passed by again, this time much closer. I could distinctly see two men in it, seated side by side. It began to make various strange maneuvers. I wondered what was going on."

The man stared at me intently, caught up in the drama, and the horror of impending disaster. I used expressive hand gestures, something I rarely do, to add emphasis as I told of my strange experience and I think I at last painted the scene for him clearly enough to convey something of what I felt.

"After their second pass over us they continued on up the freeway. When it was about a half mile from us, the helicopter suddenly fell straight down like a rock. Maybe they had an engine failure while hovering. That's what helicopter pilots fear most: If they have forward speed when the engine fails, they can autorotate to a safe landing. At first I thought it was another spectacular stunt but then came that horrible moment when I knew a fatal crash was inevitable and I could only watch it happen. It was horrible. It seemed to be in slow motion. I had several seconds to suffer vicariously with those two men who looked in the face of death—knew they were about to die. I wonder what they were thinking. Then it was all over."

"God, what an experience," murmured my listener.

"They hit hard right in the center of the freeway and destruction was total. A piece of the rotor broke off and whirled down the highway. There was nothing left but a low pile of rubble but to my astonishment it didn't burst into flames. I started to run to see if I could help, but stopped. Others were much closer and in any case I felt that nobody could possibly have survived a crash like that. There was nothing that anyone could do. I turned to the boatman beside me and said, 'Life is so temporary.' He made no reply, just nodded agreement. That was when the stewardess woke me for breakfast."

At that moment we heard a woman's amplified voice. "All passengers please fasten your seat belts and straighten up your seat-backs. We are about to land at Chicago's O'Hare air terminal. Thank you for flying United."

As soon as I could, I rushed to the news stand. "Have you heard anything about a helicopter crash?...Two men in it."

"No. The latest papers are over there." The woman waved her hand ambiguously to give me a vague hint as to where I might find them."

"It happened only about an hour ago. It couldn't be in the papers yet, but it might have been on the air. You haven't been listening to a radio?" She shook her head and stared in another direction. I bought the two latest editions, but as I expected, the news I wanted was not there. It could not have been, as I was to learn later.

During my flight to Albuquerque I told my story to everyone who would listen and to some others as well. I was obsessed. I kept repeating, "It was more than a dream. I know for certain that it happened. The helicopter fell straight down like a rock and crashed in the middle of the freeway, but didn't burst into flame."

When we landed I again rushed straight to the news stand. As before, I was told—"There are the latest papers over there." With somewhat more hope of finding what I wanted this time, I bought two more late editions but as before, found nothing.

During the final leg of my trip to San Francisco, I could talk of nothing but the helicopter crash. In my mind I kept seeing the disaster and events leading up to it. I could close my eyes and the scene would replay as clearly as the first time. I could see every detail, hear every sound. To this day I still can.

When at last I reached San Francisco, I, of course, went for the third time to a news stand and for the third time learned nothing. These many failures to get any corroboration of the crash did not at all diminish my conviction that it had occurred...but the frustration was infuriating. Not once during the day did it occur to me that my behavior was irrational though I was aware it must seem so to others.

In a rental car I began the 15 mile drive into San Francisco. I turned on the car radio, hunted for news, didn't find any and finally settled for a "good music." station. A moment later a voice said, "We interrupt this broadcast to give you some additional details of the helicopter crash. A witness is quoted as saying that the helicopter fell straight down like a rock and crashed in the middle of the freeway, but did not burst into flames." These were precisely the words I had been repeating all day.

It was not until the final edition was out that night, that I at last saw the San Francisco Examiner's big headline. "FATAL I-680 COPTER CRASH.". Yellowed with the years, I still have that paper.

According to Don Martinez, Staff Writer, the tragedy took place Friday, September 11, 1981 on the busy East Bay freeway I-680, near the town of Fremont. The water I saw was San Francisco Bay. Larry King, then NASA's spokesman, released these additional details. The helicopter was a four place

Hughes OH-6 being flown from Moffat Field to Travis Air Force Base in Fairfield, by two NASA pilots, David Barth and Richard Ritter. Barth was killed on impact. Ritter, was listed in critical condition. I don't know whether he made it or not.

To be completely factual, I must point out that the accident occurred under conditions of poor visibility. The helicopter struck 115,000 volt power transmission wires that crossed high above the freeway, cutting off the electricity of 23,000 PG&E customers. In my dream I saw neither the wires nor the haze. From a half mile away I probably would not notice or could not have seen wires in any case, and my vision penetrated the fog and haze as if they were not there. These two things then, were not apparent to me so my impression was not picture perfect. But I am bewildered by what was revealed in the vision, and by the radio reporter's use of the exact words that I had used compulsively all day—words that conveyed three seemingly unlikely facts—"fell straight down like a rock—crashed in the middle of the freeway—and did not burst into flame."

Of all people, why did I—2,500 Miles away—see this happen? I didn't know either of the pilots.

Finally, I got the shock of my life when I looked at the time of the crash given by the newspaper (8:40 a.m. Pacific Standard Time) and compared it with the time I had jotted down when awakened from my dream (5:40 a.m. Eastern Standard Time). I had seen the crash six hours, to the minute, before it happened.

THE LIFE OF RILEY

"ADVISE IMMEDIATELY BY TELEX YOUR ESTIMATED SALES FOR REST OF THIS MONTH AND FOR NEXT MONTH. NO DELAY WILL BE TOLERATED CARLOS ZANETTI."

That was all I needed. My car was in the garage again, my secretary was home with the flu, and I had not been able to reach by phone seven of the fifteen distributors in my European territory or the four most important ones in North Africa. On a sudden impulse I wrote a reply:

C. Zanetti: REURTELEX THIS DATE. YOU SILLY BASTARD. HOW THE HELL DO YOU EXPECT ME TO MAKE SALES ALL OVER THIS TWO MILLION SQUARE MILE TERRITORY WHEN YOU KEEP ME BOGGED DOWN IN MY OFFICE WRITING REPORTS AND TRYING TO ANSWER YOUR STUPID QUESTIONS? –John Riley

I did not care for the home office environment of the corporation—constant meaningless conferences, office politics, cliques, back biting, and backside covering—the endless mad scramble to make the current quarter look good, to hell with the longer range picture. I held strong opinions and was too outspoken to fit in there. I chose to work overseas as "far from the madding crowd" as I could get, making my own decisions, doing things my own way.

The company I worked for was one of the largest and most respected hi-tech electronic corporations in the world. It was the undisputed leader in the manufacture of broadcast television transmitting and studio equipment. The products were all highly engineered, complex, big ticket items, sold by engineers to engineers. I, in the Paris office, was the Regional Manager for Europe and North Africa and to do my job as it should be done, required that I make on-the-spot decisions and travel five or six days out of every week, which is what I did.

Recently the Board of Directors had decided to oust engineer oriented top management. Current wisdom of the ivory tower held that a really good sales executive can sell anything by clever arguments and force of personality. It doesn't matter whether the product is technical or non-technical. The American Management Association and Harvard School of Business had been beating the drums for this point of view with the fervency of missionaries out to save heathens, and the concept spread like bubonic plague.

The ex-CEO of a major company that sold kitchen appliances was brought in to run the corporation and with him came a swarm of high pressure stove and refrigerator salesmen whom he placed in key management positions. None of them had an engineering background and none of them knew anything about electronics.

Now the policy was to micro-manage everyone in the field, exerting the strongest possible home office control. Under the new CEO's guidance the corporation then acquired a subsidiary that manufactured kitchen appliances and proposed to sell them abroad through the same distribution organization which had been set up to sell broadcast and TV stations. The result was a nightmare and a colossal disaster.

Zanetti, a new Vice President to whom my boss now reported, had recently completed a tour of Europe to demonstrate how "a pro" makes sales. He returned in triumph after three weeks of whirlwinding, with orders for nearly a million dollars having "sold" refrigerators that had no place for wine bottles and were too big to go through European kitchen doors; and table radios that would not tune the European broadcast bands, nor run on 50 cycle power.

I soon learned the secret of this phenomenal short term success. The man talked and acted like a gangster. He didn't *sell* these things to the distributors—he figuratively held a gun to their heads and said, "This is what you have to buy right now. If you don't I will cancel your distribution agreement." In effect he was selling protection against being fired.

No distributor wanted what he was forced to buy nor could he sell it through normal channels. Some of the best money makers among them refused, were terminated on the spot, and were forever alienated. Those who gave in lost heavily and had to eventually sell off their inventory as distressed merchandise, in some cases for ten cents on the dollar.

I picked up my phone. "Kathy, I have a telex I want sent immediately and Erica is out with the flu.

"I'll come get it right away, Mr. Riley." The door opened. She took the paper that I handed her and went out. Seconds later she was back, an uncertain smile on her face.

"You *are* joking aren't you Mr. Riley? Sometimes I can't tell."

"I was never more serious in my life. Send it exactly the way I wrote it. I've had it up to here with that imbecilic son-of-a-bitch. As much as I like the company, its products, and life in Paris, I can't put up with this." I struck the top of my desk a vicious and resounding blow.

I knew I would be fired and they would pay me off to the end of the month but I intended do my best until then. I left immediately for Helsinki. The Finns, in the process of building their first TV network, were going to buy three more transmitting stations and I had already sent a proposal.

It would be my last trip for the company and I was determined to go out in a burst of splendor. I could at least make Zanetti look bad by closing an important sale at the same time as the bastard fired me in a fit of rage.

In this business you either made a multi-million dollar sale or you lost out to a competitor and had nothing to show for your efforts. There was nothing in between. That was what exasperated me about Zanetti's telex demanding to know precisely how much would be sold month by month. The man was still thinking like a department store manager.

My plane landed in Helsinki late that night. There were a few Finns on the same flight and I was the only foreigner. I knew everyone would soon be competing for taxis and, as usual, there would not be enough of them to go around. Passport Control waved through all with "SUOMI," that is to say Finnish, nationality. By the time I completed formalities, I found myself alone. There was no transportation into town. It happened every time.

Someone at the airline desk called a cab for me and advised me to wait for it outside. At least I could get away from the smell of fish oil that they used on the wooden floors. It was bitter cold and I walked back and forth under the dim light at the taxi stand, stamping my feet and beating my arms to keep from freezing as the snow swirled around me. My thoughts went back to the home office and I tried to picture Zanetti's face when he would see that telex. Who, I wondered, would they send to replace me? There were plenty who would jump at the chance. They all thought I lived "the life of Riley." There was a clique of petty, jealous men whose envy knew no bounds…men who pictured the assignment as glamorous…big expense account…fancy restaurants…luxury hotels. They saw themselves, suave and sophisticated, speaking five or six foreign languages, commuting daily to the most exciting capitols of the world—London, Stockholm, Rome, Cairo, and Paris etc.

The selected man would find to his dismay that it wasn't always like that. I thought of the time in Istanbul when every decent hotel was fully occupied. I spent four hours going from bad to worse until I finally had to settle for a room in a third class dump. The bed was filthy and they had no clean sheets or towels. The toilet was a hole in the floor. I had bought a newspaper and spread its pages to sleep on. A similar thing had happened in Damascus. I was given a room in the Semiramis that had been previously occupied by an Arab Sheik and three goats. That time I caught an infestation of skin parasites that took a month to cure. Then there was the time when my French travel agent thought I was English and told me I didn't need a visa for Nigeria. As a result I spent three days under house arrest in a small airport hotel in Lagos, waiting for a General to return from a trip and vouch for me. Fortunately I later got out of Nigeria just 30 minutes before the Biafran war started and enemy troops machine gunned 36 people in the airport departure lounge.

My feet by now were like two blocks of ice. Just as I was picking up my travel bag and briefcase to go inside to thaw out, I saw the lights of a cab approaching.

Twenty minutes later I checked into one of several ancient hotels, which was all they had at the time. Its decor was from the not so gay nineties when Finland was a part of Russia. I went to my small, dreary room and had some coffee sent up. At least I was getting warm now.

I opened my briefcase and settled at the small desk to plan my strategy for the next day. I reviewed everything I knew. Raimo Kukkula was the Chief Engineer and the sole decision maker. He fortunately spoke both English and French which was most unusual in a country where even the head waiters in the best restaurants usually knew only Finnish, a hopelessly complex language.

Raimo was a polite and friendly man—short, square, middle-aged, and balding. The trouble was that he was polite and friendly to *everyone*. The hardest kind to sell. You never knew where you stood with him until it was too late. He was known to be an alcoholic. So far he had bought one TV transmitter from me and two from a French company. The American built station was working perfectly. No outages, no complaints.

The other bidders would be German and French companies. I didn't worry about the Germans. Their equipment was bulky, heavy, and hard to maintain as well as expensive. The French could be a problem though, mainly because subsidies from their government enabled them to drop their prices as necessary to compete. If they could guess or learn your bid price, they would come in just a shade under it, but Raimo did not have to decide on price alone.

I turned on the TV receiver in my room and found that the station I had sold was transmitting a perfect test pattern. It was standard practice to do this before and after the daily program. I then checked the channels which were assigned to the French made stations. Neither was on the air. Hmmm, that's interesting I thought. Maybe they were shut down for maintenance.

I was up early the next morning and went down for breakfast—ordered eggs soft boiled so they wouldn't ladle grease on them. The bacon I pushed aside. It was thick-sliced, fat, undercooked and greasy. The coffee and toast was only fair. Most Finns were tea drinkers.

I found the Finnish Chief Engineer in his office, a short brisk walk from the hotel. After exchanging greetings and a few pleasantries, it suited us both to get down to serious talk.

"Last night and this morning I noticed that your two French made transmitters were off the air."

"Yes. One of them has been down for two weeks and I am working on the other to try to get it to meet its power specification."

"I don't understand. Why has one been down two weeks?"

"I'm waiting for some spare parts" Raimo shrugged as if to imply that it was normal.

"When did you place the order for them?"

"The day after the transmitter failed."

"My gosh, Raimo, What's the matter with that company? If *our* equipment fails we guarantee to ship needed spare parts within six hours from the moment we hear from you—if not sooner."

"Oh, really?"

Raimo looked uncomfortable and I hoped this had registered. I opened my briefcase and took out a copy of the proposal that I had already sent by mail. "But tell me how our offer compares with the others. Are you ready to award the contract to my company?"

Raimo took a deep breath and said, "The Germans were high. Yours is the low bid and the French were in the middle. You can ship from stock and the French quote eight months delivery."

Ah, I thought we've got this one in the bag.

"But I don't need fast delivery. Eight months is good enough. I've decided to get the French equipment. I'm sorry. Two men from the French company are in town now. They are due here at noon." He looked at his watch. "A little over an hour from now. We will lunch together and sign the contract after that."

I was taken completely by surprise and deeply shocked. I looked at the Chief Engineer in disbelief. "You can't be serious Raimo. Why would you do that? I've shown you in my presentation that our latest model transmitter is technically far superior to competition. I've given you a detailed comparison. Its initial cost and cost of operation are both dramatically lower than that of the French transmitters. I don't understand."

Raimo was squirming now. "Well I decided on the French equipment because they are closer—just two and a half hours flying time from here. I went down and inspected their plant last week."

"But what good does that do if they can't send you spare parts when you need them? You just told me that one of your French transmitters has been off the air for two weeks and the other can't meet its power specification."

Raimo got up to indicate that the meeting was over and held out his hand for a parting handshake. "I'm sorry. It is too late now." He looked at his watch again in a nervous gesture. "They will soon be here and I have already told them I would accept their offer. I can't go back on my word."

I was now no longer baffled. I understood that there was no way to appeal to reason. Time to change my strategy—but fast. I knew exactly how the French operated and had just heard all I needed to know. They had invited Raimo to visit their plant on the outskirts of Paris and would have paid all expenses.

After a quick walk through, they would have taken him in a limousine to the Tour d' Argent, Paris's best and most expensive three star restaurant. There they would be joined by a few more of the company's top executives and two or three beautiful, coquettish girls. He would have been served a different wine with every course and each person would take turns proposing a toast, obliging the alcoholic Raimo to drink until he was seeing double. The pièce de résistance would have been the internationally famous specialité, Canard au Sang Tour d'Argent.

Raimo would think he had died and gone to heaven. The men would have pretended to think him witty and the girls would tell him he was dashing, handsome, and sexy. All would be counting the days, they would assure him, until he could come down again. He *must* do so, and be their guest of course, whenever he wanted in the future.

When Raimo was sufficiently inebriated the girl to whom he seemed most attracted would pretend to have fallen madly in love with him. She would be what the French call an alumette—literally a match, but in free translation "hot stuff." She would make him laugh with suggestive, off-color jokes both to put him in the best possible mood and to indicate in that not so subtle way that anything goes.

After three or four hours of gorging on six courses, all that good wine, and then coffee and cognac, one of the men would look at his watch and say, "*Oh la la,* where did the day go? I have enjoyed being with you so much I lost all track of the time. But now I must leave immediately and get back to the office to sign my correspondence." The other men would pretend surprise at the lateness of the hour and make the same excuse to leave Raimo with the girls. "I am *désolé* Monsieur Raimo to have to leave, but we men will take one car and leave the other car and chauffeur for you and the girls…wherever you want to go after you decide to leave. (A wink). But take your time. Order whatever you wish. It will all be taken care of."

In Helsinki no woman would have looked with interest at Raimo since many a year, but by now he would feel quite the man about town—Don Juan himself. When finally he left with "les Girls" one needs little imagination to know where they went and what they did.

All this I knew in an instant. It was not the first time I had seen customers fall victim to French finesse.

"Well Raimo," I said, "I am disappointed, naturally, but don't be embarrassed. I can be a good loser when I have to be. Do me one favor though. At least come have a drink with me, just to show that there are no hard feelings on either side." I thought that Raimo probably had never turned down a drink in his life and he didn't this time.

"That's very good of you to take it like that. Sure I'll go with you for a quick one. Time enough for that. Good idea."

Raimo led the way to one of his favorite bars. We found a table and started to drink. Whenever Raimo's glass was almost empty, I nodded to the barman to fill it again. We drank, drink for drink. I hated that. After the second drink a small voice inside me said "that's enough. You don't want any more." Ordinarily I would have been happy to stop. Raimo and I talked and drank, drank and talked. I learned that my guest owned an island where he went on weekends to fish and drink. Usually he went there all alone, rowing out and back in a dory. We talked fishing at great length. Men who are or have been fishermen can always find plenty to say on the subject.

During this time I avoided looking at my watch to keep Raimo from remembering that time was passing. Instead I kept an eye on a wall clock behind the Finn. Twelve, that magic hour, came and went. When it was one p.m., I wondered if the Frenchmen were still looking for Raimo. I expected to see them any moment. If they were smart they would suspect that the confirmed alcoholic was hoisting a few—they had only to ask his secretary where his favorite bar was.

"Raimo, this is a good bar but don't you know any others? Let's do a bit of bar hopping and maybe we can find one with sandwiches or nuts or something like that."

"Sure, I know every bar in town. Know just the place. Come on."

My God, I thought, *after this I'll never take another drink in my life.* Raimo was no longer able to notice that I was trying to hold back. The Finn was sinking fast into a stupor. From time to time he would put his head on the table and seem dead for long periods, then he would come back to life and bellow until someone appeased with another drink. At one point around midnight, after thirteen hours of drinking, I knew that if I had one more I was going to land under the table before Raimo did. I switched to water.

The Finn was getting surly. He began to insult everyone. Most of the people paid little attention to his remarks and I gathered that they knew him and made allowances.

By one a.m. I ordered some dinner for the two of us. Because of language problems I had no idea what they would bring but assumed it would be appropriate. I enjoyed mine but Raimo in a foul temper threw his plate of food at the waiter.

By two a.m. Raimo wanted to fight everyone in the place. I felt about ready to pass out completely. This was when a woman caught Raimo's fancy. He got up, staggered over and said something to her. The man she was with took exception to the remark, jumped up, and a shouting match ensued. The decibel level increased and words hammered ear drums as the disturbance became more violent. Raimo swung drunkenly at his opponent but the man ducked, caught Raimo off balance, and gave him a mighty shove that sent him sprawling. But for good fortune this might have put the Finnish TV network off the air for some time.

I couldn't remember the rest of the evening because of alcoholic amnesia, but I woke up in my hotel room feeling abominable. According to my watch it was nearly noon. Wondering what day it was I had breakfast and aspirin tablets sent to my room and finally felt well enough to shower and dress.

I then went to Raimo's office, briefcase in hand. To my surprise the Finn was there...hung over of course. He was not just hung over; he was also deep in the doldrums.

"Look what you made me do," he said. "The two Frenchmen came to my office yesterday to take me to lunch and sign the contract. When I wasn't here they went away furious. Got on a plane and flew back to Paris. Now what am I going to do?"

"There is no problem," I said. "It just wasn't meant to be. Let me help you. All you have to do now is sign this contract. To hell with them. You'll be getting better equipment and better service and lower prices. We won't let you down."

Raimo sighed. Without protest, he scrawled his shaky signature.

I went back to my hotel and sent a telex to Zanetti. I reported the sale of three transmitting stations to the Finnish government for a total of slightly under three million dollars. But then I could not resist telling in some detail how all was nearly lost and what I had done, above and beyond the call of duty, to save the deal I checked out and boarded a flight back to Paris.

In the office the next day, Erica, my secretary said, "Oh Mr. Riley, I'm so glad to see you again. It's terrible what happened here while I was out with the flu. One of the new girls wanted to play a joke on you so she made up that awful telex and signed Zanetti's name to it. They didn't send the telex you wrote but you left on another trip before anybody could explain that it was just a prank. I do hope you have not been in contact with the home office while you were away—I mean —not knowing about the joke and all."

I should have been angry but I was too relieved. After all, I did like my job. Not all the time, for sure, but most of the time. I only wanted to check the "IN" box and go home early to find a nice dark, quiet room.

As I was starting out the door, Kathy, at the telex called me. "Mr. Riley, Mr. Riley. Wait a minute please. Here's a message that just came in for you." She pulled it off the machine and handed it to me.

RE YOUR TELEX FROM FINLAND, HOW MUCH DO YOU EXPECT TO SELL NEXT MONTH? REPLY IMMEDIATELY—Zanetti.

EPILOG

A year after all this happened, Raimo was rowing back from his island, fell into the sea and drowned. He had been drinking of course. I was very sorry to hear it. He was a good engineer and quite likeable when sober.

THE SWISS NUMBERED ACCOUNT

If you look at a map of the African continent you will notice that it resembles the front end of a rhinoceros. Its horn is at Somalia, its mouth is at Cape Town South Africa, and its right front hoof is in the North West at Dakar, Senegal. Abidjan, the capital of Cote d'Ivoir would be high on its front leg—about 300 nautical miles north of the equator—longitude the same as London. That's where Alain was and he was not too happy about it. He could hardly wait to get airborne and head for home.

Home was Geneva and he thought there was no place like Switzerland. A week of one day visits to the capitol cities of equatorial Africa: Freetown, Monrovia, Accra, Lomé, Lagos, Libreville and back to Abidjan, had done nothing to change his opinions. He wasn't complaining though. When three business men, one English, one French, and one German, came into his office and said they wanted him to fly them on a quick trip to equatorial Africa in his Cessna 421, he had asked a charter price higher than he thought they would pay. Without a moment's hesitation they had agreed. Expense account money. No problem.

Now it was time to go home, thank God. Alain filed an IFR flight plan, stowed the luggage, put aboard several large thermos bottles of coffee, a bottle of scotch, a box of sandwiches and fruit. He called UNICOM on the radio and had them send over a fuel truck to top off the tanks, drained a little from each of the sumps to be sure there was no water in the fuel, ran through his check list, and was ready to go. After he climbed into the cockpit and started the engines, he beckoned to Charlie, Maurice, and Kurt to climb aboard, then called ground control for clearance to take off.

His passengers had waited until the last minute to board because the plane had been sitting in the sun and you could have fried bacon and eggs on its metal surface. The cabin was oven temperature.

Minutes later they were climbing to cruising altitude and at last the heat and humidity of Abidjan was only a memory. It seemed no time at all before they passed over Ouagadougou in Upper Volta, with its teaming masses, and then went on to cross the bleak, God forsaken, eastern tip of Mali. Then the Sahara started.

The vast desolate waste seemed at first to not support a living creature but Alain caught sight of a camel caravan and descended to a lower altitude have a better look. A dozen picturesque Bedouins in biblical costume rode the camels and about twice that many goats and a few dogs trailed along behind. Kurt snapped some pictures. Later Alain sighted a cluster of palm trees marking a small oasis. Among the trees they could make out the tents of nomads, and again Alain flew low to let Kurt take pictures. Maurice, who knew a bit about the region and its people, explained that the tents are woven of wool, goat's hair, and esparto grass. Kurt wrote it all down so he could tell this to his wife and their little daughter when he got home.

Alain had planned to make a refueling stop in Tunis but headwinds increased fuel consumption. He decided instead on Quargla, an oasis in the Algerian Sahara desert—in the center of that country's oil and gas producing region. It was almost on course and about 400 nautical miles closer. In the early fall of 1963 the fighting between France and Algeria had just ended. The new far left socialist country, until recently hostile to westerners, should be safe to enter now for a Swiss aircraft in transit. No problem at all he thought, not realizing the seriousness of his error.

While refueling at Quargla, an Arab official approached Alain but did not introduce himself.

"Monsieur," he said, "Is it that you go to Algiers."

"No. We are going to Geneva."

"Algiers, she is far from your course?"

"Well it is a bit to the west of my course—not much though," said Alain thinking out loud. "It's just that it's a landing I had not anticipated. I should continue to Tunis according to the flight plan I filed but I *could* stop in Algiers and ask them to notify Tunis of the change. Why do you ask?"

"There eez a man here…a very important man. He must get to Algiers as fast as he can. His car she ne marche pas."

Alain on a sudden impulse decided to play the Good Samaritan. "OK. Tell him to get aboard and I will be glad to go by way of Algiers to help him." *After all,* thought Alain, *it pays to make as many friends as you can. You never can tell when you will be glad you did.*

An Arab dressed in burnoose climbed aboard and found a seat in the back of the cabin. He didn't speak to Alain nor to his three passengers.

The plane reached cruising altitude at about the time of sunset, a time of spectacular beauty in the Sahara. For a while Alain followed the oil and gas pipelines that led directly to Algiers but then climbed up over the cloud cover to 8,000 feet. The sun, a big red orb was sinking into a layer of white cotton clouds. Kurt, the amateur photographer of the group, rushed for his Leica to get some quick shots of the beautiful scene which he would take home and add to his slide collection.

Soon the lights of Algiers could be seen on the distant horizon. Alain switched on his VHF radio:

"Algiers Approach Control. This is twin Cessna HB—47296. Request vectors."

"Twin Cessna this is Algiers Approach. Squawk 0324."

Alain set 0324 on his transponder so that Approach Control could tell which contact on their radar was his.

"Twin Cessna this is Algiers Approach. Your vector to Algiers, Houari Boumedien airport, is 354. The runway in use is one eight."

Alain had tried to change his flight plan at Quargla but they told him their communications were down, so now he asked Algiers to call Tunis and do it for him. Minutes later approach control handed him over to ground control and he landed. When they were on the ground a jeep marked "SUIVEZ MOI" led him toward a designated area. He was surprised to also see three military jeeps following along, left and right. Men in the back seats of two of these were armed with assault rifles and machine guns. The third had only a driver. Alain assumed the Arab he had taken aboard had to be a man of considerable importance.

When the plane rolled to a stop his Arab passenger rushed to the door, flung it open and shouted to the men in the jeeps: "Arrest these men. They are spies. Alain was told that he and his passengers were under arrest and his plane was confiscated by the FLN—the Front de Libération Nationale.

When they tried to drag him into a jeep he lost his temper. Alain who had just turned 40 was powerfully built and in excellent condition. He had been trained by the Swiss army in hand to hand combat. Algerian Berbers are not big men and they were no match for him. He could easily handle two or three of them at a time and his rugged features, fiery temper, fog horn voice, and red hair dismayed the smaller men. Had they not been heavily armed Alain, with some help from his friends might have prevailed, but one of the Algerians fired some warning rounds just over Alain's head. Distracted momentarily he turned away from an attacker and was knocked senseless from behind by a wicked blow behind the ear from a gun butt.

The four of them and their accuser were taken to a large prison on the outskirts of Algiers, where a kangaroo court was held. The Arab in the burnoose said they had photographed forbidden areas from the air. Alain was furious but convinced that when his captors developed the films they would see their error and he and his passengers would be released. The three other prisoners were immediately thrown into separate cells so they could not communicate with one another.

Alain was singled out for brutal treatment. During the next three days they kept him from sleeping, beat him repeatedly, and subjected him to unspeakable tortures. They ordered him to sign a paper confessing that he was a Swiss espionage agent, sent to photograph secret military areas from the air. He cursed them and refused. During that period they gave him no food and almost no water.

Alain demanded to see a representative of the Swiss government but it was useless. He also asked to see someone from the Red Cross. The result was the same.

The phone rang in Alain's Geneva office and Miss Dubs, his secretary for 20 years answered it.

"This is Rene at Cointrin Airport. Is that you Miss Dubs? Yes, I recognize your voice." Fear gripped Miss Dubs like the jaws of a vise. She was very fond of Alain and lived in perpetual fear that he would have a flying accident. She had often been in contact with the airport for news of him.

"What is it? Please tell me. Something has happened to Alain?"

"Miss Dubs, I'm terribly sorry to have to tell you this but Alain filed a flight plan in Abidjan three days ago for a flight to Geneva with a stop for fuel in Tunis, and he has not been heard from since. He didn't make it to Tunis but may have been forced down in some remote area. I will inform you immediately if there is any further news. Will you be so kind as to break the news to his wife?"

Tears ran down her cheeks and her voice quavered as she stammered, "Yes, of course."

Her hands trembled as Miss Dubs dialed Alain's home. She heard the cool, impatient voice of Mrs. Rousseau.

"Yes. Yes. Speak up. What do you want?"

"Madame Rousseau, this is Mademoiselle Dubs." She was crying. "Alain is missing on a flight from Cote d'Ivoir to Geneva. They haven't heard from him in three days."

There was silence for a moment as Alain's wife collected her thoughts, then Madame Rousseau asked, "Mademoiselle Dubs can you tell me if Alain renewed his life insurance policy before he started on this trip? I know it was about to expire and I reminded him repeatedly about it."

After the first three days Alain was put in a big stone walled room with about 500 of the most dangerous, degenerate, and incorrigible criminals in Algiers. There were thieves, murderers, perverts, and all kinds of crazies. They were filthy beyond belief and so infested with vermin that they scratched until they bled. Many coughed blood—the advanced stages of tuberculosis. There is an eye disease that is prevalent in Arab countries. It causes the eye to take on a milky appearance that leads to blindness. Many were totally blind and some of the rest had only one good eye. Most of the diseases of mankind could be found in that one room. No Hell could be worse. Every few days someone died. Medical help did not exist. The latrine consisted of holes in the floor and its foul odor pervaded the air of the prison. Every day for the first month they would come for Alain and it would start all over.

"You are ready to sign your confession?"

"I'm signing nothing. I'm not a spy."

"We have all the proof we need. You know what we do with spies in Algeria? We shoot them. We are going to shoot you just like we have already shot your friends. But if you sign a confession we won't shoot you. We might even let you out in twenty years." Alain knew he would die before then.

Alain's inquisitor was very young. Just a boy. In a civilized country he would be in high school. Obviously though he had the power of life or death over all prisoners and his every order was obeyed immediately and without question. He tortured for the pleasure it gave him.

Under his uniform coat which was never buttoned he always wore the same dirty T-shirt. On the front of it was printed "Fruit of the Loom"—the manufacturer's motto. Alain didn't know his name—never found out, but you have to have a name for people so at least in his thoughts he dubbed this person "Fruit of the Loom."

When he was grilled by this mental case every denial of guilt meant a beating or hours of agonizing torture. This would go on until Alain collapsed. Then they would drag him back to the big communal room where thieves would ransack all his pockets for something of use. He had nothing.

Alain never saw Charlie, Kurt, or Maurice again and had no idea whether they had really been shot, thrown into solitary confinement, or released.

Every prisoner was Muslim and they regarded him as an infidel, a pariah. In their eyes he was lower than a snake and didn't deserve to live. Why should he eat their food? He did not deserve Allah's infinite mercy and the slop they called food was often taken from him by gangs that overpowered him, but Alain was still a very strong man and incredibly resourceful. Somehow he found a way to survive physically but his hope was gone. He was dying on the inside. Where were his Swiss countrymen? God all mighty, where *were* they?

At the end of the first month of daily torture, Fruit of the Loom had Alain brought to his office.

"Are you ready to sign your confession which I have written for you?"

"Go to hell, you moron."

"I'll show you who the moron is. You can't talk to me like that. Don't you know I can have you shot? I'll show you. Guard bring him and follow me."

Fruit of the Loom led the way out into a courtyard. Gray stone walls surrounded it. Near one wall were a series of short sturdy posts. The walls behind these posts were pocked by bullets and the posts, as well as the cobblestone paving under them, were stained with dried blood. Alain noticed that there were no bullet holes in the posts, which suggested that the victims were probably shot through the head. He tried not to throw up.

Alain's legs—in particular his knees—felt strange. He recognized the visceral signs of fear. He had felt it before a few times in his life but never as much as now. Must not show it. Must not give Fruit of the Loom any satisfaction.

"Strap him to a post and call out the execution squad."

He didn't resist this time. It was useless. He had to face the fact that he was about to die and he was determined to show them how a *man* dies. When Alain was tied to one of the posts someone put a black hood over his head. He heard the sound of their crude boots on the cobblestone courtyard. They were not even in proper step. He imagined what they looked like, the rag-tag slovenly bastards. They didn't even know how to march in smart military fashion. The squad halted about ten meters from him. *In a minute they are going to shoot me. When I die I want to go thinking the right thought. That's very important. You only die once. What must I be thinking about?* His wife and family? But he wasn't a great family man and his wife didn't love him. No. He found himself thinking of Switzerland. He would die proud he was Swiss. He visualized a beautiful snow-covered mountain, the Matterhorn, and he heard the sound of cow bells coming from the peaceful green pastures in the valley and echoing from surrounding mountainsides.

The high pitched nasal voice of Fruit of the Loom intruded on his last thoughts.

"Ready. Fire at the count of three. One...two . . ." There was a long agonizing pause. "THREE!"

Alain heard the volley of shots from ten carbines. He flinched. By reflex action or the power of suggestion his knees almost gave way under him but then he knew he could not be dead if he heard the shots. It's the ones you don't hear that kill you. Next he heard the almost hysterical laughter of Fruit of the Loom. He had not been touched. They had either fired blanks or had aimed to miss.

As they took him back to the communal room Alain thought about his mock execution. The only reasons for it had to be either simple cruelty or a desire to make him crack. They clearly needed his signed confession and maybe, for some reason, they also needed him alive—a hostage.

At that same moment in Bern, Switzerland about 500 nautical miles NNW of Algiers, a meeting was taking place in a small conference room of the Ministry of Foreign Affairs, adjacent to the Minister's office. The room was designed to be sound proof and bug proof. Only two men were present, Foreign Minister Fritz Steiger and Pierre Egli who headed Banque Suisse de Commerce Arabique, headquartered in Geneva. No notes were being taken and no secretary was present.

The conference could have taken place in either the Schwyzerdutsch or French languages in which both men were fluent but protocol dictated the former because of the Minister's ethnic background. The minister spoke first.

"Herr Egli, as you probably have guessed, I asked you to meet with me today to discuss this annoying matter with Algeria. I refer to their holding of a Swiss hostage by the name of...er...Alain something. Let me see now, where is it?" He thumbed through a file. "Yes. Here it is. Alain Rousseau. I knew I had it right. I have a good memory for names."

"Ja, Herr Minister. You will note that I also was sent a copy of the ben Bella letter which I see before you. It is no doubt that which you wish to discuss."

"Quite right. Or to be more precise, I don't *want* to but I *must*. Well, if I must, I must." The minister sighed. "Most unfortunate that the Algerians were able to capture a Swiss national to accuse of spying...and a pilot at that who can't possibly be involved or have any means of establishing his innocence. It's his word against that of their witness who it happens is a lawyer on ben Bella's personal staff."

"Herr Steiger, we are dealing with a communist country. Moreover it is one that still operates under the old Napoleonic legal code. A prisoner there is guilty as charged until he proves himself innocent. That I think is the danger for the hostage. But ben Bella heads the Algerian government. Never mind that he is a dictator who seized power when they won the war against France for the right of secession. Don't you think we must reply at the highest level—that is to say it should come from the president of Switzerland?"

"Herr Egli, you are getting ahead of the story. May I remind you that I called this meeting and I am in charge? Now I will start by reading the ben Bella letter. It is addressed to our president and a copy is directed to the Banque Suisse de Commerce Arabique—to your attention. "

"Excuse me Herr Steiger, you need not read the letter on my account. I know it by heart. I only say this with the deepest respect—to save your valuable time."

"Once again Herr Egli, I always proceed step by step. It is my way of doing things. I don't want to have to remind you again." The Minister paused to polish his glasses. They didn't need it but that was also his way of doing things. "This ben Bella clown says:

"'The Algerian Front de Libération Nationale has captured the master spy you sent into our peaceful worker's paradise. The dastardly and unprincipled man is a Swiss national going by the name of Alain M. Rousseau. He has been duly and properly tried and found guilty by the People's Court. In our country the penalty for spying is death by firing squad. Be aware that justice will be done on a date that we will decide, unless the Banque Suisse de Commerce Arabique releases to the Algerian FLN the total sum on deposit in a secret numbered account opened by Hammoud Chabab, our ex-Minister of Finance.

"'As you well know, Mr. Chabab who was Minister of Finance of the Algerian Democratic People's Republic, while acting in his official capacity, deposited in your bank an amount worth over 215,000,000 in Swiss francs. However instead of depositing this money in an account in the name of the FLN he deceitfully opened a secret numbered account and absconded to Spain. Our heroic special operatives soon found and shot him. Justice is done.

"'Now, we the rightful owners of the deposited funds, the FLN, are denied access to the account by the criminals who run the Banque Suisse de Commerce Arabique on the excuse that do not know the number of the secret account.

"'I assure you that such swindling and duplicity on the part of your dastardly criminal bankers will not be tolerated. If you want to see your master spy alive and free again, you know our conditions.'

"He rudely signs his name Ahmed ben Bella, Prime Minister, without a closing salutation. That I consider to be the supreme insult to our president and to our country." The Minister tossed the letter aside and stared at Herr Egli over the top of his glasses.

"Ja, Herr Steiger, but I must make one thing clear. We have our own rules at the bank and we must not break them. It would shake the confidence of every important holder of a numbered account in the world if we made an exception in this case."

"I completely understand your position Herr Egli and I concur with what you say. Still just between the two of us the money does not belong to the bank and it does belong to the FLN." Herr Steiger lowered his voice almost to a whisper when he said this as if the walls had ears. "I would hope these facts never become public. If they do I will deny I ever said that of course."

"Ja, of course it belongs to the FLN but they don't have the number of the account so we don't have to give them their money. Even though they stole it in good faith from France who in turn stole it from them…need I go on? But what do you propose to do?"

"That Herr Egli is what I was just going to ask you—your suggestion that is."

"Herr Minister I would be an unworthy banker indeed if I did not point out that the western world is starting to recover from a cyclical recession. Equities are grossly undervalued and headed much higher. I can make at least 30 percent a year on such investments, and possibly more, in each of the next two years." Egli took a pocket calculator from his briefcase and poked at it with a stubby finger. "In two years I can run the account in question from 215 million francs to, let's say, 363 million.

Minister Steiger's mouth dropped open in astonishment.

Herr Egli continued. "Then if we have to negotiate a compromise of some kind—say they find a way to considerably increase the pressure on us to the point where a settlement is unavoidable, we can show the account value as having been increased at a normal bank interest rate of say three percent—not more."

"By dragging things out this way we may be lucky. There is always the chance that ben Bella will have been deposed—that's par for the course in communist dictatorships—and the whole thing may be forgotten. At the very least they will be easier to negotiate with after two years of frustration and after seeing that their strategy does not work for them as they thought it would. They will understand that we hold all the cards. If the hostage dies in the meantime, they will hold no cards at all.

The Minister interrupted to say, "Obviously if he didn't exist—er, that is to say if he does not survive his imprisonment, and there is always some chance of that, the problem would go away. We must weigh the pros and the cons. Mind you I'm not suggesting that his welfare is not uppermost in my mind."

"I fully understand, Sir, that you have difficult decisions to make and your point of view must take into account what is best for the Swiss nation…and its banks of course, which is the same thing." My advice therefore is to delay. Time is working for us in every way. Now what would be the best strategy to use in playing for time? If it were me, I would take the position that the money doesn't really belong to them because there is some question whether they acquired it legally from France or whether it is considered the spoils of war. The matter may have to go to the International court in the Netherlands for resolution. But we should take that position as a bluff. We under no circumstances dare let the French, in particular De Gaulle, know anything about it. That would be a fatal blunder."

The Minister rolled his eyes heavenward and spread his hands, palm upward, as if imploring God's help to prevent such a catastrophe," and added, "I'd rather deal with the Algerian communists."

"Of course if France did try to claim ownership of the money," Herr Egli added, "ben Bella could argue that France exploited Algeria and stole the money from them in the first place—and he could make a good case for that in The Hague if it got to the International Court for decision." Herr Egli put the calculator back in his black snake skin briefcase and snapped shut the gold lock. He continued, "Once more I recommend that we communicate at the chief of state level. Our president's first move should be to tell ben Bella we are studying his letter and ask a lot of confusing questions to drag negotiations out. Next work in the ploys I have already mentioned—drag everything out at least two years. That Sir is my advice."

"Splendid. You read my mind precisely Herr Egli. All that you have said is exactly my thinking. I'm glad we agree on this matter, and by the way I have some money invested that has not been doing as well as it should. Do you think you could pass on to me some occasional good advice?"

"Certainly Herr Minister, I would be very happy to. And, might I have an occasional little favor to ask of you in return?"

"We understand each other perfectly Herr Egli. It has been a pleasure to confer with you on the best way to extricate the hostage, er, what was his name, from the predicament he is in—consistent of course with national honor and practical, as well as material, considerations."

Three months after his capture the routine of prison life was nearly driving Alain insane. He was by nature a very active man with a brilliant mind. Fruit of the Loom, after the first month, grew tired of having him beaten every day and he was now left to suffer the indignities and miseries of prison life—forgotten and friendless.

Although representatives of the Swiss government were not permitted to see him, the head of the Red Cross mission, after three months of negotiation was able to come for a ten minute visit to deliver mail, chocolate bars, and sympathy. The letter from Alain's wife and three long ones from Miss Dubs had been so obliterated by a censor that it was hard for him to make any sense of them. It was then that Alain learned of a rumor going around—that he was being held hostage for Algerian money blocked in a Swiss numbered account. Hopes of ultimate release, that had kept him going, turned to ashes.

During his imprisonment two more ten minute visits of Red Cross representatives were permitted. No news was imparted at the second meeting other than that there was no news...no report of progress of any kind in the negotiations. He got a cold, impersonal letter from his wife, a warm and sympathetic one from Miss Dubs, and a few more bars of Nestle's chocolate which he tried to eat before going back to the communal room where it would have been fought over and taken from him. Alain no longer held the slightest hope of any kind.

At the third meeting, the RC man gave Alain another letter from his wife, three more from Miss Dubs, and as many Nestle chocolate bars as he could eat in ten minutes, but he had news this time.

"Monsieur Rousseau, you have been in here two years now. I wish I could be the bearer of more hopeful news but at least I can tell you what Herr Steiger, the Minister of Foreign Affairs, has told me to pass on to you. He took from his pocket a paper on which he had scribbled during a phone conversation. I'll read you what he said:

"'I send you my warmest sympathy and want you to know that my thoughts are always with you. From the moment of your imprisonment I have done everything, I repeat everything in my power to obtain your release at the earliest possible moment. I'm sure you will understand however that no assurance of ultimate success is possible. We are dealing with a difficult adversary who thinks of nothing but the money. That is the crux of the whole problem. In the event that we fail to obtain your freedom I want you to be assured that we tried by every means possible to achieve it... Whatever happens I think that as a loyal Swiss you will be proud to know that I consider you a true patriot and a martyr and I know that you will bear with fortitude whatever fate decrees. My representative will soon meet with your captors. We can only hope for the best.'"

Deeply felt emotion brought tears to Alain's eyes. He knew that if he had to grow old and die in prison, he would never forget that stirring message from Herr Steiger and he would be forever grateful. He reached out his hand. "May I keep that paper?"

There was one final visit by a Red Cross representative. "I'm glad to be able to tell you, Mr. Rousseau, that your term of imprisonment has ended. I have brought you some new clothes and I am going to take you home."

For a while Alain was speechless. "But what about all that money in the numbered account?"

"Some compromise was worked out. I'm not sure what the facts are. We will never know because it is a state secret. I did hear a rumor. Some think that a part of the funds in question were transferred to a new secret numbered account in the name of ben Bella as an incentive for him to officially drop the matter. That is pure speculation though. Algeria and Switzerland have agreed that details will never be made public by either country."

"And what about my plane? Do I get it back? It is worth around 945,000 Swiss francs. Wasn't that negotiated in the compromise?"

"Don't even ask. Let's go now."

NOBODY BELIEVED

One of my club friends, Gus, is a brilliant engineer and he was, until his recent misfortune, well on his way up the management ladder in the Classified Contract Division of a major corporation. Gus is a wizard who designed electronic control systems for missiles. Although only in his mid-thirties, he was already under consideration for promotion to Chief Engineer of a corporate division.

As some count their money, Gus counted his calories. He updated the total on a pocket calculator almost compulsively after each cocktail and almost every mouthful of food. He did this with a frown of concentration on his face—lips pursed.

Like Marconi, his ancestry is half Italian and half Irish. He inherits the charisma of both races—the exuberant hand gestures of the former, and the endearing eccentricities of the latter. Mother Nature scalped Gus when he was in his late twenties and left him only a modest fringe benefit. He is, or was, an animated talker with a face of many expressions. An almost hypnotic charm used to emanate from his lively brown eyes. It was impossible not to like him and enjoy his company. Usually he was refreshingly open minded but I remember once when he was not. Our conversation on that occasion went something like this:

"Gus, I've noticed that engineers and scientists seem to fall into one of two groups. There are the skeptics who delight in challenging all who rely on 'old wives tales' for guidance. They look with uncompromising disdain on primitive medicine, acupuncture, ESP, UFO's, the possibility of intelligent life in outer space, and household remedies like chicken soup. Then there are those of a different persuasion who pride themselves on their open-mindedness. They believe that a true scientist must withhold his opinion on something he doesn't understand until he has investigated it objectively. Do you agree with what I'm saying? If so, which kind are you?"

"Yes, I agree that there are these two basic mentalities and maybe even a third—those in the middle ground. But it's probably true that most of us tend to one extreme or the other. I guess you'd have to classify me in the first group because I definitely don't believe in the things you mentioned, and I think it would be a waste of time to investigate any of them."

"Gus, I'm amazed. Are you aware that when Louis Pasteur first wanted to become a member of the French Academy of Sciences, he was black-balled? They derided him and called him 'Little Bugs'—ridiculed his preoccupation with germs that 'didn't exist' because they couldn't see them."

"Yes, now that you mention it, I remember hearing that, but maybe I would have sided with Pasteur if I had heard him speak. In any case, you can't put germs in the same category, for example, with ESP or UFO's."

"How can you be sure?"

"Listen, If anyone had ESP, he could own the world. Just imagine what he could do in the stock market. As for UFO's, thousands of people have reported seeing them. I get the impression that they are everywhere, but I have never seen one. If they really existed, I would see one. Most people see what they expect to see. That's a fact of life."

"But what about reputable people who report seeing these things, including USAF pilots, airline pilots, two ex-Presidents of the United States, university physics professors, control tower personnel in airports, and eminent astronomers? I personally don't know what to believe, but I'm open minded."

Gus looked around to see if any ladies were within earshot and then decided to play it safe. I had no trouble reading his lips as they framed words not acceptable in polite society.

I smiled and said, "Little bugs syndrome, pure and simple."

Gus threw his head back and laughed heartily, after which he changed the subject. I sensed that he was eager to tell me something and eventually he got around to it.

"John, I have news for you. Ellen has at last said 'yes,' and we will be married in about a month."

"Wonderful news! It's about time. Let's drink to that," I said, raising my wine glass. Gus was a very light drinker but on this occasion he was having wine with his entree. He raised his glass in toast and drank the last of it, after which he frowned, pursed his lips, took out his pocket calculator, and added

85 to his daily calorie tally.

"You've set the date?"

"Not precisely, but we plan to be married in San Francisco where her parents live. Just a small private affair...family...no guests. I'll join her there in about a month. I'm going to stay with my brother before the wedding. He lives near-by on the Oakland side of the bay."

"Well," I said, "I can't tell you how pleased I am."

It was over two months before I saw Gus again. One Sunday I happened to drop in at the club and as I didn't see any of my lunch friends, I went to the bar.

"One Mint Julip and one Caesar's Salad Charlie, and by the way, what's become of Gus? I haven't seen him in a long time—have you?"

Charlie said nothing but rolled his eyes and inclined his head in a gesture that told me, "That's Gus over there in the corner." I turned and saw a figure in the shadows slumped over a corner table. He was leaning forward with head on folded arms, and seemed oblivious to the world. I couldn't tell at first whether he was in the arms or Morpheus, or John Barlycorn, or neither of them.

Approaching, I called out, "That you Gus?"

He sat up and looked at me quite soberly, and I noticed that the highball in front of him was untouched. In an instant I could see that he was changed and not for the better. Something terrible must have happened. His eyes were dull and listless, and his demeanor was that of a man who had been to hell and back. He seemed to have aged ten years.

"Hi. I didn't see you come in."

I took the seat opposite him and ventured a discreet conversation opener. "Haven't seen you in a long time Gus. How's everything?"

"You want to know how everything is? Terrible...about as bad as it can get. Ellen has broken off our engagement. My friends are avoiding me. I not only didn't get that promotion to Chief Engineer that I was counting on—I've been fired. Other than that everything is just fine," he added with bitter sarcasm.

"My God Gus! What the hell has happened? Do you want to talk about it?"

"Not really." It didn't sound like Gus at all.

"If you don't want to explain, that's all right, but sometimes it helps to talk to a friend."

"I just wish Ellen believed in me. That's what eats me up most."

"Tell me what's bothering you Gus," I encouraged him. "Start at the beginning."

"Well.... as you know I was supposed to join Ellen in the Bay area, and we were planning to be married there at the end of October. I went up a few days before to stay with my brother in Concord, which is near Oakland. Three days before the great event, I was to drive over to meet Ellen's parents, and we were supposed to make the final plans for the wedding." At this point Gus stopped. I sensed that he had come to a psychological block, and that he might not continue—might not be able to.

"Yes, so you were going to drive over to San Francisco," I prompted. "Did something happen then?"

"Oh Brother, did something ever happen! Sometimes I think I'm crazy and sometimes I think everyone else is. Did you ever drive across the Bay Bridge going from the Oakland side to San Francisco?"

"Many times. I know the route well. I can picture it clearly."

"Well then. Here I am driving that route. I'm never going to forget the date—Friday, October 21, 1988. I come to the Oakland toll gates, and I decide to take the center lane. I pass through, and I'm on the bridge approach with four or five lanes of traffic on my right and the same on my left. It's about 0900 a.m. Everybody's in a rush to get to work, and probably lots of 'em are late. You know how it is at that time of the morning. OK, I'm a minute or two beyond the toll gate when I notice what seems to be a big black bird of some kind hovering over my traffic lane about a quarter mile ahead...just where the on-ramp of the bridge starts."

"I know just where you mean," I said.

"Well, I look at this thing and I begin to wonder why it stays in exactly the same place about forty feet over my lane. I get closer and...My God...I see it isn't a bird at all...it's an object with elliptical outline, and it's dull black and steady as a rock. I'm about three hundred yards from it now. It's silhouetted against the morning sky real clear and sharp. I take my foot off the gas and let the car slow to about 30 to have a better look. Cars behind me start honking. They're mad as hell. I can't believe they aren't looking at the thing too. Well, I roll down my window and point up at the object. I guess the cars behind take this as an unfriendly or obscene gesture."

There was a look of desperation on Gus's face now as he relived the event that seemed to have so affected him. Beads of perspiration ran down his face and his hands were shaking. He dried his sweaty palms on the front of his shirt. Clearly his memory of the event lived so vividly in his mind that he appeared to be seeing it all again.

"I look at the lanes on my left and right to see if I can cross over and stop on the highway shoulder. Damnation. It isn't possible. They're going past me on both sides at twice my speed. The car behind is tailgating me now—blinking his lights and honking. I've got to keep going. I can see the thing clearly now. I'm almost under it. It's dull black, about a foot and a half across, and maybe six inches thick. It's a small flying saucer…a UFO. Nothing else it can be."

As he spoke his hands defined the shape and thickness of the object as if it were right there before him at that instant, and I had the impression that he was holding it, touching it, estimating its weight and the texture of its surface.

"I roll down the window and lean out looking up as I go under it…the thing looks round from underneath. It's only about forty feet above me…then it's behind me, and I can't watch it anymore." He pounded the table with his fist.

"Nobody else seemed to have noticed it?" I asked, flabbergasted.

"There! I knew you wouldn't believe me. Nobody believes me."

"I didn't say that at all."

"Well, but I can tell by your question, you don't believe me. Nobody believes me." Gus had a morose scowl on his face now.

"Gus, go on with your story. What happened next?" He looked at me suspiciously for a moment. It was as if he assumed that I thought him mad and was humoring him.

"Well, when I get to the San Francisco side, I turn and go back to the Oakland side and start again for San Francisco, only this time I get in the right-hand lane so I can pull off onto the shoulder of the road when I get to the thing—only it isn't there anymore."

"What do you think it was?" I asked.

"It could be a surveillance device…probably has a microphone and camera in it. What I wonder at first is whether it's a military system under test or an object from outer space. If you wanted to test such a thing you can't think of a better place to do it than over the center lane of the bridge approach at rush hour. Nobody can stop and gawk."

"Well Gus, I guess it was something under test by our military."

"Yea, but the power source to support flight and supply the electronic equipment is a size and weight problem beyond present science. This thing is way beyond our most advanced technology. The more I think of it, the more scared I get. It had to be a probe from outer space."

"But Gus you told me that you didn't believe in UFO's."

"I didn't believe in them then because it was always someone else who saw them. Now I've seen one, and what I saw was not earth technology—after all that's right in my field. Besides, I just feel that it was extraterrestrial. It is something I can't explain, but I just know it was from outer space.

"How do you 'feel it'? How do you 'know it'? Are you saying that you have ESP?"

"You're damned right I am. You can laugh at me if you want to, like everybody else."

"I'm not laughing Gus."

Gus was getting too loud and excited now. I thought it best to change the subject. "Did you finally get to Ellen's parent's house?"

"Yea…over an hour later than I was expected. Ellen is worried sick before I get there, then relieved when arrive, and then mad at me afterward for being late. I'm nervous and jittery myself and shouldn't be meeting her parents, for the first time, shaking like a leaf and covered with cold sweat like I am."

"I tell them the whole story. Honest to God John, they back away from me like I'm some kind of nut. I can see they're sort of scared of me. They think their daughter is about to marry a lunatic. Worst of all, I see that Ellen is looking at me sort of funny too. When I finally calm down a bit and bring up the subject of the wedding, Ellen's mother, the old battle ax, says that under the circumstances she thinks I am too 'unhinged' by my experience.' What the hell does she mean by that? She says we should 'postpone' the wedding. Then she says, 'later we can see how both parties feel.' Ellen accepts her mother's decision, and there's nothing more to be said."

"I come home and tell the guys at work. Most of them laugh at me and kid me. 'Did you see any little green men?' they ask me. Some look embarrassed. One guy mentions it to the boss and he sends for me. 'Gus, he says, I've heard about your UFO, and I don't mind telling you I'm a bit disturbed. I want to hear it from you though.'"

"I tell him everything I saw, and you know what he says to me? Guess what he says."

"I wouldn't have the slightest idea."

"He says, 'Gus, I want you to take a week off…er, with pay that is. Get some rest."

"I say, 'You think I'm nuts don't you?' He does too. I tell you nobody believes me."

"I don't need it but I take the week anyway and use the time to try to straighten things out with Ellen. I get nowhere with her."

"I also make some notes and send them to the leading local newspaper with a sketch and a forwarding letter giving my credentials as an engineer. I suggest they print my report, and ask all readers who maybe saw the same thing to contact the paper. Someone writes back and says, 'This newspaper follows the same policy as the USAF. We do not publish UFO stories.' They enclose a list of about fifteen UFO clubs and investigative organizations in the USA. I send copies of my report to all of them and to personal friends I have at high levels in all three military services, but get no replies from anybody—not even from my friends.

"What I get instead is a visit by two men from a news syndicate who want my story. One carries a camera and the other carries a tape recorder. He hands me a microphone. I think, this is my chance. I can tell it like it happened. Two days later I find my picture all over the front pages of two of those supermarket tabloids, under big headlines. One says, 'MISSILE SCIENTIST SIGHTS UFO—flown by tiny men from outer space.' OH MY GOD! I didn't say anything of the sort. They even mention General Engineering. When I see it, I know the boss is going to blow his top.

"Wait till you hear what they do to me next. I go to my office on a Sunday to see how high the paper is in the 'IN' basket. I sit down at my desk. Immediately I notice that Ellen's picture is gone and in its place is this picture of a fat lady, three kids, and a pit bulldog. I look at my book case, and all my books are gone. I pull out a desk drawer, and everything is rearranged with someone else's things. Then I see a name plaque on the desk that says, 'Jerry Wright, Assistant Chief Engineer.' What the hell—that's what I am. About this time I notice a big carton in the corner, and I find my books, Ellen's picture, my framed diplomas, and all my other things in it. On top there's this envelope with my name on it. I have a sick feeling in my stomach. I open it. No letter—just this and a final pay check." Gus handed the pink slip to me. Among other things it said, "Top-Secret Security clearance revoked...psychologically unstable...possible drug or alcohol problem."

Gus paused now. He noticed his drink sitting untouched in front of him, and picked it up in a shaking hand. Like a man dying of thirst, he turned it bottom up and drank it to the last drop, spilling some of it on his shirt and tie.

I had never seen him like that before.

"Nobody believes me," he muttered, more to himself now than to me. "Nobody believes me…Nobody."

THINGS LIKE THAT JUST DON'T HAPPEN

Few things are as aggravating to contemplate as those that might have been but were not. For example there was the time when, for one brief day, I thought I had made a fortune. I was young then and a sophomore in college. The year was about 1940. It still bothers me to think of it and only now can I bring myself to put the story on paper.

My father and I were invited to dinner by my aunt and uncle and arrived a little early. While the rest of the family was busy in the kitchen and dining room I paced back and forth in the living room like a hungry animal—ravenous as usual. Soon something caught my eye. It was a violin being used to decorate the wall as if it were a mirror or a painting and, to make it more colorful, small bouquets of flowers were stuffed into its sound holes.

I will never know why I felt drawn to it. I had never been interested in violins—the piano was the instrument that captured my interest at that time. Yet I was strongly attracted to *that* violin. I stopped pacing and stood staring at it for a long time. The longer I looked the more I noticed. There was not a scratch or nick in its soft varnish that went from shades of yellow to a deep beautiful reddish brown. It seemed to be quite old but in perfect condition and I began to notice how carefully it had been made. This is the work of a *real* craftsman, I told myself.

I went into the dining room where my aunt was setting the table.

"Buddie, where did you get the violin?"

"Oh I'm so glad you like my wall decoration," she said. "Let me see now. Where *did* we get it? We've had it for years. I decided to put it to some use. Nobody in our family wants to take violin lessons."

At that moment my uncle Leigh and Dad emerged from the kitchen. They had been mixing cocktails and both held an old fashioned in each hand. Leigh was always the complete southern gentleman and his manners were courtly. With a flourish and a bow, he handed one glass to Buddie and the other to me.

"Johnny asked me where we got the violin and I have to stop and think about that. Do you recall?"

"Yes, I sure do. I found it in Father's attic after he died," replied Leigh.

I returned alone to the living room and stood staring at the violin again. On a sudden impulse I removed the flowers and held a table lamp near the instrument to better admire its workmanship. Looking at it close up I thought I saw something inside—a small piece of paper. I took the shade from the lamp and held it so that it shed its light through the sound holes at just the right angle. What I had seen was a small label that was starting to peel away from the wood. It was made of brown paper or more likely it had turned brown with age. No doubt the maker's label, I thought. Old and ready to crumble at any moment, it had come unglued at one end and was curled so that I could not see the writing on it. I adjusted the lamp's position carefully and put my face close to the instrument. By poking with a straw I was able to flatten the label enough to read it, but I had to look off to one side at an awkward angle. What I read sent a shiver of excitement through my body. It was signed in precise script, Antonio Stradovari, Cremona 1719 after which I saw a small circle enclosing a cross with AS under it. (I do not remember the exact date but this is approximately correct.)

"My God. This is a Stradovarius," I shouted. Everyone came running, all talking at the same time.

"It can't be," said Leigh. His voice showed more incredulity than excitement.

"Read that label inside. Here take this straw and use it to unroll the label which is curled. It has come unglued at one end." I held the lamp for him and handed him the straw. Leigh peered into the violin and a perplexed look spread over his face. He didn't know what to make of it.

"Pete, come here and look at this." Dad bent down and studied the label.

"Well, I'll be damned.... "

Later as we ate dinner we could talk of nothing but the Stradovarius. I recalled that I had once read an article about Antonio Stradovari and I told what I could remember of it. The rich overtone structure of his violins was equaled by no others. It would seem possible to duplicate one of his masterpieces using the same kinds of wood cut from the same part of the logs, the same patterns, the same thicknesses everywhere, the same arch and curvatures in the soundboard, the same directions of wood grains and finally the same critical positioning of the sound post. Many tried it but none attained the perfection of tone of the Stradovari violins—a unique sprightly singing tone quality. Experts suspect the master had some secret process for making and applying the varnish, others think it has to do with the way he cured the wood. The secret died with him.

There was much speculation as to what it was worth. At one point uncle Leigh said, "Johnny, I don't believe for one minute that this is a genuine Stradovarius, but if by any chance it is, I'm going to give you ten percent of what I can get for it."

"Don't say you don't believe it is genuine," I replied. "Of course it is. Why on earth would you say a thing like that?" I could not understand his unwillingness to believe his good fortune—he seemed determined not to.

"Because things like that just don't happen."

"Why not? Of course they do. Take it to an expert tomorrow and find out. Better yet, take it to several. It is genuine. I don't have the slightest doubt."

"OK, that's just what I intend to do."

"Pete, how much do you think it would be worth if it is genuine?" asked Buddie.

"Well that's a bit out of my line," my father replied, "but I seem to recall that, when a Stradovarius turned up years ago, it brought several hundred thousand dollars. Something like that is worth what you can get for it. I would think it might bring as much as a half-million dollars now."

"What will you do with that kind of money, Buddie? What do you want most?" I asked.

"I don't have to think about that. I'd like to have a nice home of our own—no more rented apartments. And I'll have the time of my life decorating it from scratch."

"You can get a beautiful home for $30,000 [1940]. What else?"

"Gosh I don't know. This is so sudden. I never thought about anything like this before." I had never seen Buddie so happy.

Everyone was excited and filled with anticipation except Uncle Leigh, who kept repeating,

"Things like this just don't happen," as if determined to convince himself that was so.

The next day was one of unbearable suspense for me. I cut classes and spent the day in the library reading up on Stradovarius violins. Finally when I knew Leigh would be home I phoned him.

"Well, what did you find out? Tell me."

"It wasn't a real Stradovarius – like I said yesterday. Things like that just don't happen."

"Who said so? Tell me everything, step by step." I immediately suspected that he had blundered. Leigh's reputation for losing opportunities was legend.

"Well, as soon as stores were open I drove down Hollywood Boulevard looking for one that sells musical instruments. When I came to the first one I went in with the violin. I said, 'This has a sticker in it that says it is a Stradovarius. Of course I don't believe it for one minute, but I just thought I'd ask the opinion of an expert.'"

"What made you think he was an expert? I'd bet ten to one he has never seen a Stradovarius in his life and wouldn't know one if he did."

"Well, he has violins there for sale. He certainly knows more about them than I do."

"And what made you think the man was honest?"

"I had no reason to suspect he's not." To Leigh that seemed perfectly rational.

"What exactly did he say?"

"Well, this guy looks at the violin and he's obviously not interested. I can see that by the look on his face. I feel stupid for bringing it in there. He smirks and says, 'Naw. This here ain't nothin but a counterfeit. How can I tell so fast? He didn't use paper labels like this here one—he burned his mark into the wood [not true]. I got a dozen or so better'n this. If ya wana sell it I ain't interested.'"

"He wasn't telling you the truth. I spent the day in the library reading up on Stradovarius violins. Stradovari did use paper labels." Leigh was deaf to my comment. He continued his story.

"OK, I said. I'm not surprised. I started out with the violin under my arm."

"Then he stopped you and made an offer?"

"Yeah. How'd you know? Just as I reached the door, the guy says, 'Tell ya what. I'll give ya a hunert dollahs fer it.' I thought that was pretty decent of him and I figured it was a lot better than nothing at all so I sold it to him."

"YOU DID WHAT?"

"Yeah, I sold it. I'd rather have a hundred dollars any day than an old violin to hang on the wall."

"You've been had. You better go out and find the best lawyer you can get, although it's probably too late now. Maybe you can buy it back. A real expert, one competent to judge an instrument of that quality would be someone like Jascha Heifetz, Yehudi Menuhin, a symphony orchestra conductor, or a professor in a university school of music. He would have judged it by its tone. That's where I thought you were going to take it. That's what you said last night."

"Johnny, I don't know any people like that."

"The man you sold it to played you for a sucker. He was not certain but he strongly suspected the violin was a genuine Stradovarius. What could he lose if he bought it for almost nothing? He is a crook who saw his chance to get a half-million-dollar violin for a hundred dollars, what would you expect such a person to say and do?"

"But Johnny, things like this just don't happen."

"Oh Leigh, for Pete's sake."

Nothing I could say would change his opinion in any way. He was born to lose, and stubborn as a mule. It seems that men who seize opportunities are rarer than the opportunities they seize.

Six months later I read an article in Time magazine. It said that a violin made by Antonio Stradovari, the 18th century master violin maker, had surfaced recently and had been purchased for $650,000 by Jascha Heifetz—or was it Yehudi Menuhin? I'm not sure which it was now after so many years. When I showed the article to Uncle Leigh, it seemed to make no impression on him at all. His comment was, "Well it could not have been the old violin I sold for a hundred dollars. 'Things like that just don't happen.'" To this day, hearing that phrase sets me off every time.

As I write this 62 years have passed since this incident occurred. Looking back now from a different perspective, I can say that I have often speculated on what drew me so strongly to the violin on the wall. What made me do the things I did that led to my discovery? I had no particular interest in violins at the time. Could it have been ESP? Perhaps, but if it was, where was it the next day when I needed it most? That's the trouble with ESP. It's never there when you need it.

PETE

"Johnny do you need any money?" There was a look of concern on the old man's face. "If you do, I can write you a check for a million dollars—I've got that much coming in every month."

Pete was in dead earnest. He lay propped up in the bed where he had been confined since his last fall three months before, his body emaciated by advancing age, hair snow white, but eyes still the bright blue they had always been…and he was now as helpless as the day he was born ninety three years before. He waited anxiously for Johnny's reaction.

Johnny hesitated. His father was clear minded most of the time, but occasionally he wandered like this in a world of fantasy. He wants to help me, he thought. I'm his only son and he wants to do something for me…something important. How can I let him down gently?

"Let me do this for you Johnny. It really is not a problem for me," the old man persisted. "Tell Addie to bring me my check-book."

Johnny started to say how much he appreciated the offer, but really didn't need the money, then changed his mind…that pathetic, earnest expression on his father's face…that did it. He understood that, for the moment anyway, the mind was not there but the heart was, as it always had been. He is confused…lost in a world of fantasy…trying to tell me how much he cares.

"Well Dad, you know I would never come to you for money, but…well yes, if you put it that way. The truth is I do need money, and I just can't tell you how I appreciate your offer. Gosh I never expected to have a million dollars, but it may be some time before I can pay you back."

The old man smiled. "You don't have to pay me back. You have already paid me back many times over. You…." He stopped. "Addie, Addie bring me my check book and a pen." His voice was shaky but full of resolve.

Addie, Johnny's stepmother, was in the adjoining room listening to the conversation and dabbing at her eyes with a handkerchief, but now she got up to do as Pete had requested. She cranked the head of the bed a little higher, placed a tray for the old man to write on and gave him a quick hug.

As his father wrote the check with trembling hand, Johnny began to have some misgivings. My God, I hope Dad won't remember this when his mind clears. If he does he will be so embarrassed. He might feel that we were humoring him when he was feeling tired and confused…letting him show how senile he was becoming.

Pete finished writing and held the check out for his son to take. "Here you are Johnny. One million dollars. Don't spend it all in one place." He was beaming now so that his eyes were mere slits. When he smiled, his whole face smiled, eyes and all. "You fill in the date I don't know what it is…not even sure of the year just now…but that doesn't matter…you can fill that in."

Johnny took the check in one hand and his father's wrinkled hand in the other. "Dad, after I cash this, I'm going to get it from you, frame it, and hang it on the wall and I'll always remember what you did for me. I can't tell you how deeply I appreciate it."

But Pete seemed to have already dropped off to sleep with a look of contentment on his face. Johnny gently cranked the head of the bed lower and sat down again beside the old man. He looked at the check and understood that it was a symbol. What does everyone dream of having? A million dollars. Probably an expert would have a ready explanation for what Pete just did. He might say that the old man in his confused state was groping for some way to express his affection and in doing it he wanted to think big, so the amount had to be one million dollars—nothing less. It was of course not a measure of what he had in the bank but the depth of his feeling for his son. Pete had always been loving but somewhat undemonstrative…now with the end approaching he probably wanted desperately to express his affection, without knowing how. But his subconscious had found a way…at last he had communicated what he felt. Yes, Johnny thought, I'm sure that's how an expert would explain it.

Johnny sat down beside the bed and looked at the old man as if to capture his image in memory while he still could. Once a year he had flown home to see his folks—home from his corporate life, that jungle, that world of cold indifference, competitiveness, and intrigue—home to California, to family, and old friends. On these occasions Dad and Addie, Johnny's step mother who was much younger than his father, had always been waiting at the arrival gate at the airport to greet him. Eventually it was just Addie, but Pete was always waiting in the car and always so very pleased and proud when he saw Johnny. This time though, he was too feeble to get out of bed.

At first his father had been perfectly lucid and they each had a Lefroig, the old man's favorite scotch, and talked of old times. They both liked to reminisce. It was always the funny things that had happened through the years that they told and retold. His father, when his mind was clear still had his penetrating wit and fun loving, kindly humor, though he was failing fast now.

After dinner Pete dropped off into a deep sleep, but Johnny and Addie talked-on, catching up on one another's news.

"Johnny, I was so glad you accepted the check Pete wanted to write for you. I know it made him happy. He offered $100,000 to Jimmy the other day and Jimmy just laughed at him. Pete looked so bewildered and hurt. I could have killed that Jimmy—making fun of him that way, after all Pete has done for him. It's hard to imagine that they are brothers; they're so different."

"Well Addie, I'll always treasure that check. It was his way of telling me how much I mean to him. Something he could never quite put into words. I'll always keep it and think of Dad whenever I see it, and I'll also remember the many happy times and good laughs we had together when I was growing up."

Addie said she had not slept well the previous night and was feeling exhausted. She excused herself and turned in early. Johnny poured another Lefroig on the rocks and sat in silence looking at his father, one by one the years dropped away until, in reverie, he was a boy again. The mist of time that slowly obscures detail seemed to clear as if wafted away by a gentle breeze. He was six and having his tonsils out. His father was there to comfort him and insisted on going into the operating room, walking beside the gurnie. Pete looked like everyone else, dressed in the sterile garb of a doctor and wearing a mask, but his familiar voice was reassuring and cheerful. It grew fainter and more distant then finally vanished as if too faraway to hear, after they put something over Johnny's nose and mouth. He woke up with an agonizing pain in his throat and felt as if he would die of thirst because of the ether used in those days and the because of the blood he had lost. He tried to drink and threw up. Soon though he was happy because his father, who knew just what to say, was there sitting beside him.

"Johnny, when you get a little older, and I make a good deal, we'll go hunting in the Yukon and Alaska. We'll hunt grizzly bears. We'll have an airplane with pontoons too and be able to land on lakes where no white man has ever been before…only Indians and Eskimos." He made a motion with his hand to represent the plane coming in for a landing on the lake.

"Will we have a boat too?" Johnny asked.

"Why sure. We'll have two boats. One will be a fast speed boat and the other will be an Indian canoe made of birch bark. It will move silently on the water so we can sneak up on the grizzlies when they come to drink from the lake." When he told of the canoe he spoke slowly and in a hushed voice that suggested the stealth of a hunter.

"Tell me about the grizzlies, Daddy. How big are they?"

"Why Johnny that's one of the biggest bears in the world. Standing on their hind legs they can reach up and scratch the bark off trees twelve to fifteen feet above the ground." This too he dramatized, standing on tip toes and reaching as high as he could.

"Wow. And what will we take to eat?"

"Why, we'll eat with the Indians of course. We'll only need to take our guns and blankets."

"Wow."

When Johnny could finally keep something down. Pete went out and got vanilla ice cream. Never before or since did anything taste so good or feel so good to a sore throat.

Pete never made that "good deal" and this great adventure was never to be, but it was important that Johnny and his father shared the dream and it formed one of many bonds between them.

Now, looking at his father he remembered him as a young man. He was quick, coordinated, powerful, and athletic. He had eyesight like an eagle. He had been quarterback on his college football team and he could throw passes that went like bullets and were always right on target. He had been a State tennis champion and a crack shot with a rifle and shotgun. He could ride a horse like a stunt man in the movies. He was a born musician—a self taught pianist who played with feeling and a superb sense of harmony. He was the hero of Johnny's boyhood and the man he most admired all his life.

Johnny looked at the hand closest to him. There was still a hint of the power it once had but it just *looked* that way…that's all…no muscles left in the arms now…just skin and bones.

Johnny thought of the hard life his father had. He had earned an often precarious living in the real estate business, selling homes of the rich and famous in Hollywood, many of whom did him out of the commissions he counted on, needed desperately, and worked so hard to earn. During the great depression you couldn't give away the Beverly Hills mansions of the stars. Almost nobody could even pay the, then modest, taxes on them. Several of his father's business friends blew their brains out and one jumped off the roof of a tall building. Somehow his father managed but they lived through the long depression never free of worry that the mortgage would be foreclosed. The real estate business was all ups and downs—a nightmare of deals that looked like he count on them but he couldn't count on anything, even after it went into escrow.

Pete was the eldest of five brothers...the head of the family when grandfather died, as they all agreed. He was the most resourceful and could never refuse a brother in need. They all had a strong sense of family. Somehow Pete never failed to help any of them when they desperately needed it, and they for their part, went to him when they had nowhere else to turn. They tried to repay their loans but it was not usually possible during the great depression.

Pete was something of an enigma. Making money seemed to bore him and yet he had extremely shrewd business judgment and seemed to enjoy helping others make their fortunes. His own needs were Spartan though and he was satisfied with a modest commission now and then to pay his bills—then off he would go on an elk hunt, or to shoot some ducks or whatever, unless his brothers got to him first with their hard luck stories.

The old man stirred. Pete was awake again. "Johnny, I want to tell you something very important. Get something to write with and take this down. I'm going to tell you how you can make millions."

Poor old Dad *thought* Johnny. Still in a fog—but I must not appear to let him down.

"OK Dad, I'm listening and ready to write."

"Well this is a deal I was working on when I got like I am and couldn't go on with it. You see, about thirty miles from here there is a marshland of over two thousand acres. Nobody wants it. You can buy it for nothing...say $20,000. Now I was reading an article on rice paddies in the National Geographic magazine. Uh. What was I going to tell you?"

"How I can make millions."

"Yea. That's right. I got the idea that I might be able to grow rice on that marshland, so I contacted an agronomist at the University. He advised having the soil assayed and I did that. It is perfect. Salt level is negligible and irrigation water is close at hand and cheap, if it should be needed, though it probably wouldn't be. Everything shows I was right."

Johnny was impressed at the imagination shown by the old man. For someone slipping into senility and experiencing one of his periods of confusion he seemed to be showing unusual imagination and practical judgment. "Where is this marshland located Dad?"

There was a long pause. "What marshland?"

"The one that could grow rice."

"Oh. That. I don't remember. Go to the County Recorder… Ventura County I think it was. Now get a paper and pen because I want to tell you how you can make millions easily." Pete then began to tell the same thing over again and he conveyed a feeling of urgency and of firm conviction. He wanted Johnny to assure him that he would act on this suggestion immediately before someone beat him to it.

"It's not the money that's important Johnny," he said finally. "It's the feeling of confidence it gives when you make it big for the first time. After that it's the good you can do with it that counts. But don't ever let money go to your head or it will destroy you as it does most people who have it."

Delusions like this must not be so bad. At least Dad feels financially secure and his imaginings help him hold onto a bit of dignity which advancing age tries to take away.

Too soon Johnny's vacation was over; he dreaded saying goodbye. He was afraid he would never see his father alive again…never again see those bright blue eyes, hear that soft southern accent, that wit, that humor which was the rarest of Pickwickian whimsy…the courtly manners of a well bred southern gentleman of another era, which so charmed all who knew him.

And this premonition was right. Soon after Johnny returned to work a telegram came. Pete was gone. He had passed away in his sleep. Johnny felt keenly the loss of his father…a personality so vibrant and loveable…one so strong of character—so full of an intangible, magic magnetism. He found it hard to adjust to life without him. He had the feeling that the world would never be quite the same again and in a sense it was true—it wouldn't.

Pete, as he often remarked, wanted to have a wake after his funeral and he said if he could be there in spirit, he would be. Though his ancestors left Ireland two hundred years ago, the idea still appealed to him and suited his basic philosophy which had its roots in happiness, optimism, and good cheer. He wanted friends and family to come and have the good things they liked to drink and eat, music of the kind he liked to whistle and play on his piano, and he wanted them to tell the old stories and have some good laughs. They did these things and tried not to be sad.

There was a stranger at the wake whom nobody knew. Yet he clearly knew Pete. He was a lawyer and he asked several of those present to please come to his office the next morning at ten o'clock. There was the formality of the will he said.

When Addie and Johnny arrived, they found Pete's three brothers already there. The fourth had died as a young man.

"I met most of you at the wake," said the lawyer, "but let me refresh your memory. My name is John Parker. I am the senior partner in the Law firm Parker, Jameson, Jackson, Drexel, and Blake. I have known Pete for well over thirty years. He was a dear friend. I can understand how you will all miss him and I sure know I will. He was a rare person. I think rarer than even you can imagine.

"When Pete was a young man of twenty-seven he came to California from Virginia with a wife and infant son 'Johnny.' I'm going to call you all by your first names because that is how I know you from countless discussions I have had with Pete.

"Well Pete went into the real estate business, as you know, because he was ruggedly independent and didn't want to work for anyone else. He also wanted to be able to go off on a deer hunt whenever he had the inclination, which of course none of the rest of us seem able to manage. One of the first things he did was to drive all over Southern California to sharpen his judgment of property values.

"There is, as you all know, a certain dome shaped hill between Los Angeles and Long Beach that rises in sharp contrast to the flat land around it. Cattle grazed there at that time. It held a fascination for young Pete. He didn't know why but he felt drawn to it as if by destiny. At first he saw it as a place where in the distant future, the most elegant homes might be built. Land values were very low and though he didn't have much money he was able to finance the purchase of a few acres of that grazing land. It then occurred to him that he should consult with a geologist he knew, to see if there were any mineral resources there. This was typical of his thoroughness. The geologist, after studying the property, said there probably was oil. The geology of the area showed the classic indications. So he and Pete, used highly leveraged financing and refinancing to buy most of the top of the hill. They talked to Standard Oil Company, presented evidence, pressed them to make test drillings, and negotiated what is called an aleatory contract, as the cows went on grazing.

"I won't keep you in suspense. That hill is what we know today as 'Signal Hill'—for decades the most valuable real estate in the world. It sat over a veritable sea of oil. The largest reserves of petroleum by far in the United States, perhaps the largest anywhere. Pete was one of the world's richest men. At the time of his death his income was about one million dollars a month net after taxes, despite much of it being channeled into philanthropic foundations that he set up. His personal holdings were astronomical."

Everyone suddenly was talking at the same time. Addie looked like she could use some smelling salts. Johnny struggled to take it all in.

"That is how he got his start, Parker continued. But he truly had the Midas touch. During his business career he turned one imaginative deal after another and was still at it when he passed on. He was not after money. Never touched any of it after he made it. Power did not interest him, nor did he see money making as a competitive game. He used to say, 'Making money is easy, if that's what interests you.' But strange as it may seem, that really didn't interest him at all, although he liked the good he could do with his money through his various philanthropic foundations.

"He was convinced that great wealth would be a curse to most people and their ruination unless they found maturity before it was given to them. With it they would know the adulation of many but could never be sure who their true friends were. For that reason he did everything he could to live like an ordinary person, and most important of all he kept the secret of his fortune from everyone. Only I, his lawyer, have known all these many years.

"When you hear his will you will get quite a lecture on how not to let money go to your heads. He will caution you to keep the friends you made when they thought you had nothing and be wary of those attracted by your wealth. He will urge you to interest yourselves in his philanthropic organizations and do what good you can with the vast inheritances bequeathed to each of you."

Mr. Parker then read the will. It would serve no purpose to repeat it here nor would it be of interest because of the tedious details and circumlocutions of legal language, in which most of it was written. It is sufficient to say that all heirs were unimaginably rich, stunned, and still trying to come to terms with reality as they filed out of the office.

Before leaving, Johnny asked to use the telephone to call his secretary in New York. "Clara is that you? Good. I have something very important I want you to do. You know that check for a million dollars that I had framed for my office wall? Well I want you to take it down and lock it in your desk. Never mind why Clara—just do it. I'll explain when I see you."

* * * * *

Printed in the United States
1382900004B/159

9 781592 864706